SHE'D NEVER FELT THIS
WAY BEFORE . . .

Beth was terrified. She was eager.

She knew she should stop him. She didn't want to stop him.

She wanted him to love her. She was afraid he never would.

She wanted forever. She would settle for now.

Although his back was to the moonlight, causing his face to be hidden in shadows, she knew he was staring at her body. She felt his gaze like an intimate caress. She resisted the urge to hide herself with her hands, lying very still, her heart hammering in her chest, her breath coming in short ragged bursts.

Why was it she didn't feel vulnerable and afraid with this man? Did love alone make so great a difference?

Books by Robin Lee Hatcher

Liberty Blue
Chances Are
Kiss Me, Katie
Dear Lady
*Patterns of Love**
*In His Arms**

Published by HarperPaperbacks

*coming soon

Dear Lady

⋈ ROBIN LEE HATCHER ⋈

HarperPaperbacks
A Division of HarperCollinsPublishers

![HarperPaperbacks logo] **HarperPaperbacks**
A Division of HarperCollins*Publishers*
10 East 53rd Street, New York, N.Y. 10022-5299

ISBN 0-06-108687-8

HarperCollins®, ![logo] ®, HarperPaperbacks™, and
HarperMonogram® are trademarks of HarperCollins*Publishers* Inc.

Cover and stepback illustrations by Jim Griffin

First printing: June 1997

Printed in the United States of America

Visit HarperPaperbacks on the World Wide Web at
http://www.harpercollins.com/paperbacks

❖ 10 9 8 7 6 5 4 3 2 1

To a few of my own "dear ladies"—
Pamela, Christine, Debbi, Darlene, and Cathy,
special friends who have enriched my life;
Michaelyn and Jennifer,
my daughters, my treasures.
God bless you all.

Dear Lady

Prologue

April 1897

"America!" The word rushed through the belly of the great steamship like the mighty winds that blew across the Atlantic. "America!"

Elizabeth Wellington grabbed hold of the hands of her two friends, her heart hammering with mingled joy and fear. "America," she whispered, testing the country's name on her lips. She exchanged glances with Mary Malone and Inga Linberg and recognized the same feelings in their eyes.

They rose together to become part of the surging crowd, hurrying to get their first glimpse of land in two weeks. Two weeks of cramped quarters, little privacy, poor food, and the smells of salt water and seasickness.

On deck, a bitter wind cut through Beth's gown and shawl, raising gooseflesh on her arms, but she paid it no heed. She couldn't have turned back anyway. Not with the other steerage passengers pressing her forward.

Inga's grasp tightened on Beth's hand. "Look!" She pointed with her free hand. "The statue!"

"Saints be praised," Mary whispered in awe. "Will you look at that. Sure and I've never seen the like, m'lady. Have you?"

For several weeks Beth had been reminding Mary that she was no longer "m'lady," that she was simply Beth Wellington, an immigrant to America like nearly everyone else on board the RMS *Teutonic*. But as she stared at the Statue of Liberty in New York harbor, she forgot to scold. She was too overwhelmed.

What would she find in this new country? Was she right to have run away from everything—and everyone—she'd ever known? From England? From Perceval? Had she made a terrible mistake, coming to America?

Beth had spent her entire life at Langford House, never venturing farther away than London for the Season. She'd grown up surrounded by the familiar, by things and people she knew as well as she knew herself. She'd known the food she would have every morning for breakfast. She'd known the mood her father was in with a single glance. She'd known the turning of the seasons and what each one would bring.

The ten days she and Mary had been in Southampton before departing on the ship, followed by the two weeks at sea, had often seemed like an odd dream, one from which she might awaken at any moment. But suddenly she realized she wasn't going to wake up, because this was real. She had severed her ties with England.

America was her new home.

"Sure and we've made it." Mary placed a hand on

her own gently rounded stomach, as if to reassure the child that was growing inside. "We're here at last."

Beth felt a tiny catch in her heart. A few weeks ago Mary Malone had been merely a maid at Langford House. In all the months—or was it longer?—she'd worked for the Wellingtons, the young Irishwoman had rarely said more than a "Yes, mum" or "No, m'lady" to Beth. It had surprised her how quickly Mary had changed from a servant into one of her dearest and best friends. If not for Mary's help, Beth would now be married to Perceval Griffith.

Married . . . and living in hell.

Inga Linberg had befriended Beth and Mary, two obviously confused and misguided travelers, while they were still in Southampton. Inga's father had helped them secure passage on the steamship, and it was Inga who had educated them on what to expect, both at sea and during the immigration process yet to be endured. Beth had become most fond of the tall, plain Swedish girl in the brief time they'd known one another.

But now they were in America, and Beth realized how much she was going to miss her friends as they each went their separate ways—Mary to wed the father of her unborn child; Inga with her family to Iowa, where her father would pastor a church; and Beth to Montana.

Montana, a place far, far from England, as far away as she could get from an arranged marriage to a man she detested.

She squared her shoulders and lifted her chin. Silently she promised herself she would face what tomorrow might bring, no matter what it was. It could be no worse than what she'd left behind.

1

Garret Steele gripped the saddle with his thighs and held on to the horn with his left hand as the big buckskin gelding beneath him set its front legs, then darted in the opposite direction in pursuit of the wily calf. The heifer was as range wild as any Garret had ever seen, but he and old Buck had been herding cows together for many years. They weren't about to be outsmarted by beef on the hoof.

Ten minutes later he had the calf roped, hog-tied, and ready for branding.

While Jake Whitaker, his hired hand, brought the hot iron from the fire, Garret removed his hat and wiped the sweat from his forehead. Then he reached for his canteen. Tipping back his head, he took a long swallow, washing down the dust.

Lord, it was hot for May. He hoped they weren't in for a long, dry summer. The cattle had wintered well, and Garret was looking forward to turning a nice profit come fall. But a drought could quickly change the face of things.

"Always somethin'," he muttered as he screwed the cap back on the canteen.

The stench of singed hair and flesh reached his nostrils, reminding him of the work still to be done before sundown. Tugging his hat low on his forehead with one hand, he stepped into the saddle. As soon as Jake freed the newly branded calf—still bleating its complaint—Garret dragged his lariat into a large coil against his thigh, then turned Buck toward the herd.

A sense of satisfaction swelled in Garret's chest as his gaze swept over the range. Satisfaction was what he always felt when he looked at what he'd accomplished in the past eighteen years. He'd been nothing but a scrawny kid, still wet behind the ears, when he'd first come to Montana, when he'd first laid eyes on this stretch of land and known he wanted to call it home.

He'd seen plenty of hard times while he'd built his herd from a few head to its present size. And he'd seen plenty of changes come to Montana, too. The railroad crawling across the plains and through the mountain passes. The coming of barbed wire. The town of New Prospects, popping up just ten miles to the south of the Steele ranch, seemingly overnight.

Yeah, things were different, but this was where he belonged. It was his home.

"Pa! Pa!"

He reined in, twisting in the saddle to watch the approach of his daughter. Janie's wild strawberry blond hair waved behind her like a banner, and her dress was bunched up around her thighs as she raced her pony toward him.

Wouldn't Muriel have a fit if she could see Janie now?

His teeth clenched as he shoved away thoughts of his dead wife.

Sliding her small bay mare to a halt, Janie said, "I finished the dishes and my lessons, Pa. Can I help now?"

He grinned even as he shook his head. "You know how I feel about you bein' out here while we're branding. This is no place for a little girl."

"I'm not so little I can't help."

He recognized the stubborn set of her jaw. And what she said was true. Janie had taken care of many of the household chores since long before her mother passed away. She'd even learned to cook, at least well enough to keep the two of them from starving. But that didn't mean she belonged in the middle of a herd of cattle at branding time. It was just too dangerous, and Garret would never risk harm to his daughter. Not ever.

"Sorry, Janie. You know the rules."

"But, Pa—"

"Janie . . . "

She scowled, her bottom lip protruding in an artful pout. "It's not fair."

He was unmoved by her theatrics. "Things rarely are."

"Can't I just—"

"Nope." He jerked his head toward the ranch house. "You get on back. I'll be finished up in about an hour."

Janie hesitated only a moment, then, with a deep sigh of the oppressed, turned her pony toward the house and rode slowly away. His daughter would probably never know how hard it was for Garret to refuse anything she asked. He'd try to rope her the moon if she wanted it.

With a shake of his head, he nudged Buck with his heels and set off to rope the last of the calves instead.

Two hours later father and daughter sat down at the rough-hewn table in the log house they called home. Janie said the blessing over the steaks that had been fried with onions and potatoes, and Garret added his own "Amen" to hers when she was finished.

"I got another letter from England today," Janie said as she cut her meat, "but it took longer'n usual getting here. Lady Elizabeth must already be married to Lord Altberry by now. I hope she'll write again soon and tell me about the wedding and the house where she's living."

Garret listened to the excitement in her voice, while feeling residual anger stirring to life. He hated it when Janie talked about England and the Wellingtons. He hated the way she fantasized about traveling abroad someday, and he blamed his deceased wife for putting the notion in Janie's head to begin with. It was Muriel who had encouraged their daughter—only six years old at the time—to write to the earl, an old friend of Garret's father-in-law. It was Muriel who had encouraged the continuing correspondence between Janie and the earl's daughter, and Muriel who had suggested Janie might one day go to England to visit Lady Elizabeth, perhaps to become her companion. It was Muriel who had dreamed of Janie one day marrying an English lord, just like those eastern society women they'd read about in the news-paper.

"I wish I could have seen the wedding," Janie went on, oblivious of her father's displeasure. "Just think. A church that can hold a thousand people. I've never even *seen* a thousand people, let alone all in one place, have I, Pa?"

"Don't reckon you have."

"It must've been something." She fell silent, and her eyes got a far-off, dreamy look.

Garret felt a tightness in his belly as he stared at his daughter across the table. She was already ten years old. In another ten years, maybe even less, she might be married. She might be out on her own by that time. Would she go as far away from Montana as England, just as her mother had hoped?

Damn you, Muriel!

Garret had a sudden vision of himself in ten years. He'd be forty-five, and all those days in the saddle and the bitter cold winters would be telling on him in his joints. He loved Montana, loved this ranch. But would he love it as much if Janie weren't around?

He gave his head a brief shake. No point troubling himself about tomorrow. Like the Good Book said, tomorrow would have enough trouble of its own.

He just didn't know how much trouble.

"Are we getting close?" Beth asked just before the wagon wheel dropped into another rut, nearly tossing her off the seat and into the road.

"'Bout there," Mr. Crew answered without missing

a beat. "This here's Steele land we're crossin' right now."

Beth gazed at the grasslands as the shadow of evening fell over it. Tall, purple-hued mountains stood above a wide, long valley, the grass and trees only now turning green after a winter's rest. At another time, she might have seen the beauty of the rugged land about her, but for now she was too wearied by travel. Two weeks on the steamship amid appalling conditions. The horrible experience of Ellis Island, where inspectors stripped a person of any dignity. The squalor of New York, a city covering over three hundred square miles and holding—she'd been told, although it was still difficult for her to believe—nearly three and a half million people within its boundaries. Next there had been a journey by train of over twenty-four hundred miles, followed by the torturous stagecoach ride up to New Prospects, Montana, on roads unfit for travel. And finally, this last assault upon her bones in a rattletrap, flatbed wagon that looked as though it would crumble into pieces at any moment.

She should have stayed in New York with Mary, she thought miserably. She could have at least waited until Mary had heard from her fiancé. Beth should have written to Janie and her father, asking if the teaching position was still unfilled, rather than rush off the way she had.

Why on earth had she taken it into her head to come to this place at the very ends of the earth? Of course, she'd had no idea it would take so long to reach Montana. What Englishman could imagine the vastness of this country? Beth Wellington certainly hadn't. Not in her wildest dreams. And certainly she'd never imagined she would arrive in New Prospects and find there wasn't a hotel or even a boardinghouse in which to stay.

Are you sure you should be goin' out there all by yourself, m'lady? she could hear Mary Malone asking. *There's sure to be all manner of wild beasties, and you've never in your life been on your own like you'll be there. Sure and you'd be welcome to stay with me and Mr. Maguire. My Seamus would not mind if you were t'join us, wherever it is we're to settle.*

Inga Linberg, speaking in her rolling Swedish accent, had added her own comments. *Come with us to Iowa. I have heard it is a fine place. Papa would welcome you into our home. You know he has come to love you like one of his own daughters, and you have become another sister to me.*

Mr. Crew spat a stream of tobacco at the ground. "Surprised Steele didn't come t'meet you in town, you bein' his guest and all. 'Course, it's brandin' time. Ranchers 'round here keep right busy once the grass turns."

Brought abruptly out of her private thoughts, Beth had only a vague idea what the old man was talking about. His English was appalling, even for an American. She thought it prudent to say nothing rather than reveal her ignorance. She settled for a nod and a shrug.

Trying to reassure herself that she'd made the right decision in coming to Montana, she recalled Janie's last letter. Beth had memorized every word of it, having read it time and time again over the past weeks.

"Dear Lady," it began like all the others,

I wish you could come to Montana to see
me. It will be years before I can visit you
in England, and Pa says he don't ever want
me to go there. Pa says he'd be too lonely
without me. I think he's lonely anyway.
You'd like it here, too. Like I told you
before, our ranch is the prettiest place in
the world.

Did I tell you the schoolmaster up and
quit? Pa's been teachin me here at home,
but he says the town has placed an adver-
tisement in some newspapers somewhere
back east to get us a new one. Trouble is,
Pa says, not many teachers want to live so
far out in the country. New Prospects is a
mighty small town compared to some.
Course, I don't care if they never find a
new teacher. I'd rather do my book learnin
at the ranch than have another teacher like
Mr. Peterson. He was sour as a pickle.
And sometimes right mean, too.

My colt's a year old now, and he's
really somethin. Pa says by the time he's
big enough to ride, I'll be old enough to
train him myself. I cant wait. Course, I'll
always love Maybelle. She's the best pony
in the world, but she's old and for babies
and I'm not a baby no more. I'll be ten on
my next birthday. That's just a few
months away. And ten is too old for ridin
a pony—

"There's the Steele place up ahead," Mr. Crew said, interrupting Beth's reminiscing for a second time.

She looked up and stared at the square log house with a narrow front porch. *That* was Janie's home? But there couldn't be more than a few rooms. There would be no place for Beth. From Janie's letters she had envisioned something much larger, something much finer. After everything she'd seen since arriving in Montana, she shouldn't have been surprised, but she was.

Mr. Crew reined in the team of horses, spat another disgusting stream of tobacco at the ground, then hopped down. He went to the rear and pulled her enormous trunk off the wagon bed.

"Need a hand down?" he asked as he dragged the trunk toward the house.

She was certain she did, afraid her knees wouldn't support her if she tried to stand on her own. Exhaustion and trepidation had stolen the last ounce of her strength. What would the Steeles think, having Beth—a virtual stranger—dropped suddenly on their doorstep? What if they refused her lodging? She'd spent almost the last of her carefully hoarded funds to pay for the stage ride up from Bozeman. There certainly wasn't enough to pay for passage elsewhere.

Suddenly the door to the house opened. Beth inhaled a quick breath, knowing her moment of truth had arrived.

The man who stepped into view was ruggedly handsome, his face and arms darkened by the sun. His hair, black as pitch, brushed his shirt collar. His eyes were a slightly darker shade of blue than the vast Montana sky, and she could see curiosity in their depths when he glanced at her. A man of at least fifteen stone, he was tall, close to a foot taller than Beth. He was also lean and muscular with broad shoulders, and he moved with power and confidence.

"Howdy, Garret," Mr. Crew said as he dragged Beth's trunk toward the porch. "This here's Miss Wellington. Reckon you forgot she was comin', so I brung her out."

Garret raised an eyebrow. "Miss Wellington?" he repeated. Then his questioning look was replaced by a darker and unmistakably less friendly one. "From England?"

"Yes." Her dry throat caused the word to sound raspy and faint.

That she wasn't wanted here was apparent in his stance and the coldness of his glare. And the feeling was mutual. Beth suddenly wished herself anywhere else.

"Lady Elizabeth? Is it really you?"

The child's voice drew Beth's gaze away from Garret Steele to the girl who'd come to stand at his side.

"It *is* you!" Janie shouted as she rushed forward, climbing up the side of the wagon like a monkey up a tree.

Before Beth knew what was happening, she was caught in an exuberant embrace. She didn't know what to do. She'd never been hugged quite like this before. Awkwardly she patted Janie's shoulder.

"What are you doing here?" the girl demanded as she pulled back. "Where's His Lordship? Is he comin', too? You've gotta tell me all about the wedding! Was everything pretty? What was your dress like?"

"Janie," her father interrupted. "You're forgettin' yourself. That's enough questions. Ask Lady Elizabeth into the house."

At the sound of his voice, trepidation returned. Beth didn't want to go into Garret Steele's house. She didn't want to stay under this man's roof when she wasn't wanted there. An image of Perceval, furious and destructive, flashed in her mind. What if Janie's father was such a man?

But what else could she do? Her trunk with all her worldly possessions was already waiting near the front door. She had no choice. At least, not for tonight.

Garret stepped forward, grabbed his daughter around the waist, and whisked her from the wagon. An alarmed cry rose in Beth's throat, but she swallowed it as Janie's feet safely touched ground. Then Garret straightened and offered Beth a hand to help her down as well. It took what little courage she had left to accept the offer.

Mr. Crew bent his hat brim toward her. "Pleasure meetin' you, miss." He glanced at Garret, bent his hat brim again, then stepped on the hub of the wagon wheel and climbed to his place on the seat, taking up the reins as he did so. "Evenin'." He slapped the leather against the broad rumps of the horses and drove away.

Beth had the urge to run after him, but Janie's hand grasped hers and pulled her toward the log house before she could act on the impulse. Unable to help herself, she lifted her eyes to meet Garret's as she moved past him. Her trepidation doubled at the look of resentment and dislike she saw in the deep blue depths.

What the heck is she doing in Montana? Garret wondered as he watched Janie lead the woman into the house. And what had made Mark Crew think he'd been expecting her? Scowling, he turned on his heel and headed for the doorway, intent on getting some answers out of Lady Elizabeth Wellington of Langford House, Buckinghamshire, England.

He found her already seated at the table, her hands clenched in her lap. Janie was hastily filling a plate with food, chattering excitedly the whole while. His daughter's delight in the presence of their unexpected guest was obvious. Her eyes fairly sparkled with joy as she waited on the woman.

There was something both regal and fragile about Elizabeth Wellington's delicate frame, clothed in a fashionable gown that had retained its elegance despite being travel stained. On her head she wore a perky bonnet of straw, feathers, and cloth flowers, a totally useless accessory, in his opinion, yet one that looked oddly appropriate on her.

As for the rest of her appearance, there was no denying she was beautiful. Thick auburn hair framed a heart-shaped face. Her complexion was smooth and pale, untouched by the sun, something most women in Montana couldn't claim. Her almond-shaped eyes were a light shade of green, like spring leaves, and she had a full, sensuous mouth, one that looked ripe for kissing.

Garret scowled at that last thought. He had no desire to kiss this woman, no matter how pretty her mouth. Lady Elizabeth Wellington was the daughter of an English earl. She was a lady of quality, a lady of wealth and good breeding.

And those were only a few of the reasons Garret had for despising her without even knowing her.

She rose from her chair. "Mr. Steele, please accept my apologies. It was never my intention to impose myself upon your hospitality."

He stepped toward the table. "What brought you here, Lady Elizabeth?"

"Please," she said hastily. "Call me Miss Wellington."

"Okay. *Miss* Wellington, what brought you here?"

She hesitated a moment, then answered in her very proper and ladylike British voice, "I came to Montana because I hope to fill the position of schoolteacher in New Prospects. Janie wrote and told me how badly a teacher was needed here, and I thought perhaps I—"

"You came all the way from England to be a *teacher?*" He almost laughed aloud. It was too absurd.

If possible, she looked even more aristocratic than before. Her reply was stiff and formal. "No, Mr. Steele. My father passed away a short while ago, and I was unable to remain in our home, as the new earl has a large family and I would have been an unwelcome burden. I chose to come to America, believing I could provide for myself as a teacher here."

"And what about that new husband of yours Janie's been tellin' me about?"

"I chose not to marry. I chose to come here instead."

"Oh, Lady Elizabeth!" Janie threw her arms about Beth's waist and hugged her, just as she'd done on the wagon. "Is it true? Are you really going to stay and be our teacher?"

The woman's demeanor changed quickly, her expression softening. She stroked Janie's hair with one hand. "I hope to, Janie. And you must call me Miss Beth. No one has a title in America."

She sounded sincere, but Garret's suspicions weren't so easily eliminated. His personal experience with women like Beth Wellington had proven they weren't to be trusted.

She glanced up at him. "I hope you will help me acquire the position, Mr. Steele."

Why should I? he wanted to ask, but once again, the delight and expectation in his daughter's eyes kept him from speaking his mind. He would have to wait until Janie was out of earshot. "Why don't you sit down and eat a bite or two, Miss Wellington? We can discuss that job later."

"But there is another matter to be settled, sir."

"What other matter?"

"I did not realize there would be no suitable lodgings for me in New Prospects. I did not know where else to go except to this ranch. That is why Mr. Crew brought me here. But there doesn't seem to be a room for me here, either."

"You can sleep in my bed," Janie interjected. She pointed toward the loft. "It's up there. You can see almost all the way to New Prospects from the window. Can't you, Pa?"

"Yes, but I'm not sure—"

"Up there?" Beth whispered as she followed the direction of Janie's hand, looking as if she hadn't the strength to climb the ladder.

For the first time, Garret realized how weary she must be and took a measure of pity—however unwillingly—on her. There would be time enough to get answers to his questions after she'd had a chance to rest.

"We'll sort things out later," he said. "You sit down and eat your supper. I'll heat some water so you can wash up, and Janie'll get her bed ready for you."

"But where will she sleep if I take her bed?"

"We'll make a spot on the floor for her in my room. We've done it before."

"But I couldn't—"

"Janie wants you to stay, Miss Wellington," he said, firmly putting an end to her arguments.

"Thank you, Mr. Steele. I am most grateful."

He shrugged off her thanks. It wasn't as if he had much choice, and it was only for a night. Tomorrow he'd find another solution. The quicker she was out, the better.

Beth awakened suddenly, swallowing a cry of terror as she sat up in bed and clutched the blanket to her chest. For a moment she didn't know where she was. But as the nightmare receded and her racing pulse slowed, the memory of her arrival at the Steele ranch returned. Remembering didn't bring much comfort, for with it came the image of Garret Steele and the certain knowledge he didn't want her in his home.

She tossed aside the bedcovers, then walked to the narrow loft window to stare outside. Pale moonlight spilled across the floor of the valley, giving the land a softness it didn't have by day.

This Montana ranch was nothing like she'd expected. She'd envisioned a quaint white house with a yard full of flowers, perhaps ivy climbing a trellis up one wall. She'd pictured everything lushly verdant with many tall trees and wide manicured lawns. She realized now that she had envisioned an English country manor, not a cattle ranch in the middle of the American wilderness. Too late, she realized she'd been incredibly naive.

But would the alternative to coming to America have been better?

No. Never.

She closed her eyes, feeling sick. Even with Perceval halfway around the world, he still had the power to frighten her. And with good reason.

She could see him so clearly in her mind, the man to whom her father had betrothed her. Perceval Griffith, Lord Altberry, was tall and handsome— eerily so—and he'd frightened her from the first moment they'd met. There had never been any depth in his smiles or tenderness in his eyes. She had always felt cold when in his company. He was a man without conscience or sympathy. His greatest pleasure came from causing others pain. She had learned that truth quickly enough.

Certainly Perceval had not proposed out of love for her. He was incapable of such an emotion. He had wanted her because she was regarded a beauty and other men would envy him. Her duty would have been to graciously decorate his arm and to provide him an heir. Nothing more. Never would there have been any love between them. Never would there have been even a moment of happiness for Beth.

But she hadn't suspected just how terrible their marriage would have been until the night before her father fell ill.

She turned from the window and sank to the floor, her back against the wall. Pressing the heels of her hands against her eyelids, she tried to keep the images from returning. But she failed.

Garret wasn't certain what awakened him, but he had an unmistakable feeling that something was wrong. He got up from the bed and pulled on his trousers, listening carefully all the while. He stepped over Janie's makeshift bed and made his way into the living room.

At the window, he glanced outside. Pale moonlight silvered the yard. Several horses stood with lowered heads in the corral. Janie's black-and-white collie, Penguin, slept undisturbed on the porch. A gentle breeze stirred the branches of the tall trees beyond the barn. Nothing seemed awry.

Then he heard it, a soft, unmistakable whimper, coming from inside the house.

He turned, hesitated a moment, then walked toward the ladder and climbed up, pausing when his gaze reached the level of the loft floor.

Elizabeth Wellington was easy to find in her white nightgown, seated beneath the window. Her legs were drawn up to her chest, her face pressed against her knees, her arms clasped around her shins. Her breathing was shallow and raspy, and every so often a mewling sound escaped her throat.

Darn her! What was she doing here, disturbing the peace of his home?

He knew well enough why she was crying. She'd taken one look at this log house and judged it unsuitable for human habitation. It wasn't the grand place she was used to living in. She thought it little better than a hovel. He'd recognized the look in her eyes. He'd seen it before.

Well, it might not be an English castle, but by heaven, it was his home. Nobody'd invited her to come here. If she didn't like it, she could get herself the heck out.

He was just ready to step down the ladder when she looked up and gasped. The look of fear in her eyes reminded him of a colt caught in barbed wire. Something had frightened her. No, something had *terrified* her.

Despite himself, he asked, "You all right?"

Her fear was palpable, like a third presence in the loft, and it seemed to have rendered her speechless.

Frowning, he climbed up the last steps and moved forward. "Miss Wellington?"

"Don't come near me! Please!"

He obeyed, recognizing the note of panic in her hoarse words. Calmly he said, "It's just me, ma'am. Garret Steele. You don't have anything to be afraid of." He took a step back. "I just thought you might be in need of something. Sounded like you were hurting. Is there something I can do for you?"

Beth dragged in a deep breath. Then, after letting it

out, she answered, "No. I'm sorry, Mr. Steele. No, I'm fine. I . . . I had a nightmare, that's all." She pushed herself up from the floor to stand ramrod straight in front of the window. Moonlight outlined her body with a white glow and hid her face from view. "I'm fine." She sounded stronger now, every inch the English noblewoman.

"Then I'll leave you be." He returned to the ladder and began his descent. He was halfway down when he heard her speak again.

"Thank you, Mr. Steele."

She was a strange one, this Lady Elizabeth. One minute she was as stiff and formal as the queen of England herself, the next she acted as scared as a helpless animal in a trap.

Garret returned to his bedroom, removed his trousers, and crawled beneath the covers on his bed. But try as he might, sleep wouldn't come again. He couldn't seem to get rid of the image of Elizabeth Wellington, huddled in a fearful pose beneath the window.

He swore softly as he rolled onto his other side and slapped the pillow over his head. The last thing he needed was to lose sleep over a woman, especially a woman like Elizabeth Wellington. She might have been wrinkled and stained by travel, but even he could tell her clothes were those of wealth and privilege. And it was his personal experience that wealthy, privileged women didn't do well in Montana. Lord knew Muriel hadn't had a good word to say about it.

He flopped onto his back and stared up through the darkness at the ceiling.

Tarnation! What woman with a lick of sense would

take the word of a ten-year-old girl, pack a trunk, and travel dang near halfway round the world in hopes of taking a teaching position in a place she'd never seen? And there she was, upstairs, scared spitless. Fool woman. She'd gotten just what she deserved and nothing more. Maybe she'd stop and think next time before running off half-cocked.

And Garret would be hanged if he was going to waste time worrying about her. He'd let her stay here a night or two. He'd even take her into town and introduce her to the mayor of New Prospects. Then the school board could make up its own mind. If they didn't want Elizabeth Wellington to teach for them, well, that was just her tough luck.

Except when he closed his eyes again, the image was still there. The image of a woman in a white nightgown, huddled in fear beneath a moonlit window.

2

The next morning, Beth gazed at her reflection in the small mirror, feeling overwhelmed by despair. There were dark smudges beneath her eyes, and her complexion looked sickly. She'd used a hint of rouge on her cheeks, but it had done little to improve her appearance.

Who would possibly want to hire someone who looks as incapable and weak as I do?

Her mouth thinned in determination. Nothing was ever as bad as it seemed at first, she reminded herself. For instance, her dark blue gown was clean and pressed. Of course, that was thanks to help from Janie. Beth had never used an iron before and wouldn't have known how to manage without her young American friend. It had become painfully clear in recent weeks that her talents in watercolors and music were not the talents she most needed when it came to caring for her daily needs.

"But I can learn to do what I must," she said beneath her breath. "I'm already learning." She placed her bonnet on her head and thought perhaps it improved her appearance, if only a little.

Beth supposed she should be grateful for the hand-some gowns and pretty trinkets that filled her trunk. While Langford House had fallen into disrepair as the earl's gambling debts increased, Henry Wellington had never stinted on Beth's wardrobe. Like the daughter of many a nobleman facing financial ruin, she had known she would be expected to save him by means of a respectable match. She had tried to accept her fate gracefully, loving her father too much to fail him.

Very pretty marriage bait you are, too. The memory of Perceval speaking those words made her shiver.

But she was free of him now, she thought as she turned from the mirror. Free to do as she pleased.

With reticule in hand, she descended the ladder to the living room. She paused at the bottom, taking a moment to draw a deep breath, steadying her nerves, thankful to be alone in the room. Much to her relief, she hadn't seen Garret Steele at breakfast that morning. And after the way he'd found her last night, Beth knew she would feel awkward when she did see him again.

The front door opened and Janie rushed into the house. "Lady Elizabeth! Are you ready? Pa's got the team hitched to the wagon."

"Yes." She squared her shoulders. "I'm ready. But you are to call me Miss Beth, remember?"

Janie took hold of her hand and pulled her toward the door. "Yeah, I remember. But I don't know why, 'cause you *are* a lady, and just 'cause you're here now doesn't change what you are, does it?"

Beth thought of England, thought of Langford House, her father, and her betrothed, thought of the sort of woman she'd been. "I want it to change what I am, Janie," she answered softly. "I don't want to be who I was in England."

The girl glanced at her with a frown. "I don't know what you mean."

"No." She squeezed Janie's hand. "No, I don't suppose you would. Perhaps someday, when you're older, I'll explain it to you."

"You sound just like Pa. He's always sayin' I can't do this or know that until I'm more grown-up. But that's gonna take *forever!*"

Beth laughed. Then she saw Garret waiting for them beside the wagon, and her laughter faded into silence.

His eyes were shaded by the brim of his hat, but she could see the grim set of his mouth and knew he was frowning as he watched their approach. But he smiled as he lifted Janie into the wagon, setting her on the wagon bed beside a black-and-white dog. Beth didn't have to know him well to see how he doted on his daughter, and as he took hold of Beth's hand and helped her up to the wagon seat, she knew with a certainty he would never insist Janie marry for any reason except love, not even to save his own life.

A totally unexpected sense of aloneness squeezed her heart and brought the threat of tears to her eyes.

"You feelin' all right this morning?" Garret asked softly as he settled on the seat next to her.

She blinked back the tears and glanced at him, but he was staring straight ahead. "Yes," she answered at last. "Yes, I am feeling well."

Garret slapped the reins against the team's back-sides, and the wagon rolled out of the yard. They traveled in silence for a long time before he asked, "You sure you want this teachin' job, Miss Wellington?"

"Quite sure, Mr. Steele."

He turned to look at her. "You won't be happy here."

Beth considered his comment, knowing he might very well be right. New Prospects, Montana, was nothing like she'd expected, and America was nothing like England. She was a fish out of water here.

But instead of agreeing with him, she asked, "Why is it you don't like me, Mr. Steele?"

Her question seemed to catch him by surprise. "Never said I didn't like you."

"You do not need to say it for it to be true, sir," she whispered before she looked away.

The length and breadth of this valley made Beth feel small and insignificant. Everything about this land, from the rugged mountains that surrounded them to the gold-green grasses rustling in the light breeze, seemed strange to her. Even the sky seemed larger and bluer than the sky over Langford House. Beth felt a wave of homesickness for England and her father and all things familiar.

"It isn't that I don't like you, Miss Wellington."

He spoke softly, and Beth guessed it was because he didn't want Janie to hear.

"It's just I don't think you belong here. Montana's hard country. Winters are long and cold. Growin' season is short and unpredictable. Depending on the weather, food can be scarce some years. Lots of folk live from hand to mouth most of the time. I've seen women grow old before their time 'cause of the harshness of this country. I've seen it kill 'em."

She glanced his way. "Is that what happened to Janie's mother?"

He seemed to flinch, then his expression turned to stone before her eyes. She knew at once she'd made a mistake. It was clear he didn't like to speak about his wife. The pain of losing her must hurt him still.

Janie's hand alighted on Beth's shoulder. "Look! There's the schoolhouse. Over there."

Beth gazed at the small, recently whitewashed building set about thirty yards back from the road. It had a bell tower rising from its roof and three windows each on two of its four sides. Some distance behind the schoolhouse was an outhouse that leaned precariously to the leeward side. It too had received a fresh coat of white paint.

What a remarkable country, she thought, not for the first time. To educate all children, regardless of class or wealth. To care so much about children learning that small towns built schools in the middle of nowhere.

Her gaze moved to a deserted-looking log cabin set in a copse of aspens and pines. "Who lives there?"

Janie answered, "Nobody now. Old Mr. Thompson used to, but he died last winter. He was a miner. Came here from Virginia City when his rheumatism made him stop diggin' in the ground. Leastwise, that's what he told me." She lowered her voice as she leaned closer to Beth. "Miss Bunny always said Mr. Thompson was mean as a skunk, but I kinda liked him. He was nice to us kids." She paused, then whispered, "Besides, Miss Bunny'd make anybody mean tempered, if you ask me."

"Janie," her father warned.

"Well, it's true," the child protested. "Ain't it, Pa?"

Garret relented. "Yeah, it is."

"Pa, what about Mr. Thompson's place? Couldn't it be fixed up for Miss Beth to live in?"

"That shack?" Garret looked at Beth, then back at his daughter. "I doubt she'd want to live there."

Beth's pulse began to race at the idea. Her own place. Not a rented room, but a place of her own. "I might want to, Mr. Steele," she said, glancing over her shoulder at the cabin. "Could it be repaired?"

"I reckon it could, but—"

"It would be close to the school."

"But I don't think—"

"Who owns it now?"

Garret's voice sounded gruff. "The mayor."

"Then if I'm given the position, I shall ask the mayor about it." She straightened on the wagon seat and smiled to herself.

Everything was going to work out. She hadn't made a mistake in coming here. Everything was going to be fine.

Bunny and Patsy Homer considered themselves the social conscience of New Prospects, Montana, and they made it their business to pass judgment on one and all. The spinster sisters—Bunny, the older of the two, was as tall as most men and skinny as a rail; Patsy was short and portly, with rolls of fat beneath her chin—had the same dour countenance and a knack for sticking their noses in where they didn't belong. As proprietresses of the town's general store, they were quick to pick up any gossip to be had and just as quick to pass it along to others. Therefore Garret was dismayed to find the sisters seated in the waiting area of Mayor Owen Simpson's office.

He shouldn't have been surprised, of course. Owen's office in the First Bank of New Prospects was always busy, what with him being the banker, the mayor, *and* head of the school board. But Garret had been hoping he wouldn't have to talk to anyone or introduce Beth until after she'd decided to go back to England. Unfortunately, before he could back up and close the door again, the sisters had spied Beth waiting on the boardwalk behind him.

Bunny's eyes lit with interest as she craned her neck to get a better look at the newcomer. "Good day, Mr. Steele," she said with one of her most gracious—and irritating—smiles. "What a pleasant surprise. We so rarely see you in town."

Sighing inwardly, he removed his hat and motioned Beth and Janie into the office. "Good day, Miss Bunny, Miss Patsy. Is Owen in?"

"Yes," Patsy answered. "He's with Gloria Pruett at the moment. Her husband's lost the loan payment again, you know? Lord knows how she puts up with such a shiftless man."

"I hadn't heard." He closed the door.

"And how is your little Janie?" Bunny patted his daughter on the head.

"Just fine, as you can see."

The sisters looked at him expectantly. "Perhaps you could introduce us to your guest," Bunny suggested when he didn't do so without prompting.

He saw no way to avoid it or he would have done so. "Miss Wellington, this is Miss Bunny Homer and Miss Patsy Homer. They own the New Prospects Mercantile. Ladies, this is Beth Wellington. She's come to town to be the new schoolmarm, if the school board agrees to hire her."

Patsy rose from her chair and folded her hands just below her ponderous breasts. "How do you do, Miss Wellington?"

"I'm well, thank you, Miss Homer. And you?"

Patsy's eyebrows rose, and her nose wrinkled in just a hint of a sneer. "You're not an American."

"No, I came here from England."

Janie piped up, "Her father's an earl. That's an English lord, and she's a lady. She used to live in a big stone manor called Langford House, and she was supposed to marry Lord Altberry, but she came here instead."

It was Bunny's turn to stand. "Your father's an earl? Well, gracious me." Her expression was one of disbelief. "And you're a schoolmarm, Miss Wellington? Or should I say, *Lady* Wellington?"

"Miss Wellington will do quite nicely," Beth answered.

Garret wished he could pull her aside and warn her about this pair of vipers. Then again, it wasn't his responsibility. He'd already gone out of his way for her. If she wanted to live in this town, let her figure out for herself whom she should trust and whom she shouldn't.

Patsy nodded toward Bunny. "It just so happens my sister and I are on the school board." She plunked down on her chair, making the wood creak. "Please,

Miss Wellington, sit down and visit with us while we all await Mr. Simpson."

Garret figured this was a good time to make himself scarce. "You ladies'll have to excuse me. I got things t'do here in town. Janie, you comin'?"

"If it's all the same t'you, Pa, I'd like to stay with Miss Beth."

"Suit yourself." He set his Stetson over his hair. "Ladies." Then he made his escape.

As soon as the door closed behind him, he paused to take a deep breath of crisp spring air, mighty thankful he wasn't the one about to face the inquisition. If those two crones didn't send Lady Elizabeth Wellington hotfooting it back to England, then he didn't know what would.

Come to think of it, this was probably the best thing that could've happened. Those snoopy sisters would put Beth through her paces. She would quickly see she didn't belong in New Prospects. She would go back to England, and Janie would forget about her and the other nonsense Muriel had put into her head.

Yes, sir, it couldn't have worked out better than this. Maybe he'd learn a new appreciation for Patsy and Bunny Homer after this day was done.

Yes, sir, maybe he would at that.

Owen Simpson lost his heart the moment the auburn-haired beauty was ushered into his office. A bachelor for all of his thirty-one years, he'd never once considered taking a wife, being convinced that most married men were either unhappy or unfaithful—and usually both.

But all of that changed when he met Beth.

"Miss Wellington is seeking the position of New Prospects' schoolteacher," Patsy Homer added when she'd completed her introductions.

"You're planning to stay in Montana?" His heart leaped with joy. Ignoring the thudding in his chest, he offered her his hand.

"I hope to, Mr. Simpson."

At another time, he might have wondered what Garret's daughter was doing with this woman, but at the moment it didn't matter. He couldn't seem to think straight, to think of anything beyond the way looking at her made him feel.

As Beth withdrew her hand from his, she said, "If I can find employment and a place to live, I should very much like to stay in New Prospects."

Bunny Homer settled onto the wooden chair nearest the office door. "Miss Wellington's father, the *earl* of Langford"—Owen knew he was supposed to be impressed, given Bunny's emphasis on the title—"and Muriel Steele's father were friends. Miss Wellington has been corresponding with little Janie for several years."

"Miss Wellington's father died a short while back," Patsy said, taking over from her sister, "and she has no other family in England, dear girl. So she decided to come to Montana to visit Janie. She's a guest at the Steele ranch, and she'd like to stay on as our school-marm."

Owen might have felt alarm had Beth been staying in the home of any other man in the area. But not when the man in question was Garret. Owen was probably the only other person in New Prospects who knew the entire story about Garret and Muriel Steele. He also knew it would be a cold day in hell before the rancher had anything to do with the fairer sex.

"Unfortunately," Bunny continued, "Miss Wellington doesn't have her teaching certificate. Such a pity, too. I'm sure she would have made an adequate teacher, but I suppose she shall have to move elsewhere and find another means of support. There are few enough opportunities here."

Owen made up his mind then and there that Beth Wellington would be hired. It didn't matter to him in the least whether or not she had the qualifications to teach or what any of the other school board members thought. One of the benefits of being the mayor—not to mention the banker who controlled loans for the majority of people in the area—was folks pretty much always agreed with him when he spoke his mind.

"Do sit down, Miss Wellington." He motioned her toward a chair close to his own. "Tell me why you wish to teach the youngsters of our fair town."

She offered him the faintest of smiles, then took her seat while he did the same.

With hands folded in her lap, she looked him straight in the eye. "The answer is quite simple, Mr. Simpson. I like children. I was educated at the Hanford Society's School for Young Ladies and excelled in academics. I was particularly interested in literature and history and have adequate ability with mathematics." Beth glanced toward the Homer sisters, then back at Owen. "I didn't know until today I would need a certificate, but I am certain I could pass the exam. I would like the opportunity to try, at least."

She had the prettiest voice he'd ever heard. He'd never thought much of British accents. Too highfalutin, as his mother would have put it. But Beth's voice was different. It enchanted him, made him wish she would continue speaking for hours.

"I promise you, I would be a good teacher."

"I'm sure you would, Miss Wellington, and we will be delighted to give you an opportunity to do so."

Patsy cleared her throat. "Perhaps we should meet with the other board members this afternoon and settle the matter."

Owen had the feeling Beth was holding her breath, but he knew she couldn't possibly want to get the job any more passionately than he wanted her to stay in New Prospects. "I agree. Miss Wellington, I'll make certain you have our answer before evening." He would also make certain the answer was a positive one.

Once again Patsy cleared her throat, more loudly this time. "I hate to bring up a matter of such a delicate nature, but I feel I must. Surely Miss Wellington cannot mean to remain at Mr. Steele's ranch. A friend of the family she may be, but . . . Well, certainly you can see how it would look to folks hereabouts."

"Indeed," Bunny added with a note of urgency. "It would be highly improper for her to stay there any longer. Mr. Steele is alone, after all, except for little Janie." She clucked her tongue. "No, she can't stay there."

Owen knew Bunny Homer had designs of her own on the rancher, and that was the reason for her concern—especially given the loveliness of the Englishwoman. Still, he couldn't argue with the Homer sisters' logic.

"We have a spare room above the store." Patsy gave her head a firm nod. "Miss Wellington must stay with us."

"I am most grateful, Miss Homer, but I could not impose—" Beth began.

"Nonsense," Bunny interrupted sharply. "My sister is quite right. You're probably not aware of how we Americans do things, Miss Wellington, being a foreigner and all, but it's usual for the schoolmarm to board with one of the families with children. Since you have yet to be hired, it is too soon to ask for such privileges, and you certainly cannot stay with Mr. Steele until you have your certificate. He *is* an unmarried man, you know, and your stay would be unchaperoned. Even in England such a thing must be frowned upon."

I have a very large and beautiful home, Owen thought as he stared at Beth and envisioned her sitting in the front parlor, serving tea in his grandmother's best china.

"I had no intention of remaining at Mr. Steele's ranch," she said, interrupting his musing. "I wanted to ask about the Thompson place."

He frowned, puzzled. "The Thompson place?"

"I was told you own the property, Mr. Simpson. Is that correct?"

"Yes, I do, but—"

"I should like to rent it from you. I should like to live there. It's close to the school and would be ideal once I am teaching."

"But it's just a shack!" he protested.

"And you may not be the teacher," Patsy added hurriedly. "The board may not hire you, even if you do get your teaching certificate."

It was Patsy's comment that changed Owen's mind. "Tell you what, Miss Wellington. You stay with Miss Bunny and Miss Patsy for now. If the board's decision is to hire you—on the condition of that certificate, of course—I'll let you live in the old Thompson cabin, as long as it's sound. I won't charge you rent. It'll be my contribution to helping New Prospects obtain a teacher."

"That's very kind of you, Mr. Simpson."

"Not at all, Miss Wellington." He smiled as he imagined their future together. "Not at all."

3

Wednesday, June 2, 1897
New Prospects, Montana

My dear Mary,

I do so hope this letter finds you well, and
that by this time you have been reunited
with your Mr. Maguire. As for me, I
arrived safely in New Prospects, Montana,
two days hence. It is very different country
from England. I have traveled through
vast plains and over the highest of mountains to get here, and I should fail dismally
were I to attempt to describe it to you. It is
both terrifying and beautiful. A rugged
splendor, as it were. Certainly, this country is much larger than anything I dared
imagine when you and I first embarked on
our adventures together.

When I arrived in New Prospects, I was

dismayed to discover there were no appropriate lodgings available to me. I was forced to impose upon Janie's father for a place to stay that first night. It was most apparent Mr. Steele was not overjoyed with my company. Now, however, I am residing in a room above a shop in town, the New Prospects Mercantile, which is owned by two unmarried sisters by the name of Homer. Miss Bunny and Miss Patsy, they are often called. They have been kind to me, although I cannot say I think we shall ever become friends.

I truly desire a home of my own, and in truth, there is hope for just such a place, a small log cabin near the schoolhouse, which is a short distance outside of town. The cabin is owned by the mayor, and he seems willing to let me live in it, should the roof prove sound.

Many of the homes and buildings around New Prospects are made of logs, but in town, the buildings are framed and most are whitewashed. The streets are wide but dry and dusty, and I suspect they are nearly impassable when it rains. I suppose I shall find out soon enough.

Dear Mary, I am woefully ignorant and, at times, quite frightened by the strangeness of this place and these people. Their speech is often foreign to me, but with effort, I am learning to understand what different words mean.

Imagine my trepidation when I was told
I am required to have a teaching certificate
before the town can hire me. I do so wish
you were here with me, for you and our
dear friend Inga shored up my courage so
often during the weeks we were together.

But I should tell you about Janie Steele.
She is a delight and an even more precious
child than I had imagined from her letters.
She is a pretty little thing with pale red-
gold hair and blue eyes. She has made me
feel most welcome and less lonely. I am
enormously fond of her. As for her father,
as I already said, he allowed me to stay in
his home, even though it was apparent he
was not pleased to find this stranger at his
door. I believe he still suffers over the loss
of his wife, Janie's mother, for he does not
like to speak of her.

I shall spend the coming days studying
McGuffey's Readers, which were provided
to me by the mayor in preparation for the
certification exam. I shall have to travel to
the county seat to be tested. The parents
here are anxious for their children to be in
the classroom for the summer session,
which should have begun in May, so I
shall take the exam as soon as I am able.
Exam dates are set by the county superintendent of schools, and I have yet to ascer-
tain when the next one shall be. I am told
the exam takes all day and is quite gruel-
ing. If I should pass, my certificate shall

only be valid for one year, then I shall
need to be tested again.

I pray to God I shall pass, for I do not
know what I would do otherwise. There
does not seem to be much call in this
country for English gentlewomen who can
paint with watercolors or do needlepoint.
Perhaps I could learn to be a dressmaker if
I cannot teach.

But I shall not allow myself to think
upon failure. I am determined to obtain
my certificate and to teach. The more I am
around Janie, the more I realize teaching
children is my calling, not simply a means
of earning a living.

Have you heard from Inga? I have not
received letters from either of you, of
course. I miss you both a great deal. Please
write soon and let me know how you are
faring and how you have found your Mr.
Maguire.

With affection,
Your friend Beth Wellington

"This room's even smaller than my loft," Janie said of
the cramped attic quarters. "You shoulda stayed with
us at the ranch."

Beth shook her head. "I could not do so."

"Don't see why not," the girl muttered.

"It simply would not have been proper, Janie."

She glanced about the small room with its narrow

bed, the faded rag rug on the floor, the pitcher and bowl with chips in the edges, and the lifeless gray curtains at the window. It was true. There wasn't much to be said for this room. It lacked light and gay colors.

"But this is only temporary," she said aloud, both for Janie's sake and her own. "Just until Mr. Simpson has the cabin ready for me."

Her young friend picked up a book from the table beside the bed. "What're you readin' *McGuffey's* for?"

"I'm preparing to teach. These books are unfamiliar to me, and I must study them so I may be a good teacher when the time comes."

"Won't come soon enough for me."

Beth reached out and brushed a wisp of pale hair back from Janie's face. "But your letter said you liked studying at home. And I suspect your father is a good teacher."

Janie shrugged. "Good enough, I 'spose. But Pa expects too much sometimes."

Beth remembered one particular evening when she was about Janie's age. She envisioned her own father with clarity, younger and still handsome. He hadn't yet squandered his wealth and had been dressed to the nines, preparing to escort a duchess to some society ball. When he'd seen Beth standing in the doorway of her bedchamber, he'd given her a distracted pat on the head and told her to be a good girl. Then he'd left, and she hadn't seen him again for over a week. It was as if he'd been unable to bear the sight of his daughter, perhaps because she'd resembled the late countess. But that excuse hadn't made Beth any less lonely for her father's attentions.

Looking at Janie once again, Beth wondered what it would have been like to be cherished by her father. To have him care for her so much that he would sit with her at a work-worn kitchen table and teach her to read and to do her sums. Her heart ached for another chance to earn her father's love, but that chance had died with him.

Turning her back toward Janie, she blinked away wistful tears. "You didn't tell me what brought you to town," she said, managing to make her voice sound normal.

"Pa had t'bring the hired hand in t'see the doctor. Mr. Whitaker thinks somethin' might've been broke when his horse kicked him." Janie touched Beth's elbow. "You know how to ride, Miss Beth?"

Feeling once again composed, she glanced down at the girl. "Indeed I do. At one time, Langford House had one of the finest stables in the shire." She paused, remembering, then added, "My father dearly loved to foxhunt."

"Don't know nothin' about foxhuntin', but Pa and some of the other ranchers had to hunt down a grizzly a couple winters back."

"A grizzly?"

"You know. A bear. They're so big they can kill a man with just one swipe of their paw. Every so often, one of 'em wanders down outta the hills."

"Oh, my."

With a sudden change of topic, Janie asked, "How're you gettin' along with the Homers?" She rolled her eyes expressively. "Aren't they awful?"

"They have been most generous to me."

Janie wrinkled her nose. "Don't you trust 'em. You'll be sorry if you do."

"That's enough, Janie," Beth rebuked mildly.

"But—"

"You shouldn't talk so of your elders. These women were under no obligation to offer me a place to stay, and until I am employed, I have no means with which to compensate them. I shan't have you speaking ill of them when all they have shown me is kindness and hospitality."

Janie looked as if she might attempt further argument, then just as suddenly she grinned and grabbed Beth's hand. "Come on. I'll take you t'see Maybelle. She's just down the street a ways."

Beth allowed herself to be pulled along, out of her attic room and down the narrow back staircase, past the second-floor apartment of Bunny and Patsy Homer, and out the rear door in the mercantile's storage room, which opened into the alleyway. Once outside, Janie guided her to the boardwalk, then toward the doctor's office, where her bay-colored pony was tethered beside her father's wagon.

"Here she is," the girl said proudly. "This is Maybelle."

"Oh, she's a very fine pony, Janie."

Just then the door to the doctor's office opened, and Garret Steele stepped onto the boardwalk. He stopped when his eyes met with Beth's. As always, she felt his disapproval.

He gave a brief nod. "Miss Wellington."

It wasn't as if she cared whether or not he liked her. She wasn't a guest in his home any longer. She had the tentative approval of the school board to become the new teacher. The mayor had promised her a house in which to live. She had made a few acquaintances in town, and she couldn't love Janie more if she were her own little sister. She had no need of the man's approval or his esteem.

"Good day, Mr. Steele," she said, returning his nod.

"You settled in with the Homers?"

"Yes."

"Pa, you should see where they stuck her. Up in the attic in the ugliest little room. Wouldn't you think they could've—"

Beth stopped Janie's objections by laying a hand on her shoulder. "I quite like my room. It's very private, and I have a fine view of the mountains."

Garret wished he could put a stop to his daughter's obvious adoration for Beth Wellington, but he didn't know how to do it. As he stared at the two of them, the Englishwoman and Janie, he felt resentment churning in his gut.

What is it she wants here, anyway?

There was too much that didn't add up about Beth, he decided. At first he'd thought her simply an empty-headed female who had come to America on a whim. Now he wasn't so sure. But it still didn't make sense. She didn't belong here. She would never belong here. And he'd bet the ranch she wouldn't stay long enough to do more than cause trouble. Eventually she would tire of the hardship of this life, and she would go back to where she came from, back where she belonged. Or she would find herself a rich American to marry, someone who could give her the

life of ease to which she was accustomed. Which
would suit Garret just fine. It would mean she'd be
gone from here, she and her influence with Janie.

Beth leaned down, bringing her head closer to
Janie's. "I should get back to my studies. Thank you
for showing me Maybelle."

"You gotta come out to the ranch sometime so I
can show you my colt, too," the girl responded. "He
doesn't got a name yet. Maybe you can help me think
of one."

Beth glanced up, her gaze meeting Garret's. "I
should like to do that, Janie," she replied softly, then
straightened. "Good day, Mr. Steele."

"Ma'am."

He watched her depart, noting how she seemed to
glide rather than walk. There was an elegance about
all of Beth Wellington's movements, about her voice,
about her appearance. No matter what she did, one
could always tell she was a lady.

Then he remembered the way she'd looked huddled in her nightgown, her eyes filled with terror.
What would cause a woman like Beth to be so
afraid?

He gave his head a shake. It didn't matter to him,
whatever it was. She wasn't his concern. And he'd be
hanged if he'd let her become his concern, either.

"Garret!"

He turned around to see Owen Simpson hurrying
toward him along the boardwalk.

"Didn't expect to see you back in town again so
soon," the mayor said as he came to a halt a few steps
away.

"Neither did I." Garret jerked his head toward the

doctor's office. "Jake thought maybe he'd busted his leg, but looks like he got lucky."

"Glad to hear it. Listen, I've got a favor to ask of you. I just received a telegram from the superintendent down in Bozeman. They're holding an examination for teaching certificates next Wednesday. I need someone to take Miss Wellington down there for the day. I'd do it myself, but I'll be in Billings on business. I thought, since you're her friend . . . "

She's no friend of mine, he wanted to answer. But he couldn't. Especially not with Janie standing beside him, listening to every word. Instead he said, "It's a busy time of year for me, Owen."

"I know, and I wouldn't ask, but you know how badly we need a new schoolteacher. I thought she'd be more comfortable with you than with someone she doesn't know. I'd ask Miss Patsy and Miss Bunny, but that's a long trip for three unescorted ladies to take."

He wanted to refuse, but he couldn't seem to find the right reason.

"Listen, Garret. I'd never forgive myself if something were to happen to Miss Wellington. I'd consider it a personal favor if you'd do this." His voice lowered a notch. "I'm not about to let her leave New Prospects."

Owen's words caught Garret completely by surprise. He'd never known his friend to give much notice to a piece of calico before. Was it possible . . . No, surely not. Owen was a confirmed bachelor. Garret had known him for years now, and the banker had only two interests—making a success of his bank and helping New Prospects grow and prosper.

The mayor grinned. "You're the only man I'd trust to take her down there, spend all that time on the road with her. Anybody else but you might have ideas of his own."

"You tellin' me you got designs on Miss Wellington?"

"That I do."

"Well, I'll be."

"So you'll do it?" Owen persisted. "You'll see she gets down to Bozeman and back?"

Garret removed his hat and raked his fingers through his hair. "Guess I will, if it's that important to you."

"It is. I assure you."

Watching Beth Wellington's approach through a front window of the mercantile, Bunny Homer pressed her lips together and clenched her hands at her waist. Bitterness twisted her stomach into a giant knot. It wasn't fair, she thought as she studied the woman's flawless beauty.

Ever since his wife died—actually long before— Bunny had been waiting for Garret Steele to notice her, but he would never do so with *that woman* in town. Somehow, some way, she had to get rid of Beth Wellington.

"This is all Owen Simpson's fault," she said as she tossed an angry glare at her sister.

Patsy sniffed indignantly. "Owen was only looking out for the children of this community."

"Hogwash! He's smitten with her, and any fool could see it." She said it just to be cruel. After all,

Patsy had been pining after the banker almost as long as Bunny had for Garret and with much less success, in Bunny's opinion, since Owen hadn't been encumbered with a wife.

Patsy met Bunny's gaze. "Perhaps we should decide what exactly we're going to do about it instead of standing here arguing."

"She seems determined to stay. Do you suppose it's simply because she hasn't anywhere else to go?"

"I don't know. She's terribly fond of Janie Steele."

"That dreadful child," Bunny muttered.

Thoughtfully Patsy tapped her index finger against her chin. "There must be some way."

Bunny watched Beth turn down the alley leading to the back entrance of the building. *You're not going to spoil my chances, Miss High and Mighty. I'm not letting Garret slip away from me again.*

Bunny Homer had been just eighteen years old the first time she'd seen Garret, when he had come into her father's general store in Bozeman to buy some supplies. She hadn't known who he was or where he was from, but she'd decided she'd do anything to be his wife. He hadn't noticed her, of course. No man ever had.

A few years later, after his business failed, Clarence Homer had moved his wife and two unmarried daughters to New Prospects and started up the mercantile. Bunny would never forget the day Garret had walked into that new store. She'd nearly dropped to her knees right there and thanked God for her father's financial troubles, for bringing them to that small nothing of a town. And then Muriel Steele had followed her husband into the store, destroying Bunny's hope.

Well, no one was going to take away that hope again, she thought with determination. Especially not some Englishwoman who didn't belong here. She didn't care how beautiful Beth Wellington was. Garret was going to be hers. He was *meant* to be hers.

"Maybe we can make her *want* to leave," she said, more to herself than to her sister, "but it has to be done carefully." She glanced at Patsy. "Very carefully."

Beth had just sat down for supper with Bunny and Patsy when a knock sounded at the door. Patsy went to answer it.

"I hope I haven't come at an inopportune time, Miss Homer," Owen Simpson said from beyond the door, "but I was looking for Miss Wellington."

"She's here with us, Mr. Simpson. We were just about to have our evening repast. Would you care to join us?"

"No, thank you very much. But if I might have a word with Miss Wellington?"

There was a pause, then Patsy answered, "Of course. Do come in."

Beth rose from her chair as Owen entered the room, hat in hand. He nodded first toward Bunny, then met Beth's gaze.

"Good evening, Miss Wellington. I'm sorry to disturb your supper. Might I have a moment of your time?"

Beth hesitated, feeling uncertain, afraid of what might have brought him here to speak to her. Then, knowing she couldn't avoid it, she walked over to where Owen was standing.

"I have news of the next certification exam," he told her in a low voice.

Her pulse quickened. "Already? But that's wonderful. When is it to be?"

"Next week. On Wednesday."

"Wednesday? But what if I am not ready so soon?"

Discreetly he touched the back of her hand with his fingertips. "I have every confidence in you."

At first the look in his hazel eyes was merely kind. Then, as the silence lengthened, she saw something else there—the special look of a man interested in a woman in a much more personal manner. She felt a jolt of panic as the image of Perceval flashed in her memory, as she remembered Perceval taking her hand and squeezing her fingers until she thought they might break.

And then the moment passed. The image vanished. She wasn't in England. She wasn't betrothed to Perceval or anyone else. Owen Simpson might be interested in her, but she was under no obligation to return his attentions unless she chose to do so. It was up to her.

He cleared his throat. "I have to go down to Billings on business next week, so I can't offer my services to get you to Bozeman, but Garret Steele has agreed to take you down and bring you back."

"Mr. Steele?" She couldn't have been more surprised if he'd told her Saint Nicholas was going to escort her to a Christmas ball.

"Yes. I thought you'd be more comfortable with an old family friend than a stranger."

She thought of the way Garret frowned whenever he looked at her. Old family friend? Not hardly. He tolerated her, at best. But perhaps she should think of this as an opportunity to change his opinion of her. Not that she cared for herself, one way or the other. But for Janie's sake . . .

"You'll need to go down on Tuesday and return on Thursday. Trip takes too long to do it all in one day. I've already taken the liberty of reserving a room for you and another for Mr. Steele in a respectable hotel for those nights."

Beth glanced over her shoulder at the two women waiting at the table. When she looked back at Owen, she dropped her voice almost to a whisper. "But I haven't enough money to pay for a hotel, Mr. Simpson."

"You needn't worry about that. The school board will advance you the money out of your first month's wages."

"But—"

"It's what we would do for any prospective teacher, Miss Wellington."

She was getting a headache. It was beginning to pound with a steady thud right behind her eyes. What if she failed to pass the exam? What would she do? Where would she go? And in addition to all those worries, she would have to spend hours upon hours in the company of a man who had disliked her on sight and who no doubt hoped she would fail and leave town.

"I'd best be on my way," Owen said, then offered her a warm, encouraging smile. "We'll talk again before I leave for Billings."

When he was gone, Beth turned to face her hostesses. In a shaky voice she said, "The certification exam is next week."

The sisters exchanged quick glances. "So soon?" Patsy said. "My, my."

"Shall we have our supper before it grows even more cold?" Bunny suggested as she waved her hand over the table.

Beth hurried to her chair. "I apologize."

"No need for that." Patsy folded her hands. "Sister?"

Bunny closed her eyes and bowed her head. The other women followed suit, listening as Bunny spoke a quick blessing over the meal. When Beth opened her eyes, she found both of the sisters watching her.

"Are you nervous about the exam?" After spooning an ample portion on her own plate, Patsy passed a platter of mashed potatoes to Beth.

"Quite."

"I'm sure you'll do fine." Bunny took a small helping of canned beets. "And how are you to get down to Bozeman?"

"Mr. Steele will escort me. Mr. Simpson has already made the arrangements."

Bunny dropped the serving spoon on the floor. As she bent to pick it up, she said, "Really? But my sister and I would have been happy to take you down in our carriage." She straightened. "Wouldn't we, Patsy?"

"Indeed."

"We insist," Bunny said firmly.

"That's very kind of you, Miss Homer."

"Not at all." Bunny smiled that odd, half-frozen

smile of hers. "We will talk to Mr. Simpson about it first thing tomorrow."

Patsy leaned forward, her expression serious. "I think there is something you should know about Mr. Steele. Far be it from me to carry gossip, but given your friendship with the Steele family, I feel it's my duty."

Beth's headache was growing worse.

"His wife, poor dear, once told me he was fond of the drink. And when he was drinking, he sometimes became . . . violent."

"It's true," Bunny chimed in. "Muriel told me so, too. She was a very unhappy woman because of it." She clucked her tongue and shook her head. "Such a shame. Such a shame."

Beth didn't know why, but she felt a strong urge to argue in Garret Steele's defense.

Patsy lifted the bread plate toward Beth. "I do hope you won't think we are just carrying tales. But it would be unfair of us not to warn you about him. You are, after all, a stranger in our midst and in need of guidance. I hope you will allow my sister and me to help you in whatever way we can."

4

The New Prospects Methodist Church stood at the corner of Main and Second. One of the first buildings erected after the founding of the town, it was filled each Sunday by the faithful of the community.

Garret and Janie arrived just as services were beginning and took their customary seats at the back of the small sanctuary. Reverend Hezekiah Matheson paused in his opening benediction just long enough to cause members of the congregation to crane their necks to see who had joined their midst at the last moment. Not that any of them were surprised to see it was the Steeles. It almost always was.

Garret scowled at Hezekiah, but all the minister did was smile before he resumed his blessing over that morning's service. No one enjoyed teasing others as much as Hezekiah Matheson, a practice Garret had told him more than once was inappropriate for a minister of the gospel. Hezekiah always laughed in response and never altered his ways.

After the benediction, the congregation rose for a song of worship, accompanied by Stella Matheson on the church organ. Singing in church was one of Garret's secret pleasures, and he joined in with gusto. He didn't pretend there was anything special about his voice, although he thought it was probably a step above the "joyful noise" Hezekiah talked about. But it wasn't how he sounded to himself or others that made him like the singing so much. It was the way it made him feel. As if there weren't any problems for him to worry over. It wasn't often he got to feel that way, so he enjoyed it while he could.

The congregation was well into the second verse of the hymn before Garret became aware of a different voice among them. A woman's voice of such crystalline perfection that he was forced to stop his own singing just to listen. The voice wasn't strong or loud, yet it seemed to rise above all the others.

Janie tugged on his hand. When he looked down, she whispered, "It's Miss Beth."

He nodded, knowing she was right.

"It's beautiful."

Again he nodded, for there was no denying the truth.

Garret heard little of the service after that point. Beth's singing stayed with him, echoing in his memory, touching him in some indescribable way. It was as if he'd discovered something important about Beth Wellington. But he was unable as yet to identify what that something was.

At the close of the service, Hezekiah introduced Beth to the members of the congregation. When she stood, as the minister bade her to do, a sudden and most unwelcome jolt of desire coursed through Garret. It would have been troublesome at any time. To feel it in church seemed a sacrilege. Reluctantly he admitted a man would have to be a saint not to respond to her rare comeliness.

And Garret was obviously no saint.

Silently he swore at himself. Was he a complete idiot? Hadn't he been down this road before? Hadn't he learned his lesson after all those years with Muriel?

Garret took hold of his daughter's hand and drew Janie outside, but before he could make a clean get-away, he was stopped by Owen Simpson.

"Good weather we're having, isn't it?" the mayor commented with a glance toward the clear blue sky. "Hope it holds for your trip down to Bozeman."

Garret muttered under his breath. He'd forgotten about his promise to take Beth to the county seat.

"Listen, Garret," Owen continued, mindless of his friend's inner turmoil, "I leave first thing tomorrow morning for Billings. I thought I should tell you the Homer sisters came to see me last Thursday. They tried to convince me it would be better if they took Miss Wellington down to Bozeman, but I disagreed. As I already told you, that's no trip for three unescorted females. I made it clear to them it was you who would see Miss Wellington there and back. I thought you should know, just in case they come to you after I've left town. You know how persistent Miss Bunny and Miss Patsy can be."

"Yeah, I know."

"I don't want to take a chance on losing our teacher before she's even begun. Truth be told, she's the only applicant we've had for the position. Not many willing to come to a town like ours, I guess, especially with the low salary we offer."

Damn! Garret had been hoping to convince Beth to leave New Prospects. Now he realized that if he did, the children would remain without a teacher. Who knew for how long?

Owen gave Garret a friendly slap on the back. "Well, I'm going back inside. I don't want to be the only one who doesn't welcome Miss Wellington to New Prospects." That said, he hurried into the church.

"Shouldn't we say hello to Miss Beth, too, Pa?"

"I don't reckon she needs to hear it from us."

"But—"

"Come on, Janie. If I'm gonna be gone the better part of three days this week, I'd best see to my chores while I can."

Beth was surprised by her keen disappointment when Garret and Janie slipped out the back of the church without so much as a by-your-leave. It shouldn't have mattered to her that he couldn't exhibit the most common of courtesies.

Yet it did matter.

In truth, Garret had been too much on Beth's mind for days. Perhaps it was due to what Patsy and Bunny had told her about his fondness for strong spirits and, according to the sisters, the violence that resulted. Beth knew firsthand what a dangerous combination alcohol and a mean temper could prove. Perceval had taught her that lesson well. She should have been relieved by Garret's disinterest in her.

Yet she wasn't relieved.

She'd told herself many times the only reason she thought of him at all was that he was Janie's father. Janie was the only friend she had within twelve hundred miles, so naturally she was concerned for the child's welfare.

Yet she didn't believe that was the only reason she thought about Garret Steele.

"Would you care to join me this afternoon, Miss Wellington?"

"I'm sorry." She was surprised to find Owen standing before her. "What was it you said, Mr. Simpson?"

"I was wondering if you'd like to ride out with me to the Thompson cabin. I thought you might like to see the inside of it before you decide for certain to live there. The roof is going to need some work, but otherwise, I'm told it's sound enough."

"But we're expecting Miss Wellington to dine with us," Patsy Homer interjected quickly.

"Then we'll go after she eats," Owen answered. "I don't mind waiting."

"Perhaps you would like to join us, Mr. Simpson?" Bunny asked. "We've a pot roast cooking even now."

Although he answered Bunny Homer, his smile was for Beth. "Thank you. I would like that very much."

It occurred to Beth that the mayor was actually a pleasant-looking gentleman. He was of average height and coloring, with a relaxed demeanor and a gentle voice. Other than a moment of anxiety when she'd first realized he was interested in her as a woman, Beth was quite comfortable in his presence. She liked him and hoped they could be friends, once he recognized she had no intention of ever becoming some man's chattel. She had left England to escape such a fate. She wasn't about to enter into it willingly here.

"Well," Patsy said in a stilted tone, "if our dinner is not to be ruined, we had better get home." Then, in a surprisingly agile movement for one of considerable bulk, she slipped in between Owen and Beth and placed her hand in the crook of Owen's arm. "Come along, Mr. Simpson. I trust you like potatoes and onions with your pot roast?" Then she drew him away before he could make a sound.

Nearly two hours later Owen was finally able to make his escape with Beth. For a while he'd wondered if he would be smothered by Patsy's attentions before he could leave. The woman was as subtle as a sledge-hammer—and about as heavy and unattractive.

Very unlike the beguiling creature riding beside him in his fringe-topped surrey. He glanced toward her now.

Beth was holding on to the brace of the canopy with her right hand as she stared across the grass-lands toward the rugged mountains in the distance. Just looking at her caused his stomach to tighten and his throat to go dry.

Was he crazy to think he might be able to win her affections? Probably, he answered himself, but he was sure as heck going to try.

"Mighty different from England, I imagine," he said into the silence.

After a moment, her pretty mouth curved into the tiniest of smiles. "It is indeed."

"Do you miss your homeland?"

She nodded. "Sometimes. But I am not sorry to have come to America."

"I'm not sorry you came, either." Owen felt himself coloring like a schoolboy and was relieved she wasn't looking at him. Nervously he cleared his throat. "Well, here we are," he said as the horse pulled past the schoolhouse and up to the cabin.

The old Thompson place looked even shabbier to him today. He couldn't imagine Beth staying in it for one night, let alone living here for any extended period. He wished he could convince her to give up the idea. Even better, he wished he dared ask her to marry him and live in his fine house in town. But he sensed it was too soon for that.

He got out of the surrey, then offered his hand and helped Beth to the ground.

"I've hired a man to work on the roof, but he said it would be a week or two before he could get to it." He opened the door and motioned for her to enter.

As she went in she asked, "What about the roof?"

"It leaks." He pointed toward the rough-hewn timbers set on log rafters that made up the roof. In a few places, a glimpse of blue sky could be seen. "I don't know what Thompson did when it rained. Probably set out buckets and just let it run."

Beth said nothing as she moved around the one-room cabin with its hard-packed dirt floor. There was a cast-iron stove for cooking and heating and two shuttered windows for letting in sunlight and fresh air in good weather. Nails hammered into the log walls served as the only clothes wardrobe. A rickety table in the center of the room looked as though it would topple over should it hold anything heavier than a teacup. Cobwebs filled the corners of the room, and mice droppings were in evidence wherever he looked.

"Miss Wellington, I really think you should give up this idea. I never should have agreed to—"

She whirled to face him. "You cannot withdraw your offer, Mr. Simpson."

"But this place isn't suitable for you."

"I shall make it suitable. It needs only some cleaning and a few pieces of furniture."

"But—"

"Please, Mr. Simpson. I'm asking you not to withdraw your offer."

"All right." He shook his head, regretting his acquiescence but unable to resist her plea. "It's against my better judgment, but if that's how you want it . . ." He let his voice trail into silence even while renewing his vow that she wouldn't live there for long. He would personally see to it.

Beth was grateful for Owen's reluctant agreement. She didn't want to argue with him. She knew she couldn't explain why it was so important to her to have her own place in which to live.

It certainly wasn't because she coveted this particular cabin for a home. She had never seen anything so stark and mean in her lifetime. Even the servants at Langford House had better accommodations than this. Nor was it because she thought it better than the attic room the Homer sisters had provided for her. It wasn't, not by any stretch of the imagination. She would only have been able to tell him this was where she *needed* to be, and even she found that a weak explanation.

"May I see the schoolhouse now?" she asked before Owen could revive his argument.

He remained silent a few heartbeats, then answered, "Of course. Come with me." He took hold of her arm as they stepped outside. "Folks in New Prospects are rather proud of their school," he said conversationally as they walked across the expanse of bare ground.

The one-room, wood-framed building had a shingled, gabled roof with a vestibule added onto the front entrance. Banks of three windows lined both the east and west sides of the rectangular schoolhouse, and a stovepipe chimney was visible at the north end.

"You're probably wondering why the school is out here instead of in town." Without waiting for her reply, Owen continued, "New Prospects got its start from two men who brought their families into the area with them. Jacob Smith and Robert Blackburn by name. They established a supply depot for the miners up north—it's the mercantile now—and pretty soon, other settlers followed. Blackburn, who'd built his home out on this parcel of land, wanted the town to move this direction, so this is where he built the school. But he dropped dead of a heart attack right after the school opened, and his widow moved back to Ohio with their children. The town of New Prospects remained where it began. Only no one wanted to see this schoolhouse go to waste, so here it stayed."

Beth glanced over her shoulder at the rickety cabin. "Was *that* the Blackburn house?"

"No, that wasn't it. The house burned down back in about eighty-six. Thompson built his cabin on the old site. Mrs. Blackburn was his sister, and she deeded the land over to him, except for the school-house, which she gave to the town."

Eighteen eighty-six. Only eleven years ago. Such a brief time, really. By comparison, the nearest village to Langford House was hundreds of years old and inhabited by direct descendants of those who had first peopled it. The villagers lived in the same cottages their ancestors had built. Even their sheep and cattle and chickens were the offspring of the animals their ancestors had kept. There was something comforting about such a long history.

Yet the newness of this land made it seem fresh, exciting, and full of promise. It was rugged and untamed, full of potential, waiting to be shaped by those who settled it. Beth felt a quickening in her heart. She was here soon enough to become a part of Montana's history. Nothing was guaranteed. Nothing was done as it had always been done. There were no traditions one had to follow.

She tried to imagine what her father would think of this place but couldn't. The earl had been a man steeped in convention. He would never have considered leaving Langford House.

"Come on." Owen stepped forward, drawing her with him. "Let's go inside."

They climbed the five steps leading to the front door. A key was hidden behind a loose board near the door casing. Owen retrieved it and unlocked, then opened, the door.

The small vestibule, Beth suspected, served both as a buffer against the frigid winds of a Montana winter and as a cloakroom for coats, mittens, and lunch pails. Beyond this entry area was the main room of the schoolhouse. Beth felt her heart skip a beat as she stepped into the doorway and saw the neat rows of desks facing the front of the classroom.

My classroom, she thought with a mixture of excitement and trepidation.

A large Windsor wood stove stood just to the left of the teacher's desk. Blackboards, wiped clean, filled the majority of the north wall. On the east wall was an enormous map of North America, and an American flag hung from a pole in the nearby corner. Window shades were drawn on the west side of the building, shutting out the glare of afternoon sunlight.

Speaking more to herself than to Owen, she said, "When I was growing up, I never thought to do anything of value with my life." She stepped toward the center of the room. "I was expected to marry well. That was all."

"Is marriage of such little value?"

She glanced over her shoulder. "No. Not for most women."

"And for you?"

Beth looked away. She ran her fingertips over the marred surface of the nearest desk, stirring up the dust that had settled there in the many weeks the school had been closed.

"I'm not certain," she answered at last. "I only know I didn't wish to marry a man my father had chosen for me simply because it was expected."

"Miss Wellington?"

She turned with a gasp, startled by his unexpected nearness. She hadn't heard him cross the room to stand behind her.

"Why did you come to America?"

"For many reasons."

"I hope you'll come to trust me with those reasons," he said softly, his gaze searching hers.

Owen Simpson seemed kind and gentle, and Beth felt unthreatened in his presence. She suspected he was intelligent, and she knew he was successful at his own business. He was handsome without being a dandy. Perhaps she could learn to trust him.

But when she thought of Owen, her heart didn't skip a beat the way it did when she thought of Garret Steele. Garret was unlike any man she'd known before—rougher, more unrefined, less educated. A man strong enough to snap a lesser person in two. A man of frowns and dark moods. A man who still mourned the death of his wife and who cherished his daughter. A complex man, she suspected, and one who did not encourage her friendship or her trust.

"What is it you're thinking?" Owen asked softly.

She blinked, chagrined by her wandering thoughts. "I'm sorry. I didn't mean to ignore you."

"I can see I'm not going to get any answers today." He took hold of her elbow. "I think I'd best get you back to town now. We've probably given folks enough to gossip about for one afternoon."

"But we have done nothing," she protested.

He laughed more loudly. "That's one thing you'll have to learn about small towns, Miss Wellington. You don't have to do much to get folks talking."

5

Tuesday, June 8, 1897
New Prospects, Montana

Dearest Inga,

What a delightful surprise it was to receive
a letter from you yesterday and to learn of
your safe arrival in Uppsala, Iowa. The
parsonage sounds wonderful, and I am
certain the people of your new town will
quickly grow to respect and admire their
new pastor, just as I did. Please give your
father my best regards.

I posted letters to both you and Mary
last Wednesday. Perhaps you are reading
yours even as I write this. I hope so.

It is early morning. I could scarcely sleep
a wink last night for worry and excitement. I am traveling again today, back to
Bozeman, Montana, where tomorrow I

shall take the examination for teachers. I feel ill equipped. Everything I learned at the Hanford Society's School for Young Ladies seems to have fled right out of my mind, leaving behind nothing of real value.

I often struggle to understand the simplest phrases of my new neighbors. What English meant in England is often not the same here in Montana. You are fortunate to have moved into a community where many of your neighbors are from your native land.

Janie and her father are accompanying me to Bozeman. I suspect Mr. Steele is less than pleased to have this responsibility thrust upon him. I am also quite certain he only agreed to the mayor's request to escort me out of an obligation to the children of the community and especially for Janie. Mr. Steele loves his daughter a great deal, and that love is apparent in everything he does. Only with her have I seen him smile a true smile. He is a darkly handsome man, given to scowls, but he noticeably brightens when he is with his daughter.

I made the acquaintance of a number of people following church services on Sunday. I particularly liked the minister's wife, Stella Matheson. She seems most pleasant. Perhaps I shall find myself with another friend. But, oh, how I do miss you and Mary. There are times I think I can hear your voices, times when I can still feel the swell of the deck beneath my feet, and I expect to turn and see you standing nearby.

I must close and prepare for the day. Do extend my affections to your parents and sisters. The next time I write, I hope I shall be sharing the good news of my success in Bozeman.

Fondly,
Beth Wellington

Garret wasn't looking forward to the trip to Bozeman, but Janie was. Once he'd told her she could go along, she couldn't stop talking about it. Or about Miss Beth. He figured that was why he thought of the Englishwoman so often between the church service on Sunday and the moment he drove his rig up to the front of the mercantile on Tuesday morning.

It had happened to him at odd times during the last two days. All of a sudden, he would imagine he could hear her singing. Or he would wonder if her lips tasted as sweet as they looked. Or he envisioned her lying in bed beneath him.

And it was the last of these images that haunted him the most. He'd done just fine without a woman for a long time. He'd learned a man could curb his baser urges if he wanted to. And he'd wanted to. Even Muriel had posed no temptation in those last years before she died.

He swore as he rubbed a hand across his face, as if to erase the bitter memory of his wife from his mind. "Go tell Miss Wellington we're here," he told his daughter in a gruff voice.

"Sure, Pa." She jumped down from the wagon and ran around the corner of the store.

Janie had been gone only a minute when the front door of the mercantile opened and Bunny Homer stepped onto the boardwalk.

"Why, Mr. Steele, I didn't know you were out here."

It was a bald-faced lie, and he knew it. He wasn't anybody's fool. He knew Bunny figured he needed a wife and had decided she was the perfect female for the job. She'd set her cap for him when Muriel was hardly cold in her grave. Bunny was wrong, of course. The last thing in the world Garret needed was a wife. Although if he had any hankering for one, she would probably be just the sort he'd consider. Bunny Homer was about as attractive as a scarecrow in a corn-field—tall and skinny, with a face as long as a horse and a toothy smile that grated on his nerves, as did her gossiping, meddling ways. A husband wouldn't have to worry about her running off with some other man. Nobody'd want her.

Bunny drew closer to the wagon. "Is this the day you're taking Miss Wellington to Bozeman?" She tried to sound as if she didn't dang well know the answer.

"Yeah." He hoped Janie and Beth would hurry.

"My sister and I offered to take her, you know. I think it was tremendously unfair of Mr. Simpson to impose on you this way."

He tilted his head back, squinting up at the sun. "Well, I suppose it doesn't hurt to get away with Janie for a day or two. She's lookin' forward to the trip."

"You do dote on that child." There was a disapproving edge in Bunny's brief reply.

Garret glanced back at the woman, catching a glimpse of something akin to anger before she altered her expression to one of simpering flirtation.

If she had any idea how ridiculous she looked . . .

"What she needs is a woman's firm hand, Mr. Steele. Fathers are often too lenient with their daughters. You don't want Janie to grow up wild."

Before he could give Bunny Homer a piece of his mind, Janie and Beth appeared, hand in hand.

"We're ready, Pa! Look. Doesn't Miss Beth look pretty?"

"She sure does," he answered before he could stop himself.

She was wearing a green-and-white-striped confection with enormous puffed sleeves, a high collar, and a narrow waist. A dainty straw hat, trimmed with flowers and a tuft of ostrich feathers, nestled in her auburn hair. In her hand she carried a closed silk parasol.

A splash of color brightened Beth's cheeks, and Garret realized he was staring at her with open admiration.

Hell's bells!

Setting his jaw, he got down from his seat and helped first Beth, then Janie, into the wagon. When he regained his place, leather reins in hand, he looked toward Bunny Homer, who had watched the entire process from the boardwalk. Her mouth looked as if she'd been sucking on a lemon.

"I'll have Miss Wellington back on Thursday," he told her, giving his hat brim a small tug. Then he slapped the reins against the team's rumps. "Giddup there."

As the horses set off down Main Street, Beth opened her parasol and leaned the rod against her shoulder. "I appreciate this, Mr. Steele."

She sat a bit stiffly on the seat beside him, her eyes locked on some distant point ahead of them. The edges of her parasol fluttered in the breeze, causing shadows to dance across her cheek. He didn't know how she did it, but she seemed to get prettier every time he looked at her.

She glanced at him, held his gaze. She didn't speak, and neither did he. For just an instant he felt something much stronger than physical desire tugging at his heart.

Luckily Janie chose just that moment to begin telling Beth about the new puppies that had been born the night before. Garret turned his attention back to the road and shoved the unwelcome feelings away, unrecognized and unacknowledged.

Beth was thankful for Janie's presence on the journey. Given how silent and sullen Garret Steele always seemed to be, she knew it would have been a miserable day without the child's light and easy chatter.

They'd been on the road perhaps an hour or so when Janie asked Beth to tell her about England.

"What would you like to know?" She glanced over her shoulder.

Janie was kneeling on the wagon bed, her arms folded on the back of the seat. She looked up at Beth with sparkling blue eyes. "Everything. Tell me about Langford House first."

"Langford House," Beth repeated softly. It seemed like years rather than months since she'd seen her ancestral home.

"Yeah. What's it like?"

Surprised by unexpected homesickness, she was unable to answer for a few moments. When she did, her voice sounded strained. "The house was built in sixteen eighty by the first earl of Langford. It's small by comparison with many English country estates, but I always thought it more comfortable and less drafty that way. Certainly we required fewer servants to care for it."

A good thing, too, Beth thought. In the years before her father's death, the house staff had dwindled to only two—Mrs. Crumb, the housekeeper, and Mary Malone, the maid.

"The house is made of stone and has three stories. The main hall on the first floor was where my parents entertained when I was little. My mother held the grandest soirees."

"What's a soiree?"

"A party. With music and dancing." Beth remembered hiding in the shrubbery outside the hall one night when she was five or six years old, watching as the dancers twirled around and around while the musicians played. By the time she was a young woman, there had been no more soirees at Langford House.

"Go on," Janie urged. "Tell me more."

She sighed, shaking off memories of those happier times, then continued, "The second and third floors of the house hold the family apartments and bed-chambers for guests. The servants' quarters are in the basement. The kitchen is in one of the pavilions." Anticipating Janie's question, she explained, "A pavilion is a small building connected to another. The other pavilion holds the chapel."

"A chapel? You mean you've got your own *church?*"

Beth smiled wistfully. "Well, it isn't as big as a church, but in its day, it was quite beautiful. I always found it a comforting place to be. So still and serene. I spent many an hour there when my father was ill and again in the days after he died."

A lengthy silence followed.

"It must have been hard to leave it," Garret commented.

She was surprised to hear his voice instead of Janie's. "Yes, it was difficult. But as I told you, I had no choice. I had no wish to be a burden on some distant relative. And if I had stayed in England, I would have been forced to marry Lord Altberry. I could not do that. I . . . I did not love him."

"Then why were you gonna marry him in the first place?" Janie inquired in her usual blunt style.

"Because my father wished it. In England, that is the way it's done. Lord Altberry was a wealthy man, and my father needed the marriage settlement he offered for me. After Father died, I realized I needn't go through with the marriage if I could find some means to make a living. I thought I would go into service as a governess or a nanny. Then Mary told me she was coming to America and invited me to join her. It seemed the perfect solution. I was educated and believed I could be a teacher. In England, I would have been pitied for my change in social status, but not here. Here I had hopes of making a fresh start."

"And that's when you decided to come to New Prospects to be my teacher," Janie finished for her.

She was warmed by the girl's earnest smile. "Yes, that was when I decided to come here. I remembered your letter about losing the schoolteacher. I was certain I would be a good teacher, and I . . ." Her voice fell to a whisper. "I was in need of a friend in my new country. I knew I had one here."

Janie frowned. "But what happened to your friend Mary?"

"She came to America to join her intended. She stayed in New York City to await Mr. Maguire's arrival. I expect she is quite happily wed by now, although I have yet to hear from her."

Janie stood up and impulsively kissed Beth's cheek. "Well, I'm glad you're gonna be my teacher, and I'm always gonna be your friend."

"Thank you, Janie," she whispered.

"Pa's gonna be your friend, too. Aren't you, Pa?"

Without looking at Beth, he answered curtly, "Sure."

Bozeman, Montana, the county seat, is located in the fertile Gallatin Valley in the midst of the Rocky Mountains. It was named for the frontiersman John M. Bozeman, and because of its proximity to Yellowstone National Park, many adventurous visitors passed through the town on their way to the park, most of them arriving on the Northern Pacific Railroad. Every fall, cattle from the Steele ranch, as well as from other ranches in the valley, were driven to Bozeman for shipment to points east. Thus Garret was familiar with the town and drove straight to the hotel where they were to stay for the next two nights.

After signing the register, Garret paid for their rooms from the money Owen had sent with him, courtesy of the New Prospects School Board. Then he handed one key to his daughter and the other to Beth. "You two get settled while I see to the horses. Then we'll get something to eat." Stepping outside, he paused and took a deep breath of air. It had been a long day, made more so by Beth's close proximity.

He'd made up his mind when he'd first set eyes on Lady Elizabeth Wellington—actually, long before he'd first seen her—that he didn't like her. She was exactly the sort of woman he wanted to avoid. She was the daughter of privilege, a woman of society. In addition, she was exceptionally beautiful. Both were good reasons in his book for disliking her.

Only, as much as he wanted to, he didn't dislike her. Instead she made his blood run hotter than it had in years, made him feel randier than a cowpoke fresh off the Chisholm Trail after a long drive.

He gave his head a slow shake, wishing he could shake Beth from his thoughts. He'd already thought on her too much as it was. Listening today as she patiently answered Janie's questions had told him far more about her than he'd wanted to know. Perhaps he'd learned even more from the things that had gone unsaid.

With a sigh he climbed into the wagon, then drove the team toward the livery at the edge of town. Tommy Summers, the owner's teenage son, helped unharness the horses.

"Give them a good rubdown, will you, Tommy?" Garret requested as he tossed the youth a coin.

"Sure thing, Mr. Steele." The boy stuck the money in his pocket. "I'll git right to it."

Garret strode out of the barn and started walking back to the hotel. When he reached the Rusty Bucket Saloon, he hesitated a moment, wondering if a drink might help wash Beth Wellington from his mind. But he thought better of it. A clear head would serve him better. In his younger days he'd tried drowning his anger, frustration, and disappointment in whiskey. He'd discovered soon enough that an alcohol haze didn't make the problems go away. It hadn't helped any back then when he was trying to forget Muriel. It wouldn't help him forget Beth now.

Wait just a dang minute! What was he thinking? Beth was nothing to him but a troublesome influence on his daughter. That was all. She was a stranger, come from England, with plans to teach school in New Prospects. Other than doing this favor for Owen, Garret didn't plan to have anything more to do with the woman.

He cursed as he hurried on toward the hotel. He'd be hanged if he would fall prey to Beth's pretty charms or the sadness that appeared every so often in her eyes. He'd be better off to take advantage of one of the whores out at Mad Maddie's place, get the wanting out of his system. Maybe Jake was right. Maybe doing without a woman as long as Garret had wasn't natural. Maybe all he needed was a tumble beneath the sheets, and then he could start thinking straight again.

Heck, yes. That was just what he was gonna do. Visit Mad Maddie's. Right after Janie was asleep, he'd slip out of the hotel and take himself down to the other side of town, where the madam's two-story house was set out of sight of the respectable citizens of Bozeman.

Beth had just finished changing her travel-dusty dress and smoothing her hair when a knock sounded at the door of her hotel room. Assuming it was Janie, she opened it without hesitation. But instead of the young girl, she found a uniformed porter holding a large bouquet of hothouse flowers.

"Miss Wellington?"

"Yes."

"These are for you, miss." He held out the flowers, stiff elbowed, his face growing red as he stared at her. "There's a card, too. Stuck in the top there."

She took hold of the vase. "Thank you." She backed into the room and closed the door, then set the bouquet on the table. Flowery scents perfumed the air as she reached for the card and opened it.

My thoughts are with you as you take the exam. You'll do wonderfully well. I haven't any doubt. Owen Simpson.

She lifted a sprig of forget-me-nots and held the sky blue petals up to her cheek. It was thoughtful of

Owen to do this, she told herself, yet she couldn't deny she'd entertained the briefest of hopes that the flowers were from Garret Steele.

But how foolish could she be? Garret would rather be anywhere than with her. Everything about his manner when they were together told her so. He tolerated her only because of Janie.

"I wonder what Muriel was like," she whispered as she returned the forget-me-nots to the vase. "What made him love her so?"

As she glanced up, she caught sight of her reflection in the looking glass above the dresser. The face staring back at her bore more than a slight similarity to the small portrait of her mother, which the earl had carried in his pocket watch until his death. Now she carried both watch and portrait in her reticule, reminders of the happy years of Beth's childhood when Anne Wellington had still been alive.

The countess had been born a commoner—Anne Morgan, daughter of a country vicar—but she had also been what was known in her day as a diamond of the first water. Beth had heard the story over and over again as she grew up, perhaps because her resemblance to her mother caused others to remember Anne. She'd been told how the young earl was smitten when he'd seen her mother picking wildflowers in a country meadow as he was racing his four-in-hand along a deserted stretch of road. After only a year, by sheer perseverance, he had overcome the objections of his own father and the vicar and had married Anne. And they had been happy, the earl and his commoner countess.

Even society had eventually fallen under Anne's charming spell.

Was it any wonder Beth had believed in true love, that she had expected to one day fall head over heels for her own Prince Charming and be carried away to some magical castle in a distant kingdom? Except those childhood dreams had been eroded by time and stark reality.

Beth turned from the mirror, wondering at the strange meanderings of her thoughts. One would think she still had hopes for finding that prince.

Pure and simple nonsense. She had no such illusions about men. There were no princes. Even her own father—whom she'd loved a great deal—had not been who she'd once thought him to be.

"I should be thinking about the exam," she scolded herself as she pulled on her gloves. "This is no time for preoccupation with things of the past." Stiffening her spine, she opened the door and left her room.

Once downstairs, she paused in the doorway to the hotel restaurant. The dining room was filled to capacity, and multiple conversations combined into a general din. She searched the crowd for Janie and her father but couldn't find them.

Then, just as she was about to give up and turn away, she saw Garret rise from his chair beside a table in the far corner. He looked so amazingly virile and handsome, his dark hair washed and combed back from his face. Her heart gave a little leap, and instinctively she lifted her hand to wave at him.

He means nothing to me, she reminded herself as

she followed a path between the tables, making her way toward where Garret and his daughter were waiting. Nothing at all.

She could only pray it was true.

6

Garret leaned back in his chair, arms folded across his chest, and watched as his daughter consumed the ice cream in a glass bowl, enjoying watching her almost as much as she was enjoying the rare treat. By the time Janie finished, she had a creamy mustache across her upper lip and a smudge of chocolate syrup on her chin.

"You shoulda had some, Pa," she said as her spoon clattered into the empty bowl. "It was good."

"That's all right. You had enough for both of us." He held out a napkin. "Here. Wipe your face."

After a quick rub the mustache was gone, but the chocolate was still in evidence. "How d'ya think Miss Beth is doing on that exam?"

"Don't know." He moistened the napkin in his water glass, then rubbed her chin with it. "I expect she's doin' well enough."

"It'd be awful if she wasn't gonna be my teacher."

He frowned. "We've done right enough so far."

"Oh, Pa," she said, her tone exasperated. "It ain't the same and you know it."

He rose from his chair, eager to change the subject. "Come on. I want to have a look at some horses while we're here. No point wastin' the trip."

As they walked through town, Garret's thoughts stayed stubbornly on the Englishwoman. He'd tried just about everything to rid her from his mind. Everything except visit Mad Maddie's. For some reason, after they'd had supper last night, he just hadn't been able to bring himself to go there.

Maybe it was because of the way Beth had smiled at Janie while listening intently to the child's bright chatter. It made his chest tighten just remembering it. Janie's mother hadn't hardly ever smiled at her, let alone listened to her that way. Muriel had been too concerned with her own wants and needs to care about those of her daughter.

He glanced toward the county courthouse. Beth would be about halfway through the test by now. Was she doing okay? She'd looked mighty nervous when he'd seen her this morning. Nervous and lovely. He'd offered to walk her to the courthouse—because Owen had asked him to—but she'd declined. She'd said she would be fine on her own.

I was in need of a friend in my new country. He could still hear the sad tone of Beth's voice as she'd whispered those words to Janie yesterday. He could understand that. Everybody needed a friend now and then. If all she really wanted was to teach and take care of herself . . .

But who was he kidding? A beautiful woman like Beth Wellington wouldn't long be satisfied with a log cabin for a home and the hard day-to-day routine of life out west. She would soon enough be setting her cap for some man to rescue her.

And if she did, what would it matter to him?

Nothing—except Janie would be hurt when Beth went away, and he was darned tired of seeing Janie hurt.

"Pa?"

"Hmm?"

"You're squeezin' my hand."

He glanced down at his daughter. "Sorry." He loosened his grip. "What d'ya say we buy you a new dress while we're here?"

"A new dress?" She looked at him as if he'd lost his mind. "I don't need a new dress."

"You'll need one when you go back to school."

"I'd rather git me a new pair of stirrups."

Garret smiled. "Maybe we'll do both."

She grunted. "Can't afford both," she said, sounding like the adult. She was right, too, but that didn't make the truth any more palatable.

He thought of his wife again. Thought of the way Muriel had thrown his failures in his face. Thought of how she'd accused him of never buying her anything new, accused him of being petty and stingy. She'd always wanted more than he'd been able to give, no matter how hard he'd tried to please her. Would Janie one day look at him in the same way? Would she one day be eager to leave the ranch and get as far away from him as possible, just like her mother?

"Come on. We'll see if the hardware store's got some stirrups for that saddle of yours. And then we'll buy you that new dress, too."

* * *

Beth's footsteps were joyously light as she emerged from the courthouse. For the first time in weeks, she felt carefree and unafraid. She paused for a moment on the top step, turning her face toward the sky and breathing a brief, "Thank you."

Then she turned toward the hotel. She knew Janie would be eagerly awaiting news, and now that she felt optimistic about the results, she was just as eager to share the news. She wondered how Mr. Steele would feel if she succeeded.

Her heart skittered. It shouldn't matter, she told herself.

But it did matter. Far more than she wanted it to.

"Miss Beth! Miss Beth!"

She turned toward the sound of Janie's excited cry and watched the child dart across the street.

"How'd you do? Are you gonna be my teacher for sure now?"

"I won't know until tomorrow morning, but I hope so."

Janie hugged Beth. "I'm so glad."

Beth slid her hand over the child's silky hair. It took her somewhat by surprise, how warmed she felt by Janie's show of affection. "As am I."

"You hungry?" Garret asked as he joined them. "Janie and I were on our way to have an early supper. You can join us if you'd like."

Her stomach felt odd, although she didn't think it was from hunger. Still, she nodded. "Thank you, Mr. Steele. I would like to join you."

Janie took hold of her hand. "You'll never guess

what we did while you were takin' the exam. Pa bought a couple of mares, and I got some new stirrups for my saddle." She wrinkled her nose. "I even got a new dress t'wear t'school and another for church."

"I'm sure they are quite lovely dresses."

"Oh, they're okay, I guess," the child replied as they started walking, "but I don't see why girls can't wear trousers to school like the boys. It's right hard to play baseball in skirts."

"Baseball?"

"You know. The game."

Beth shook her head. "No, I'm afraid I don't know."

"You mean they don't play baseball in England?" Janie's eyes were wide with disbelief. "Can you believe that, Pa? They don't play baseball in England."

Garret seemed amused by his daughter's incredulous tone. Or perhaps it was Beth's confusion that caused him amusement. "Baseball is a bit like your cricket," he explained as if he were speaking to a child.

"Oh." She'd never seen cricket played, either, but at least she'd heard of it.

"Well, you're gonna have t'learn," Janie continued. "You might have t'be the umpire sometimes at recess."

Beth caught the glimpse of a challenge in Garret's eyes before he looked away. It made her all the more determined to succeed. "Then you must teach me," she told Janie. "As soon as we get back to New Prospects, you shall teach me how to play baseball."

I'll show you, Mr. Steele. I will be the best teacher the children of New Prospects ever had. I don't know why you want me to fail, but I'm not going to.

Bunny Homer peered at the clock on the top shelf, then checked the watch pinned to her bodice. Both of them told her it would be another thirty minutes before she could close the store for the night. It wouldn't come any too soon. This day had been interminably long.

No matter how hard she'd tried, she had been unable to rid her mind of thoughts of Garret Steele and Beth Wellington together in Bozeman. Heaven only knew what might have happened between them while they were there! One couldn't trust a foreigner to behave in a proper manner. For all she knew, Beth had shared a room with Garret. Her cheeks grew hot just thinking about the possibilities.

And then there was that dreadful child of his. Janie was besotted by the Englishwoman. If not for the girl, it might have been easy to drive a wedge between Garret and Beth, but as it was . . .

"There must be something I can do," she whispered to herself.

From the stairway at the back of the store, Patsy said, "There is."

Bunny gasped and whirled around. "Oh, good heavens! I didn't hear you come down. Whatever are you doing, lurking on the stairs?"

"I wasn't lurking, sister dear, and I couldn't help overhearing you, either. There is something we can do about Miss Wellington." She raised a pudgy hand.

"Don't bother to deny you were thinking about her. I know you too well."

"Can you say you've been thinking otherwise yourself?" Bunny retorted.

"No indeed. Miss Wellington has been much on my mind this day. And I think I've come up with the perfect solution to our dilemma. It is really so simple, I'm surprised we didn't think of it sooner. We brought Miss Wellington here simply to keep an eye on her, but we're missing a wonderful opportunity. We don't dare speak against her, not with Mr. Steele and Mr. Simpson so determined to hire her as the new schoolmarm. But she's a foreigner, Bunny. She doesn't know our ways. It's evident in so many things she says and does. All we need do is plant a few misconceptions about what is acceptable and she'll do the rest herself."

Bunny imagined the possibilities and then began to smile. "But of course. Oh, Patsy, it's brilliant." She grabbed her sister by the shoulders. "If we could make Miss Wellington look foolish, no one would want her teaching their children. Remember the look on her face when we told her Mr. Steele is a drinking man? She believed us and was alarmed. We could mislead her about others, too."

"Yes! There was that rumor about the reverend's wife and a bordello. No one else believed it, but Miss Wellington might. Can you imagine how she might behave toward Mrs. Matheson if she were to hear it?"

In a rare moment of genuine agreement, the sisters hugged.

When Patsy stepped away, she said, "I never cared much for Stella Matheson anyway. Too self-righteous,

in my opinion. It would serve her right to be ostra-
cized."

Bunny scarcely heard what her sister was saying as
her thoughts sped back to Garret Steele. He would
thank her one day for the trouble she was going to
now. He would thank her for rescuing him from that
foreigner. Men were too innocent of a beautiful
woman's wiles to recognize the danger they were in.
It was up to Bunny to make certain Garret didn't fall
prey to them a second time.

Garret wasn't sure how it happened, but during
dinner he found himself growing more relaxed
around Beth Wellington. Perhaps it was hearing her
tell, in answer to his daughter's persistent interro-
gation, about the ocean voyage from Southampton
to New York City, followed by the arduous trip
across country by rail. Or perhaps it was the way
she responded to Janie, with patience and a warm
smile. Whatever the reason, he found there were
some things to admire about the woman beyond
mere appearances. For one, she was not the empty-
headed female he'd at first thought her to be. She
may not have shown the best of judgment, coming
to New Prospects without the guarantee of a job,
but she was no one's fool, either. Of that he was
becoming convinced.

"What do I miss about England most?" Beth said
softly, repeating Janie's latest question. Her eyes took
on a faraway look. "That's difficult to say. The green-
ness, I think. Everything is quite brown and gray over
here by comparison. England is much more green.

But then, your skies seem to be much bluer. I suppose that's a fair exchange."

"You think you'll ever be sorry you didn't marry Lord Altberry and stay there instead of coming here?" Janie queried.

Her expression became almost brittle. "No, I shall never be sorry about that."

Garret couldn't help wondering about this Lord Altberry. Beth had said earlier that she hadn't loved him, but now Garret suspected there was more to it than that.

"What about Miss Malone and Miss Linberg? What are they like?"

Beth smiled again. "I think Mary is a lot like you, Janie. Small and pretty, with a zest for life and an iron will. Nothing ever seemed to frighten her."

"Is that true about me, Pa?"

Beth's gaze lifted toward Garret. He felt a strange connection pass between them, as if she'd actually touched him.

"Yeah, it's true," he answered Janie.

"What about Miss Linberg? What's she like?"

"Inga has the gentlest spirit of anyone I've ever known. Without her help, I might not have been allowed to enter the country."

"Why not?"

"I did not have a guarantee of employment. I might have been turned away, a single woman with no family in America."

"Don't seem fair."

"Perhaps not," she said, her expression growing distant. After a long silence, she gave her head a small shake and met the child's gaze once more. "Now it's time for you to tell me something about yourself, Janie."

"Like what?"

"Anything you want. Something you've never told me in one of your letters."

Janie screwed up her mouth and closed her eyes. Watching her, Beth smiled. It was the sort of look Garret had noticed most mothers wore when their children did something they found adorable. It caused his chest to tighten in response.

Janie opened her eyes again. "I don't know, Miss Beth. I think I've told you everything already."

Beth's glance shifted toward Garret. "Then perhaps your father would like to tell me something?"

Lord, a man could just about lose himself in her eyes. Their color reminded him of new leaves budding in the spring.

"Tell her about when you were a boy, Pa," Janie insisted with fresh enthusiasm. "Tell her how you lived in Kentucky and how you came to be in Montana."

He dropped his gaze to his empty supper plate, bothered by the way looking at Beth made him feel. "I doubt she wants to hear that."

"You're quite wrong, Mr. Steele. I should very much like to hear it." Her voice was gentle, encouraging.

He couldn't help himself. He looked up again. "I'm not much of a storyteller, Miss Wellington."

She smiled—that same patient, tender smile she shared so often with Janie—but said nothing.

"Go on, Pa. Tell her."

Surprisingly, he found himself talking without

more urging. "I was born in Kentucky, the first year of the War Between the States. My pa was killed by the Yankees before I was born, and it was just Ma and me on our farm until I was thirteen. That's when Ma took sick and died. The farm wasn't worth much, and I'd never been keen on bein' a farmer anyway. So I put what things I could in a pack and lit out for the West, where I learned to be a cowboy."

Janie touched his arm. "Tell her about when you first came here."

"That was late in the summer of seventy-nine. We'd just brought up a herd of cattle from Texas, and I wanted to do a bit of exploring before I headed back down south."

"But when he saw the valley up there by New Prospects," Janie interrupted, "he knew he didn't ever want to leave again. Ain't that right, Pa?"

"That's right, Janie. That's just how it was."

"Tell her how you thought the sky was like a big blue canopy and the mountains like . . . like . . . What'd you call 'em, Pa?"

"Sentinels," Garret replied reluctantly.

"Yeah, sentinels. That's a guard, Miss Beth. He thought the mountains were like guards to protect us."

Beth was silent for a moment or two, then said, "That's quite poetic, Mr. Steele."

He shrugged, feeling embarrassed and uncomfortable.

"I think I shall feel more safe with that image in mind," she added softly.

"Yeah . . . well . . ." He cleared his throat as he stood. "I guess we'd best get us some shut-eye. We've a long trip ahead of us again tomorrow, and we won't get as early a start as I'd like since we gotta wait for those test results." He reached for the back of Beth's chair and pulled it away from the table.

When he took hold of her arm, Beth felt an odd flutter in her stomach and her breathing became shallow and quick. She glanced quickly at Garret, then away, made even more unsettled by the brief eye contact.

"Go on with your story, Pa."

"What else do you want me to tell, Janie?"

"Tell her how you built the house and how you lived there all alone until you met Ma."

With Janie between them, they left the restaurant and walked toward the hotel. Beth didn't look at Garret again, but she was aware of him as she'd never been aware of anyone before.

"Pa nearly didn't get the cabin up before the first snow came," Janie said as she took hold of Beth's hand. "Go on. Tell her, Pa."

He was silent a few moments, then began. "Janie's right. I nearly didn't make it. I'm lucky I didn't freeze to death that first winter. It took longer than I thought it would to fell enough trees and cut 'em and hew 'em so they'd fit together. I'd never built anything before, 'cept a chicken coop when I was a boy, and I did plenty wrong. But somehow I managed to get it done and had me enough wood chopped t'see me through the winter." He whistled softly. "I'd never seen a winter like that first one. Blizzards where you couldn't see a foot in front of your face. Winds that blew for days on end. Snows so deep, sometimes they drifted up to the roof of the cabin."

Beth tried to imagine snow so deep but couldn't. She'd rarely seen anything more than a dusting of snow at Langford House.

"Only way I survived, I guess, was pure stupid luck, but I was too young and full of myself to admit it. Come spring, I headed back to Texas and brought me up a small herd of cattle of my own. Wasn't much, but it was a start. Jake came to work for me the next year. I hired him not so much 'cause the place needed another pair of hands as 'cause I wasn't looking forward to a second winter with just myself for company."

"Pa says that readin' is how most cowpokes manage t'get through the long winters of Montana. That's how come we don't have Texas longhorns on the ranch no more. He read up about some other breeds and he went to California to buy a Hereford bull. That's how he met Ma."

Beth sensed Garret's reluctance to continue with the story. Despite herself, she cast a covert glance in his direction. His profile was rigid, his jaw set.

Janie, however, carried on, oblivious of her father's discomfort. "My grandfather was a real rich man, and he had a big, huge house in San Francisco. My ma used to tell me all about it. Anyway, he invited Pa back to the house after he'd looked at the bulls he had for sale, and that's when he met my ma. They were married before he came back to Montana. Isn't that right, Pa?"

"Yes." The single word was clipped, telling Beth far more than any lengthy explanation would have.

He had loved and lost, and the pain was still too great for him to bear. She had seen it with her own father. Losing Anne had destroyed Henry Wellington. He had sought to fill the void left by her death in other women's beds, in strong spirits, and in the gambling hells of London. He had seemed to forget most of the time that Beth even existed. Until, of course, he'd realized he was on the brink of financial disaster and that he'd needed his daughter to marry well to save him.

But losing Muriel wouldn't destroy Garret. Because unlike Beth's father, Garret cherished his daughter. His love for Janie was what kept him going. That and, perhaps, the memories of his wife.

Tears stung her eyes unexpectedly. She couldn't help it. She wished she could have been loved like that—both as a child and as a woman. She wished she still believed in her own Prince Charming, riding up on his handsome white horse to rescue her from some tall tower.

But those were children's fairy tales, and real life was something very different indeed.

7

It was late in the afternoon by the time the Steele wagon rolled into New Prospects. Beth was relieved to see the mercantile. She longed for the solitude of her room. It had been an exhausting day.

She had started it after a disturbing night. First she had dreamed of Perceval, a dark nightmare full of shadows and threats. She'd seen his face, heard his voice, felt the old familiar fear. They'd been in England, but not at Langford House or the Griffith estates. Instead they'd been in some sort of stone tower. She'd known she was a prisoner and there was no way out, no means of escape.

Then Garret had ridden to her rescue, a knight of old on a prancing white horse. He'd been clad in chain mail that had gleamed brightly in the sunlight, chasing away the shadows as well as her fears. Perceval had disappeared, too, gone forever, driven away by her handsome Prince Charming.

She'd awakened just as Garret had been about to seal his victory with a kiss.

The dream had left her uneasy in Garret's presence, as if she feared he might read her thoughts. Even the news that she had passed the exam and was now certified to teach the children of New Prospects hadn't eased the unsettled feeling.

The journey back to the small town north of Bozeman had seemed interminable. Garret had hardly spoken more than a dozen words the entire time, answering his daughter's questions with one-word replies of "Yeah" or "Nope" and never elaborating on anything. She'd wondered if he'd been rendered sleepless by strange dreams, too, then had scolded herself for such foolishness.

As the wagon pulled up in front of the mercantile, Bunny and Patsy Homer stepped out onto the boardwalk. They smiled and waved in greeting, and Patsy asked, "How did you do on the exam, Miss Wellington? Did you get the results?"

"Yes. I passed."

"How wonderful," Bunny said, her gaze flicking toward Garret as he stepped in front of Beth and hopped down from the wagon.

"Miss Wellington." He held out his hand to her, then, when she took hold of it, helped her to the street. "I'll get your satchel."

"Thank you, Mr. Steele."

Bunny waved for them to come toward her. "You must all come inside and have some lemonade to wash down the dust."

"That's kind of you, Miss Homer," Garret answered, "but Janie and I need to be gettin' back to the ranch. I've been gone too long as it is."

Hurriedly Beth added her own refusal. "I hope you

will forgive me if I, too, decline your invitation, Miss Homer. I'm weary beyond words." She took her satchel from Garret, careful not to let their fingers touch. "Thank you again, Mr. Steele," she whispered. With a quick glance toward the wagon, she added, "I shall see you in school on Monday, Janie."

"Good-bye, Miss Beth," the girl called after her. "I had a really good time. I'm sure glad you're gonna be my teacher."

Beth didn't dare look toward the Homer sisters as she stepped onto the boardwalk, afraid one of them would insist she come to their apartment. Her head was beginning to ache, along with the rest of her body. It wasn't until she'd reached the back stairway that she realized Bunny had followed after her.

"Is something amiss, Miss Wellington?" the woman asked, not with concern but with a note of suspicion.

Beth stopped on the bottom step and turned to look at the woman behind her. "Amiss?" Why did the woman's question bother her so? "I don't know what you mean."

"You seem upset." She peered at Beth with narrowed eyes. "I was wondering if anything happened to distress you."

"No. I am tired, that is all." She turned and began her ascent, feeling a desperate need to escape.

"Miss Wellington?"

She stopped again. "Yes?"

Bunny showed her a modest smile. "I hope you know my sister and I desire to be your friends. Should you ever need someone to confide in, please come to us."

She was instantly ashamed of herself. Bunny had done nothing but be kind and courteous. Her concern seemed genuine, but Beth had been ascribing other unspecified motives for her questions.

"I shall remember that," she said, returning a smile. "And I do thank you for all you've done for me. You have been most generous."

Bunny's smile grew into one of her toothy and most unappealing grins.

"I'll be happy to tell you and your sister about the exam tomorrow, if that's convenient for you. But now I'd prefer to lie down."

This time the woman didn't object. "Of course. You do look tired. Go and rest. If you need supper brought up to you, you just say so."

"At the moment, I don't think I could eat a bite, but thank you for offering. Good evening."

She hurried up the stairs and let herself into her small room. Late afternoon shadows filled the attic, making it seem gloomy, almost haunted. As soon as Beth set down her satchel, she hurried to light the lamp and dispel the dreariness. Then, with a deep sigh, she sank onto the bed.

"What is wrong with me?" she whispered.

It was peculiar, the way she felt. Not simply weary. Something more. Something indefinable. Or perhaps something she didn't wish to define.

She lay back on the bed, staring up at the peaked ceiling, her arm thrown across her forehead. "I passed the exam," she said aloud. "I am able to support myself. I have achieved what I set out to do. I am independent and free. There is nothing to trouble me now."

But she *was* troubled. Deeply so. Why?

She envisioned him again, Garret Steele on a white horse. And then she knew what was troubling her.

She was losing her heart—to a man who was still in love with the wife he had buried.

Supper was a quiet affair at the Steele ranch. Even Janie was unusually subdued, and she didn't argue with her father when he told her it was time for bed before the sun had set.

Garret tried going to bed early, too, but sleep just wouldn't come. He simply lay on his bed while pieces of conversation from the last three days kept repeating in his mind, bringing up bad memories from the past and warning of possible troubles in the future.

He hadn't liked being reminded of Muriel, but he'd sworn Janie would never guess he'd learned to hate her mother long before she died. Pretending didn't come easy to him; lying was even harder. It was always better for him to clench his jaw and say as little as possible.

Maybe he wouldn't have hated Muriel if she'd ever been good to Janie, but she'd been so blasted withdrawn and cool with her only child. Uncaring for anyone other than herself to her dying day, that had been Muriel Slade Steele.

If you were any kind of a man, we wouldn't have to live like this!

He could still hear her shouting those words at him. If it hadn't been for her pregnancy, he would have sent her back to Huntington Slade and let her father deal with her. Garret had been fed up, tired of it all. He'd have given her a divorce, just for the asking. He'd have taken whatever blame she'd thrown his way. But then had come the night of Janie's birth. When Muriel went into labor, Garret had sent Jake for the doctor, but before they could get back to the ranch, Janie had arrived. Garret had held that squalling, red-faced infant in his arms and had forgotten every reason he'd had for wanting to send mother and baby to San Francisco. From that moment on, Janie had become his reason for everything.

He swore as he sat up in bed. He didn't want to remember those years between Janie's birth and her mother's death. If the first years of his marriage had been bad, the last years had been hell. Muriel had sworn to make them so—and she'd succeeded.

He uttered another curse, then got out of bed and pulled on his trousers and boots. Shoving his arms into his shirtsleeves, he left his bedroom and went outside.

A blanket of stars spilled across the heavens, those closest to the nearly full moon fading in comparison with the brighter light. A gentle night's breeze caused tree limbs to whisper as they rubbed against the side of the house. A coyote's howl drifted across the range, followed by the *whoo, whoo* of an owl.

Garret sat on a bench near the front door of the cabin. Penguin came padding over from his favorite spot near the corner of the house. Placing his muzzle on Garret's thigh, the collie looked at his master with doleful eyes.

"I don't like this, fella," he said as he stroked the dog's head.

He reminded himself that the Steeles had done fine

on their own, just father and daughter, but the memories persisted.

Huntington Slade had died two months after Janie's birth without ever seeing his granddaughter. Geraldine, his widow, had soon after married a man who'd stolen her fortune and escaped to Europe, leaving her destitute. Garret had invited his vain, spoiled mother-in-law to live with them in Montana. She had declined, and neither he nor Muriel had ever heard from her again.

To be honest, Garret feared Geraldine Slade might still be alive, that she might have recovered her money, that one day she might come here and try to take Janie from him. If Muriel had ever told her mother the truth . . .

"Damn!" he whispered, then stood and walked toward the corral, Penguin following at his heels. "Heckfire an' tarnation!" he added, louder this time.

He'd given no thought to any of this in ages. It was because of Beth Wellington that it was resurfacing. He wished she'd failed her teacher's exam. If he'd had any sense, he would have given her some money the day she'd arrived and sent her someplace else. He'd have made sure she wasn't around Janie. Janie liked her too much.

And Garret? He'd been reminded of how long it had been since he'd shared a bed with a woman.

He cursed silently again, admitting it wasn't just any woman he needed. If it was, he could have paid that visit to Mad Maddie's down in Bozeman. No, it was Beth Wellington he wanted in his bed, Beth Wellington whose image made his blood run hot.

Worse yet, he thought as he leaned against the corral fence, he was beginning to like her.

Perhaps even admire her.

He looked down at the collie. "You'd've thought I'd learned my lesson with Muriel, wouldn't you?"

Penguin cocked his head to one side, looking puzzled.

"Yeah. Me too."

Beth awakened slowly, her head still aching. It had been a long and torturous night, filled with more disturbing images, whether she was awake or asleep. There had been her father, a once loving but weak man. There had been Perceval, cruel and abusive. And there had been Garret, strong but still devoted to the memory of his wife.

The last image had tortured her the most.

That she'd found herself falling in love with Garret Steele had been completely unexpected. That she would be foolish if she allowed those feelings to continue was indisputable. That she must put them behind her was a necessity.

She rose from her bed and performed her morning ablutions with unusual haste, eager to set her mind on other things. She decided to skip breakfast with the Homer sisters. Instead she gathered the cleaning supplies she had purchased for just this day and set off on foot toward the schoolhouse.

The brisk walk in the cool morning air seemed to cure her headache, making it easier to think. Mentally she made a list of the things she must accomplish before Monday morning. In addition to ridding the school of accumulated dust and cobwebs, she had to notify all the families with children that the summer session would begin in three days. She also needed to plan her lessons for her first day.

It would be wise to visit the families tomorrow, she decided, her footsteps slowing as her mind began to race. Yes, that was a good idea. If she could meet them individually beforehand, she would be more prepared when she faced her class on her first day as a teacher. She would need a horse and someone to give her directions.

She immediately thought of Garret. He'd been in this valley longer than anyone. He had to know all the families and where their farms and ranches were. And she could probably borrow a horse from him as well.

Deep inside, she admitted there were other reasons for her wanting to ask his help in this matter. She wanted to see him again. She wanted to test these feelings that persisted in her heart.

And then what shall you do?

She recalled the Homer sisters' warning about Garret. But as quickly as the memory came, she dismissed it as idle—or even vicious—gossip. She had witnessed real violence in the person of Perceval Griffith, and she knew without question that Garret Steele was not capable of it.

But even if he weren't capable of the same sort of brutality, could she possibly know him well enough to love him?

No, of course not.

And even if she did, what good could come of it? He wanted no part of her. True, he'd ceased to scowl at her quite as often during the trip to and from

Bozeman, but he was no more inclined to care for her than he had been before. His heart belonged to the woman he'd lost. His words and actions made that clear.

Stopping in the middle of the road, Beth stared at the mountains surrounding the long, wide valley. Rocky peaks, tinged a purple hue, jutted up against the sky. Sentinels, Garret had called them, and so they seemed. She felt at home here, safe here, more than she had ever felt at Langford House. She was not about to allow herself to destroy that peace and safety by losing her head over a man.

Resolutely she shoved all thoughts of Garret into a secret place in her heart and closed them away.

Hours later Beth stood at the entrance to the schoolroom and observed her handiwork. Sunlight streamed through windows that sparkled both inside and out. There wasn't a cobweb left to be found anywhere, and dust had been obliterated from desktops and floor. Not even a trace of chalk remained on the blackboards.

She felt inordinately proud of her accomplishment. She supposed it was because she'd never done much physical labor before. Mrs. Crumb, the housekeeper at Langford House, had never allowed Beth to help her and Mary. It didn't matter that the staff had been drastically reduced and it was impossible for only two servants to keep up with the housework. She still wouldn't let Beth lift a useful finger. A lady didn't stoop to such menial work, the woman had always told her.

"Hello."

She let out a tiny yelp of surprise as she turned toward the voice.

Owen Simpson stood in the open doorway. "I thought I'd find you here." Doffing his hat, he moved through the vestibule. "Looks like you've been busy today."

She nodded. "Yes." She glanced over her shoulder at the schoolroom, and her smile returned. "Yes, I have been busy."

"Amazing."

She looked at the mayor, but instead of admiring her cleaning efforts, he was staring at her. She felt her cheeks grow warm. "I . . . I thought I should get ready to begin classes on Monday. Did you know I passed the certification exam?"

"Yes, Miss Patsy told me. I went there to see you."

She couldn't help it. She wished Garret would look at her the same way as Owen was at this moment.

Quickly she turned away from him and walked into the center of the room. "I thought I should try to visit the parents of my students tomorrow."

"That's an excellent idea. I'll take you in my carriage."

She ran her fingers across the surface of the nearest desk. "I can't ask you to do that. You have only just returned from your business trip and must be tired."

She heard his footsteps on the wood floor as he crossed to stand behind her. "You don't have to ask me. I want to do this."

There was nothing to do but accept his offer. "Very well. And thank you."

"Now, will you allow me to see you back to town?"

She turned and met his gaze, feeling suddenly tired, like a wilting flower. "That would be most appreciated, Mr. Simpson. It's a long walk."

He started to say something more, then seemed to think better of it and closed his mouth.

He didn't have to speak. Somehow Beth knew what he'd wanted to say to her, and she was relieved he hadn't. Her own feelings were in too much confusion already. The last thing she wanted was to hear a declaration of any personal sort from this man.

Owen reached for the bucket of dirty water. "I'll empty this for you. Then we can be on our way."

Beth waited until he was gone, then gave the room one last look before walking out, closing the door and locking it behind her. As she descended the steps, she glanced over at the small log cabin that was to be her home, then toward the mayor, who was now waiting for her beside his carriage. "Mr. Simpson, I believe I would like to move out here next week."

"But the roof—"

"It doesn't appear we are about to get rained on. I think it will provide me adequate cover until your man can make his repairs."

"I'm not so sure that's a good idea."

"But I am sure."

For some reason, that made him grin. "Very well, Miss Wellington. Next week it is."

8

Sunday, June 13, 1897
New Prospects, Montana

Dearest Mary,

I write to you with wonderful news. I have passed the examination, and I am now certified to teach the students of New Prospects. It was of great surprise to me that I was able to take the examination as quickly as this. I had feared I would be forced to wait many weeks, and in the meanwhile, I would of necessity be reliant on the charity of others. Thankfully those fears were not realized.

Tomorrow is the first day of the summer session with my pupils. I spent last Friday scouring the schoolhouse in preparation. The building stood empty for several months, and the dust and cobwebs had nearly taken over. You would have been quite proud of me, Mary. At least I like to think you would have been. I am certain Mrs. Crumb, however, would be horrified to learn I have taken to washing floors and windows "like a common scrubwoman." As for myself, I found there is a large measure of satisfaction in hard, honest labor. It is just as well I feel that way, for the cleanliness of the schoolroom is the responsibility of the teacher, so I shall be mopping and dusting with some regularity.

Yesterday, I visited the homes of many of my students. For the most part, I have felt welcomed by the members of the community. A few, I believe, are not pleased to find an Englishwoman will be teaching their children. They seem to forget their own families have not long been in this country. Many can probably trace their roots to England, perhaps even to Buckinghamshire itself.

However, as I said, most have welcomed me, and I believe I shall get on quite well here. I believe it for many reasons. The first one is because I have fallen under the spell of the mountains. Janie's father calls them sentinels, and such they are. They surround this valley, a valley that is both wide and long, so one does not feel closed in by those same mountains. Only protected by them.

I suppose I should share with you that I seem to have won the regard of the mayor of New Prospects. His name is Owen Simpson. He is a pleasant-looking fellow, not as tall as Janie's father, but tall enough to command the respect of other men. He has been most attentive since my arrival in New Prospects. Sometimes I fear too attentive. I do not feel ready to cope with such things as of yet. You often told me I would one day feel differently, but the time is not here.

Mr. Simpson owns the cabin near the school where I will be living soon. Although my last letter expressed hope that my current hostesses and I would become friends, I feel less inclined to believe it now. For some reason which is difficult to explain, I am somewhat hesitant to trust everything they tell me. A few days ago, they shared things about Garret Steele which I cannot believe. Perhaps it is because he is Janie's father that I choose not to credit their gossip. Or perhaps it is because, after Lord Altberry, I'm certain I could spot the same behavior in others. Whatever the reason, I feel in my heart Mr. Steele is a good man. Regardless, I will be glad when I am able to move into my own little house.

I trust my letters are finding you well. I hope they have also found you with your

Mr. Maguire. I think of you often and pray
God is keeping you safe and happy.

With affection,
Your friend,
Beth Wellington

Beth's stomach was aflutter with butterflies as she
stood at the front of the classroom, watching her
students filing through the doorway on Monday
morning.

The youngest among them were the six-year-old
Matheson twins, Rob and Mike, sons of Reverend
and Mrs. Hezekiah Matheson. Her oldest student,
Trevor Booth, was sixteen. The son of a farmer from
the northern-most end of the valley, Trevor was a
good ten inches taller than Beth and probably
weighed twice what she did. That he resented being
in school with so many younger children was obvious
from the bitter look in his eyes.

Janie Steele—God bless her—sat at one of the
front desks, giving Beth the courage she needed to get
through her first day simply by her presence.

When she'd confirmed all her students were in
attendance, Beth offered what she hoped was a confident smile. "Good morning. I am your new teacher,
Miss Wellington."

"Good morning, Miss Wellington," the Matheson
boys chorused, sounding as if they had rehearsed the
words—probably at the behest of their father—before
coming to school.

Her smile broadened. She had done some rehearsing of her own. "I know you have been without a teacher for a number of months. We shall spend this first week together becoming acquainted while I learn where each of you is in your readers." She purposely met the gaze of each student while she spoke. "I trust you have each taken your seat according to grade level. If you have not, then I shall ask you to move to a different desk at this time."

She paused, giving them an opportunity to comply. No one moved.

"Very well." She motioned toward the blackboards. "As you can see, for those of you in the second through fifth *McGuffey's Readers,* I have indicated which lessons I want you to begin with this morning. Please read silently and write the answers to any questions on your slates. I will work first with those pupils who are in the *McGuffey's Primer* and the first *Reader.* Will those pupils please raise their hands?"

Trevor Booth stood. "I don't got a slate pencil, so I can't answer no questions."

"You do not *have* a slate pencil," Beth corrected, "so you cannot answer *any* questions."

"That's what I said."

She didn't need any experience as a teacher to recognize the challenge in his posture or his tone. This boy was going to be a problem unless he understood Beth was in charge and would not brook misbehavior in her classroom.

"Sit down, Trevor," she said in a firm, calm voice that belied what she was feeling inside. "I shall allow you to use my slate pencil."

"Don't got no slate, neither." He remained standing.

Someone snickered.

Beth's stomach twisted into a knot. "Fortunately for you, I have an extra slate as well. And the proper way to say what you just said is, 'I don't have a slate, Miss Wellington.'" She walked toward the boy, refusing to quaver beneath his hostile glare, even when she had to look up to meet his gaze. She set the slate and pencil on the desk in front of him. "Please remember to return these to me at the end of class today."

Trevor leaned toward her and whispered, "You make a fool of me, you'll be sorry."

She didn't know how she managed to hold her ground. "I have no intention of making a fool of you, Trevor. You seem quite capable of doing so yourself. However, if you allow me to, I shall be happy to help you learn many new things."

"Yeah?" His gaze slid to her breasts, and he grinned suggestively. "There's a thing or two I'd like ya t'teach me at that."

"That is quite enough!"

Still smiling, he sank onto the chair. "Sure thing, Miss Wellington."

Beth returned to the front of the classroom, feeling the eyes of the other students on her, knowing that whatever she did today would set the tone for the days and weeks to come. It could mean success or failure. It could even mean her job.

Drawing a deep breath, she turned to face the children. "I know my speech is different from yours. I'm new to your country, and there are times I will make mistakes because I am not familiar with all of your customs. I trust you will help me realize when I have made a mistake." Her gaze returned to Trevor Booth.

"But I also expect you to treat me with the same respect you would give any teacher. I will not tolerate otherwise."

Inside she was shaking like a leaf. She could only hope she didn't show it on the outside.

"Now, please open your readers and begin your lessons."

Garret didn't always come for Janie at the end of the school day. His daughter had been riding Maybelle to and from school by herself for the past two years. But since he'd needed to go into town for a few supplies, he'd decided to stop by and ride home with her.

At least, that's what he'd told himself.

Janie's face lit up with a smile when she saw him waiting for her. She ran across the schoolyard to where her pony was tethered. "Oh, Pa," she said breathlessly when she stopped beside his buckskin. "You should've seen Miss Beth. She did real good. She's gonna be my favorite teacher ever. Trevor tried to bully her like he does everybody else, but she didn't back down or anything."

He looked at the other students pouring out of the school. It took only a moment to find the Booth boy, moving with a swaggering gait toward his big plow horse. "What do you mean, bully her?"

"You know. It's just sorta the way he says things. And the way he looked at her. Creepy like."

He watched Trevor swing his leg over his mount's broad back. Then he glanced toward the schoolhouse. For a reason he chose not to analyze, he knew he had to see Beth, to make certain she was all right.

"Wait here," he said as he dismounted. "I'll be back in a few minutes."

Long, purposeful strides carried him across the yard and up the steps to the front door. He hesitated at the entrance, listening. All was silent inside. He went in and paused once again at the rear of the classroom.

Beth stood with her back to him, cleaning the day's lessons from the blackboard, her arm moving in round, rhythmic sweeps. No one else was in the room, and nothing seemed out of order. He didn't know what had made him think otherwise.

Just as he was about to turn and leave unnoticed, Beth dropped her arm to her side and leaned her forehead against the blackboard. First there was a slight tremble of her shoulders, then he heard a quiet sob.

She's crying.

He should have left in a hurry. He should have run out of the schoolhouse as fast as Janie had minutes ago. He should have done a number of things differently.

What he did was walk toward her, saying as he drew near, "Miss Wellington?"

He heard a quick intake of breath, then she swiped the tears from her cheeks with her wrist before turning around. "Mr. Steele. You surprised me."

"Rough day, huh?"

She offered a weak smile. "A little."

"Janie said you were great."

"Janie is my friend."

"She's also honest."

"I hope it's honesty and not simply kindness."

"I heard you had a bit of trouble with the Booth boy."

"He was testing me. I believe we came to an understanding."

She said it with confidence, but Garret thought he caught a glimpse of fear within the depths of her green eyes. He couldn't blame her. Trevor had always been a troublemaker.

He touched her shoulder. "Mr. Peterson had problems with Trevor, too, but Peterson was a mighty stern disciplinarian. That's what it'll take. You'll let me know if . . . well, if you need my help."

Darn! That was the last thing he'd meant to say. He didn't want Beth Wellington running to him when she couldn't handle her own students.

She stepped backward, out of his reach. "I'm certain that won't be necessary."

He stared at her for what seemed a long time, finally admitting to himself she was nothing like Muriel. She wasn't going to turn tail and run away when things got a little difficult. There was more to Beth than mere beauty. She wasn't a spoiled female who would demand to be called Lady Elizabeth by servants and peers. She had a quiet strength, a determination of spirit. Very much against his will, he admired her.

Then he realized he was just the slightest bit disappointed she'd been so quick to refuse his offer of help.

Beth stepped around him and gathered the books on her desk. "If you'll excuse me, Mr. Steele, I really should start back to town. I've a great deal of work to do this evening. Lessons to plan."

"'Course." He cleared his throat. "Didn't mean to keep you."

She met his gaze again, then showed him the most delicate smile he'd ever seen. "Thank you, Mr. Steele. I hope you know how much I appreciate all you and Janie have done for me. You have been so kind, and I—"

"No need t'thank me." But he was glad she had anyway.

He let her lead the way out of the school, then waited at the bottom of the steps while she locked the door. He was just about to offer to give her a ride back to town when Owen Simpson drove up in his carriage.

Just as well, he thought as he placed his hat on his head. He didn't have any intention of being anything other than, at most, a friend to Beth Wellington. Owen, on the other hand, had made it clear he was more seriously interested in the new schoolmarm. Better Garret just stay clear altogether.

"Howdy, Owen," he called as the mayor disembarked from the carriage.

"Garret." Owen's gaze flicked to Beth. "Good day, Miss Wellington."

Garret touched the brim of his hat. "Well, if you'll both excuse me, Janie and I need to get back to the ranch."

As she watched him stride across the yard and mount his horse, Beth felt as if she might never see him again. As if she had just lost something precious.

Ridiculous, she told herself. He's only going home. Besides, he's not mine to lose anyway.

When Janie waved at her, she waved back, forcing

herself to smile, suppressing the wish to go home with Janie, to prolong her visit with Garret and avoid reality for a short while.

"How was your first day, Miss Wellington?" Owen asked.

She felt a twinge of guilt for her thoughts. "I believe it went well, Mr. Simpson."

"Good. Good. Glad to hear it." He glanced toward the departing father and daughter, then back at Beth. "I was just returning to town. Thought you might appreciate a ride."

She wanted to do as Owen had done. She wanted to watch Garret as he rode away, wanted to keep watching until he was out of sight. But she managed to resist the temptation. "Thank you. I would appreciate it."

He took the books from her arms, then walked beside her toward his carriage. "It's a long walk to and from town for you to make every day. Perhaps you would allow me to drive you out each morning and back to town at the close of school."

"I couldn't impose."

"But it wouldn't be an imposition."

Beth knew what he was leading up to. She prayed he would stop before it was too late.

"Miss Wellington—"

"Besides, I shall be living out here in the cabin soon."

"Nonetheless—"

"And I'm planning to buy a horse of my own, just as soon as I can afford to."

He set her books on the floor of the carriage, then faced her. "You do make it difficult for me, Miss Wellington," he said with a wry smile.

"Difficult?"

"Surely you must realize I have strong feelings for you."

Don't say it. Please don't say it. I'm not ready yet.

"Miss Wellington, I hope someday you will return those same feelings."

She dropped her gaze to the center of his chest, wishing all the while he weren't standing so close. "We hardly know each other, Mr. Simpson," she whispered after a lengthy silence.

"That doesn't always matter."

She met his gaze again. "It's much too soon."

But not so soon she hadn't already lost her heart to someone else.

"I promise not to rush you"—he hesitated, then said her name softly—"Beth. Just give me a chance. Keep an open mind." He offered an engaging grin. "Lots of folks seem to like me. Although I suppose it could be 'cause I'm the town banker."

She smiled at his small jest. "I doubt you have had to purchase your friends, sir."

"Then that must mean there is hope for us." He cupped her elbow with his hand and helped her into the carriage.

"I'm sure we shall become friends," she answered at long last. She hoped he would understand what she was telling him.

But his reply did nothing to reassure her. "We shall be more than friends, dear lady. On my word, we shall."

9

Garret shoved the pitchfork into the collection of straw and manure covering the floor of the stall. Judging by today, summer had arrived in earnest, bringing with it unusually hot temperatures for June. The barn was still, without so much as a breeze to lessen the heat or blow away the dust he'd stirred up. Sweat trickled down his spine and dampened his shirt beneath his armpits.

A man working as hard as he was shouldn't have been plagued with thoughts of a woman. At least that was his opinion. Nonetheless, he was thinking about Beth, just as he had all week long. Maybe it wouldn't have been as bad if Janie hadn't come home every day from school, yammering on and on about Miss Wellington and what a great teacher she was and how all the kids loved her and how Trevor Booth was still causing her grief but that Miss Wellington was handling him just fine.

Tomorrow, Janie'd told him, Beth was moving into the old Thompson cabin. Reverend and Mrs. Matheson had given her a bed and bedding. The widow Perkins had donated a table and chair. Every family with children in school had donated household items for the new teacher.

"We gotta do somethin', Pa," his daughter had said at supper last night. "It ain't . . . I mean, it *isn't* right if we don't do somethin' for her, too."

What she'd said was true, of course, but he'd be darned if he could think of what they could do for Beth. No, that part wasn't true. He could think of plenty of things. An ivory comb for her hair. A pretty green hat the same shade as her eyes. A necklace with topaz stones to lie in the hollow of her throat. Plenty of ideas, but all of them too personal. Those were the gifts a suitor gave to the woman he was courting. Or the gifts a man gave to his wife.

"Blast!" Garret stuck the pitchfork into the muck and left it standing there as he strode out of the barn. He stopped in the middle of the yard and looked up at the sun.

It was the weather, that was all. Just the heat and the dust and the sweat. It was enough to make any man crazy after a while.

A horse snorted, drawing Garret's gaze toward the nearest corral. Several geldings and mares stood inside the fenced area, tails swishing, and heads hung low. In the corral next to it was Janie's sorrel yearling, one of the finest colts ever born on the Steele ranch, and that was saying something. Garret was proud of the stock raised on his place. He hadn't achieved it overnight. He'd worked hard to breed the best, both cattle and horses.

Beth needs a horse.

Of course. He should have thought of that sooner. The schoolmarm ought to have a horse, especially living out so far and all alone. She'd need a means of transportation to go after supplies in town and to call on the parents of her students. And there was nothing personal about a horse. Just a neighborly sort of thing to do. That's all.

He walked toward the larger of the two corrals and stepped up on the bottom board to have a better look at the animals inside. Some were only green broke. Others had been trained to work cattle, and that training couldn't be wasted to make one of them a lady's mount.

Then he spied the flaxen gelding he called Flick because of the way the horse flicked his tail just before he made a sudden turn. Flick had been a good little cow horse in his prime, but now he was due some rest after many years of working cattle. The gelding was intelligent and calm, with a soft mouth and easy gait. He'd make a fine horse for a lady.

Garret checked his pocket watch. Two-thirty. Still an hour and a half before school let out. He could take Flick there and then ride home with Janie. He wouldn't be doing anything out of the ordinary. He would simply be doing his part, along with the rest of the community, in providing the schoolteacher with the necessities for doing her job. No more and no less.

He stepped down from the corral, then strode over to the water pump and gave it a couple of hard yanks to start the water flowing into the trough. He splashed his face, then stuck his head under the stream. Straightening, he used his kerchief to dry his neck and face.

"Hey, boss."

He turned to watch Jake ride into the barnyard.

"We got us some trouble on the east range," the cowhand said as he dismounted, still favoring the leg he'd injured over two weeks before. "Looks like another grizzly's takin' a likin' t'beef."

Garret frowned. In the eighteen years he'd been in the area, he'd only had trouble with two of the mighty beasts. Usually they stayed farther up in the high country, away from humans and all traces of civilization. They had their territory and seemed to stay in it. But when they came down out of the mountains, they were trouble. Big trouble. He could lose a lot of cattle in a hurry, and so could many of the other ranchers in the valley.

Jake removed his hat and whacked it against his thigh a couple of times, sending up a small cloud of dust. "Found remains of three cows. One was a fresh kill. Figure the bear's stickin' close."

"We'd better get together a hunting party. Head out at first light." He glanced toward Jake's leg. "You up to another day in the saddle?"

"I'll be right enough by mornin'. Just need a bit of liniment t'ease the soreness. These old bones ain't ready for the rocker just yet."

Garret glanced toward the corral. "I was just headed over to the school. I'll ride into town afterward and spread the word."

Standing at the front of the classroom, Rosie O'Toole read aloud from *McGuffey's Third Eclectic Reader.* "Once when there was a famine, a rich baker sent for twenty of the poorest children in the town, and said to them, 'In this basket there is a loaf for each of you. Take it, and come back to me every day at this hour till God sends us better times.' The hungry children gathered eagerly about the basket, and quarreled for the bread, because each wished to have the largest loaf. At last they went away without even thanking the good gentleman." Rosie looked up from the book with an expression of uncertainty.

Beth smiled at her. "That was very good, Rosie. Thank you. Janie, would you like to take the next two verses?"

The girl jumped to her feet. "Sure, Miss Beth."

Beth gave her head a slight shake.

"I mean, Miss Wellington," Janie corrected.

Someone whispered, "Teacher's pet."

Beth suspected it was Trevor Booth who'd spoken, but she pretended not to hear him. She'd had her fill of confrontations today. And to tell the truth, Trevor frightened her more than she wanted to admit. There was a simmering rage deep inside that boy, not mere mischievousness as was true of the other high-spirited lads in her class.

"But Gretchen," Janie began reading, "a poorly-dressed little girl, did not quarrel or struggle with the rest, but remained standing modestly in the distance. When the ill-behaved girls had left, she took the smallest loaf, which alone was left in the basket, kissed the gentleman's hand, and went home. The next day the children were as ill-behaved as before, and poor, timid Gretchen received a loaf scarcely half the size of the one she got the first day. When she came home, and her mother cut the loaf open, many new, shining pieces of silver fell out of it."

"Very good, Janie," Beth said, using precisely the same words and tone she'd used with Rosie. "Jonathan, would you please read the last two verses?"

Her first week in the classroom had taught Beth as much as she'd taught her students. She'd told Owen Simpson she would be a good teacher. Much of her statement had been bravado and wishful thinking, born of a need to support herself in her new country. But it had turned out to be true. She *was* a good teacher. The children liked her, and she liked them even more. She loved their individuality, their uniqueness. She'd found something special in each one of them—with one possible exception.

As Jonathan Perkins scuffled slowly toward the front of the classroom, Beth continued mulling over the problem of Trevor. He'd defied her in many small ways this past week, and so far she'd managed to stand up to him. He had given in each time. But what would she do when the day came that he didn't give in? And she had no doubt such a day would come.

Resolutely she pushed aside that worry and gave her full attention to the work at hand as the Perkins boy began to read aloud.

"Her mother was very much alarmed, and said, 'Take the money back to the good gentleman at once, for it must have got into the dough by accident. Be quick, Gretchen! Be quick!' But when the little girl gave the rich man her mother's message, he said, 'No, no, my child, it was no mistake. I had the silver pieces put into the smallest loaf to reward you. Always be as contented, peaceable, and grateful as you now are. Go home now, and tell your mother that the money is your own."

When the reading of *The Little Loaf* was finished, Beth questioned the children on the moral of the story.

It was Janie, as was so often the case, who raised her hand first. When called upon, she said, "I think it means if we're honest and don't cause trouble, good things'll happen to us in the end."

"Good. Anyone else have an opinion?" Beth asked, encouraging others to speak up. "Jonathan?"

The boy screwed up his mouth thoughtfully, then replied, "My ma's always talkin' about livin' right, even when everybody else is doin' wrong. She says there isn't no reason t'be . . ." He paused and scuffed his toe against the floor. "She says there's no call t'be sinnin' just 'cause others are."

Beth nodded, pleased as much by his participation as by his answer. It was usually somewhat of a miracle just to get Jonathan to put together five words in a row. Thus she decided not to correct his grammar this time.

"Anyone else?" When no one volunteered she said, "Very well. For Monday, I want you to read lesson number seven." She returned to stand behind her desk. "May I have your attention, class. It is now three forty-five. Because you have all done so well this week, I believe you deserve an early dismissal. I shall see you again on Monday. You may go now."

In a flash, they were out of their seats and rushing from the schoolroom amid a cacophony of voices. In a matter of minutes the room was empty, save for

Beth. A few minutes more, and she had only silence for company.

She sank onto the chair behind her desk, smiling as she acknowledged her own sense of satisfaction and accomplishment. But she also admitted her weariness. She was ready for some time to herself. It had been a strain, preparing all the necessary lesson plans every evening while trying to be courteous to the Homer sisters.

She closed her eyes and let out a lengthy sigh. It would be so nice to be on her own again. Bunny and Patsy had been hospitable, yet she was never quite comfortable with them. Perhaps it was their tendency to gossip about others in the community. Beth could scarcely believe Stella Matheson, the minister's wife, had once lived in a bordello. Nor would she have guessed Catherine Perkins had borne a child out of wedlock. The sisters had also suggested Owen Simpson hadn't acquired his wealth by honorable methods, although they hadn't been specific. And, of course, there was their suggestion of Garret's fondness for strong drink and an anger ready to explode when he gave in to it.

She doubted them, even while a small part of her wondered if there could be a grain of truth in the stories they'd shared oh so delicately. After all, hadn't Stella said to her earlier in the week that the American West was a place where people could start over, where past mistakes didn't matter, where what a person wanted to keep private was left private? Could the woman have been admitting she had a past to be forgotten?

Beth heard footsteps on the stairs and glanced up,

expecting to see Owen. The mayor had come by the school on one pretense or another every day this week, always offering her a ride back to town and always trying to talk her out of moving into the Thompson cabin. She'd accepted his rides but refused to change her mind about living near the school.

But it wasn't Owen she'd heard approaching, and she felt a shiver snake up her spine when Trevor stepped into the opening to the vestibule. He filled it with his bulky, muscular build.

"Did you forget something?" She forced her voice to sound calm.

"Yeah. I had somethin' t'say t'you."

She rose from her chair, resting her knuckles on the desktop, trying to look confident. "And what is that?"

"I'm no schoolboy. I don't need no more of your book learnin'." He approached her. "But there's a thing or two I'd like t'teach you." His meaning was clear in the way he moved as well as in the leering expression he wore. He was correct. He wasn't a boy. He was a young man—a dangerous one, it suddenly seemed.

"That's enough, Trevor."

"No, it ain't."

She glanced toward the door, real fear taking hold. It was a familiar thing, this feeling of vulnerability. Perceval had taught it to her. And after she'd learned it, he'd been able to control her with nothing more than a glance, a gesture, the tone of his voice.

"He ain't comin'."

She looked back at him. "Who isn't coming?"

"The mayor. I seen his buggy broke down, down

the road a piece. He's walkin' back t'town right now."
Trevor laughed, low in his throat. "It's just you and
me, Teach."

She took a step backward.

"I could do anything I liked, and nobody'd be the
wiser 'cause you wouldn't dare tell 'em. Know why?
'Cause you're not from around here. Folks don't take
t'your kind. That's what my pa says." He came closer.

Beth took another step backward. "Trevor, you
forget yourself. I'm your teacher and—"

"Like I said, it's just you and me, Teach."

"You're wrong about that, boy. Now get away
from Miss Wellington."

Trevor whirled in the direction of Garret's voice.
In the same moment, Beth pressed her back against
the blackboard.

The teenager let loose with a vile curse. "You got
no right t'tell me what t'do!" he shouted.

"Wrong again." With a few swift strides, Garret
crossed the room and grabbed Trevor by the collar.
With a jerk and a shove, he propelled the boy toward
the doorway.

Beth tried to follow but found her legs wouldn't
obey. She started to shake, shake so hard that she
could no longer stand. Slowly she slid down the wall
until she sat on the floor, her knees drawn up to her
chest, her arms clasped around them.

She had no idea how long she was there, staring at
the empty doorway, before Garret reappeared. His
face was lined with worry as he walked across the
room, then knelt on the floor in front of her.

"Beth, are you all right?"

She nodded, but it was a lie.

"He won't bother you again," he said gently. "Trevor Booth is finished with his schooling."

He rubbed his right knuckles with the fingers of his left hand, and she wondered if he'd hit the boy or if she simply wished he had. She tried to say, "Thank you," but no sound came out of her throat.

Garret sat and leaned his back against the wall next to her. "It's not your fault. He's pure trouble. Always has been."

She couldn't stop shaking, couldn't say anything to explain her behavior.

Unexpectedly he put his arm around her shoulders and pulled her near. "It's all right, Beth. It's all right." He pressed her head against his chest and stroked her hair.

After a long while she whispered, "He didn't hurt me. He didn't even touch me."

Garret said nothing.

"I should have handled it better. He's just sixteen. Just a boy."

"He was threatening you like a man."

She drew a deep breath, then straightened away from Garret, leaving the protection of his arm. "I was his teacher. I should have known how to handle the situation." She lifted her chin and met his gaze. "You mustn't tell anyone what happened. I could lose my position."

He stared into her eyes for a long time before saying, "It wasn't just Trevor, was it? That wasn't all that caused you to be so afraid."

Beth didn't know why, but she felt compelled to answer him honestly. "No, it wasn't."

"That first night you came to the ranch. You had a

nightmare or something. You were afraid then, too."
His voice lowered. "Was it me? Did I frighten you,
Beth?"

She shook her head. "No, you don't frighten me."
That was partially a lie. The feelings she had for him
frightened her. But that wasn't what he'd meant.

"Then what is it?"

"Lord Altberry," she answered, feeling a familiar
tremor at his name.

"Your fiancé?"

"Perceval was not a kind man." She finally broke
free of his gaze, turned her head to stare sightlessly
toward the window. "He liked to make others feel
weak. He liked to dominate."

"He hurt you." There was a note of outrage in his
statement.

"Yes, but never so anyone could see. Certainly not
so my father could see."

"Why didn't you tell him? Your father, I mean."

Because he wasn't like you, she was tempted to
say. Instead she answered, "There were many reasons. They seem difficult to understand in America,
but they were not so strange in England. Father was
the one who had arranged the marriage, and I
couldn't disappoint him. I thought there was something wrong with me. If I were only a better person, a
different person, then Perceval wouldn't become
angry with me. I thought it would get better once we
were married. Or at least, I told myself so."

She was silent for a short while, remembering, and
Garret once again waited without interruption.

"It was the night before my father fell ill when
everything changed. Father and Perceval had been

hunting all day, and when they were through, they celebrated with brandy after supper. Perceval's moods were mercurial in the best of times, but when he drank . . ." She shook her head slowly, feeling a familiar knot forming in her stomach. "I tried to excuse myself, but he wouldn't let me go. He liked to keep me nearby whenever he visited Langford House."

Beth swallowed the bitter taste in her mouth. "I had become quite adept at imagining myself elsewhere whenever he began drinking, and that's what I was doing. In fact, I was thinking about Janie and her latest letter. . . ."

"Elizabeth?"

The sound of her name dragged her abruptly from her memories. She looked up to find Perceval standing next to her chair, watching her with an icy glare, his eyes glazed by intoxication.

"Are you purposefully ignoring me, my dear?"

Beth shook her head, her throat gone dry.

He smiled heartlessly. "See that you don't." He cradled her chin in the palm of his hand. The touch was gentle yet held a warning—no, a promise—of pain. . . .

"Perceval hated it when I failed to pay proper attention to him. He . . . he took pleasure in the pain of others. He enjoyed frightening me." She shuddered. "And he frightened me often."

"If you'd rather not tell me—" Garret began.

She continued as if he hadn't interrupted. "He was dreadfully intoxicated that night. After he'd made certain I was listening to him, he asked Father for another bottle of brandy. When he stepped toward the fireplace, he tripped over one of Father's hunting spaniels and fell to his knees."

"Bloody hell! Miserable cur!"

"He was up in an instant. He was unharmed, but he was furious. He began kicking the dog. He kicked it again . . . and again . . . and again." She felt cold. Her voice dropped to a whisper. "He was out of control. He kept shouting and cursing, and the dog was howling in pain. I couldn't bear it."

She covered her ears, as she had on that horrible night, but it seemed as if she could still hear Perceval's vile curses and the animal's pitiful cries.

"When the dog died, I knew I couldn't marry Perceval. I knew I had to convince Father to face ruin rather than give me to him. I was sure he would understand, that he wouldn't force me to marry against my will after what had happened." She swallowed, the lump in her throat making it hard to speak. "Because if I had married him, I knew I'd never know a better life—or death—than that poor dog."

Garret swore softly.

"Father became ill the next day and died not long after," she added as she lowered her hands from her ears. "Perceval handled all of the necessary affairs. He arranged for the funeral and contacted the new earl. Afterward, he insisted we wed quietly and soon." She swallowed, then finished, "But I came to America instead."

"Now I understand."

She blinked away the memories, suddenly reminded of where she was and whom she was with. She turned her head to look at Garret.

"It took a lot of courage for you to do what you did," he said.

"I ran away."

"Maybe. But sometimes running away is the smartest thing to do. Sometimes it's the most courageous thing to do." He pushed himself up from the floor, then leaned down and offered her his hand.

Placing her fingers in his palm and feeling his grip tighten, she forgot the bad memories, forgot about Trevor Booth, forgot everything except for the way she felt when she was with this man. More than anything in the world, she wished he could learn to love her in return.

"In all the commotion, I almost forgot I came to give you something." Gently he pulled her to her feet.

Standing, she found herself face-to-face with him, her body mere inches from his. She could see the dark stubble of his beard beneath his sun-bronzed skin, wondered what it would feel like were he to kiss her and rub his roughened cheek against hers. Her pulse quickened, and her mouth went dry. The wanting of that kiss was overwhelming.

"Come on." His voice sounded husky, strained. "I'll show you what it is."

Mutely she followed him, her hand still captured in his.

"I thought, with you living out here all alone, you ought to have a way to get around." He stopped and motioned with his free arm toward two horses, tethered nearby. "The small one is Flick. He's yours."

Garret took pleasure in her obvious surprise, although he was sorry when she let go of his hand and descended the steps without him. Still, he was glad he could do something to bring her joy after the story she'd related to him. It was bad enough Trevor had threatened her as he had. But when Garret thought of the things that blasted Englishman must have done to her . . .

"He's a fine animal, Mr. Steele," she said as she ran one hand over the gelding's withers and back. "I really shouldn't accept him. He's much too valuable to give away."

"I want you to have him."

There had been a moment, inside the school, when he'd nearly kissed her, when the desire to possess her had almost cost him his hard-won self-control. And although he understood her better after what she'd told him, it didn't change the facts. She was still a beautiful woman who was used to the finer things in life. And he was still a Montana cattleman with a simple log house, struggling to make it from one year to the next, always hoping for a strong market when he sold his cattle in the fall just so he could make it through another winter, another spring and summer, repeating the same cycle over again.

"It's no wonder Janie is such a generous child," Beth said, looking up at him. "She's learned it from her father."

He might have kissed her then, despite his misgivings, if he hadn't still been at the top of those steps. Fortunately, before he could react to the impulse,

Owen drove up in what looked like the doctor's buggy.

Garret descended the stairs and untethered his horse. "I'd best be on my way," he told Beth as he stepped into the stirrup and settled onto the saddle. Then he glanced toward Owen as the other man approached. "We've got another grizzly killin' cattle on the east range. I'm on my way into town to form a huntin' party. If you see anybody, spread the word, will you?"

"Sure," Owen replied to Garret, but his gaze was locked on Beth.

As Garret rode away, he couldn't help thinking that Owen Simpson had a lot more to offer a woman like Beth than he would ever have. Shoot, he didn't even want to offer a woman anything. He liked things as they were, just him and Janie. Things were simpler that way. Uncomplicated. The way he liked them best.

He glanced over his shoulder. Owen was standing close to Beth as they talked to one another. Owen was courting her. Owen had staked his claim, almost from the first day she'd arrived. Owen had a fine house on the edge of town and was a prosperous businessman. He was college educated. Owen would have plenty to offer Beth. She wasn't ready yet, but she would be, given time.

Garret straightened in the saddle, telling himself to forget Beth and what had happened to her back in England or even what had happened to her just this afternoon. He had enough worries of his own, foremost of which was a grizzly to kill before he lost any more cows.

Beth Wellington wasn't any of his concern.

And that was the way it was going to stay.

10

On Saturday morning Owen drove Beth and her possessions, including the furniture and other household goods the citizens of New Prospects had given to her, out to the Thompson cabin in a wagon he'd borrowed from the livery. Beth had already spent time earlier in the week cleaning her new home from top to bottom. Now all that was left was to settle in.

When the school came into view, she remembered what had happened the day before with Trevor Booth. Residual fear caused her to catch her breath. What if the boy were to return? What if next time Garret didn't come to her rescue? What if . . .

She forced out the air from her lungs while scolding herself silently. She wasn't going to live in fear. It was fear, not Trevor's threats, that would make her helpless.

She turned her gaze from the schoolhouse to the cabin. That was when she spied Janie, seated on the top rail of the small corral, stroking Flick's head. Maybelle stood nearby, grazing on tufts of grass.

Beth's mood brightened at the sight of the child. "What are you doing at school on a Saturday?" she asked as the wagon rolled to a stop.

Janie hopped off the fence. "I came t'help you move in. Hello, Mr. Simpson. You're helpin', too, huh?"

"Yes," he answered, frowning slightly. "Does your father know you're here?"

"He's off huntin' down that grizzly with a buncha men. Don't worry. He knows I'm here. 'Fore he left this mornin', I told him I was gonna help Miss Beth."

Beth's heart skipped a beat. "Is it dangerous?" she asked Owen. "This hunting of grizzly bears?"

"Not really. They've got the dogs, and most of the men are good shots. They've done this before." He climbed down from the wagon, then helped her do the same.

She had other questions, but she forced herself not to ask them. It wouldn't do for anyone to guess how she felt about Garret Steele, that it was him and him alone she was worried about.

"How d'ya like Flick, Miss Beth? Ain't . . . I mean, isn't he a great horse? Wish I'd been here when Pa brought him to you. If I hadn't gone home the long way so I could talk to Pearl, I'd have seen him on the road and come back with him. I think it's great you'll have a horse of your own now. Maybe we can go ridin' sometime, you an' me."

Beth smiled, thankful for Janie's chatter. "I'd like that." She forced away unwelcome thoughts of the girl's father and concentrated on the present. "Shall we help Mr. Simpson with my things?"

"Sure."

With the three of them working, it didn't take long to move the items out of the wagon and into the small house. Then, while Beth and Janie unpacked the trunk and put items away, Owen climbed onto the roof and spread a canvas tarp over it, just in case it rained before the roof repairs were completed.

As usual, Janie kept up a steady banter. She talked about her colt and Maybelle. She talked about the new litter of pups. She asked endless questions about England and Langford House and what it was like to sail across an ocean and ride across America on a train.

Beth responded to Janie's stories and questions as she moved about the room, hanging dresses on nails in the wall or setting dishes on a board shelf near the stove. And before any of them knew it, they were finished.

"Gosh, Miss Beth. I can't hardly believe it's the same place. Didn't look this nice when old Mr. Thompson lived here."

Beth smiled as she surveyed the room, from the vase filled with wildflowers in the center of the table to the lace curtains at the windows to the quilt covering her bed. "It does look nice, doesn't it?"

"Sure does."

She gave the girl's shoulders a squeeze. "Thank you for all your help. I never would have accomplished it so quickly without you."

Janie shrugged. "I like helpin' you."

"So do I," Owen said from behind them.

Beth turned. "You shall never know how very much this means to me, Mr. Simpson."

"I think I do." He glanced at Janie. "We probably

ought to leave Miss Wellington alone, allow her to enjoy her new place in peace."

Janie didn't budge.

"Your father might be back from the hunt. He'll be wondering about you."

"He knows where I am."

Beth felt like laughing. It was obvious what was happening. Owen was trying to be rid of the child so he could have Beth to himself, and Janie was having none of it. She leaned down, bringing her face closer to Janie's. "Mr. Simpson is right. I would like some time to myself. Thank you for coming to help. You made the work so much more enjoyable."

"Weren't no trouble." Janie wrinkled her nose as she glanced toward Owen, then back at Beth as she whispered, "Is he leavin', too?"

Beth straightened and met Owen's gaze. "Yes, Mr. Simpson is leaving, too. I shall see you both in church tomorrow."

Reluctantly Janie said good-bye and left.

Owen waited until the girl was riding away before he said, "I was wondering if you might have supper with me tonight, Miss Wellington?"

"I'm sorry. I don't believe that would be wise. You have already helped me a great deal. People might get the wrong impression."

"You mean they might think I'm courting you."

"Yes."

"But I am."

She thought of Garret, thought of how it had felt when he'd placed his arm around her shoulder, of how comforting it had been to press her face against his chest and listen to the strong, steady beat of his heart. How she yearned for it to be Garret who wanted to take her to supper, to allow folks to know he was courting her.

But it wasn't.

"Miss Wellington?" He took a step closer. "May I call you Beth?"

Garret had called her Beth yesterday after he'd sent Trevor packing. He'd knelt on the floor beside her and said her name softly. She suspected he hadn't even realized he'd used her given name. He hadn't meant it as an endearment.

Owen Simpson did.

"It's much too soon," she answered softly.

"Is it because of the man you were engaged to in England? Are you still in love with him?"

"No."

He touched her arm. "I would be a good husband to you. I could give you anything you wanted. I am not rich, but neither am I poor. I'd provide well for you. If you wanted it, I wouldn't even object if you continued to teach. I've known I wanted you for my wife from the first time I saw you. You are so beautiful, Beth."

She turned away. "It's too soon." *But it wouldn't be if you were Garret.*

"You think I'll give up. I won't."

"Mr. Simpson—"

"Call me Owen."

She faced him again. "Mr. Simpson—"

He drew closer. "My name is Owen."

She loved children, and in her heart she knew she wanted to have some of her own. That had been the one bright thought when she'd imagined herself married to Perceval. She would have had children, and she would have loved them, even though they were his. But when she'd left England, she'd left behind the dream of being a mother. Now, here was a good man, offering to give her a home and a chance to have those babies.

"Owen," he prompted. "Go on. Say it."

She looked into his hazel eyes, saw the kindness there, saw his affection for her. Wasn't that enough? Wasn't that more than most people had?

But she wanted more.

"Owen, I don't think—"

He kissed her. She let him go on kissing her, hoping she would feel some spark of desire, some quickening of her heart. He was a good, kind man. He had treated her with nothing but respect. If she wanted children, she could do much worse than Owen Simpson for their father.

But there was no spark of desire or quickening of her heart, no matter how much she wanted those feelings to exist.

Owen drew back, then touched her cheek with his fingertips. "All right, Beth. I'll give you a little more time to get used to the idea. But like I said, I'm not going to give up. I'm a determined man. I know what I want. I want you to marry me, and one way or another, I'm going to get you to agree to it."

The hunting party climbed higher into the mountains as the day went on, the men traveling in pairs, looking for fresh signs of the grizzly. Garret rode with Hezekiah. The reverend, a crack shot with a rifle, had taken the lead a short while before and was about twenty feet ahead of Garret as they followed a rocky trail up a steep incline.

At the top, Hezekiah reined in his horse and waited for Garret to reach him. "You see any sign of it?"

"Nope." Garret removed his hat and wiped the sweat from his brow with his shirtsleeve.

"I think we might as well turn back. If it's gone up this far, it's no danger to the cattle."

"It'll be back. Once a grizzly gets used to easy kill, it always comes back for more. If we don't keep after it, I could lose a lot more of my herd, and so could the others."

Hezekiah nodded. Then he glanced toward the western horizon. "Look at that. There's a storm brewing."

Garret followed the other man's gaze. Thick clouds darkened the sky over the distant mountains and threw long shadows across the valley floor. For some reason, he thought of Beth. She'd moved into the cabin today, the cabin with the leaky roof. He wondered if she'd be all right.

In truth, Beth hadn't been far from his mind all day. The oddest things would make him remember the way she'd looked, the way she'd felt in his arms, even the clean fragrance of her hair. It had been a long time since he'd felt as angry as he had when he'd overheard Trevor Booth's threats. It had taken every ounce of his self-control not to beat the young bully to a bloody pulp. And after he'd heard Beth's confession about that lord or count or whatever he was, Garret was thankful he hadn't. She'd seen enough violence.

It had been much easier when he'd thought Beth was nothing more than a spoiled, pampered, self-indulged female whose only concern was getting her own way. It had been much easier to ignore her, to wish her elsewhere. But there was more to Beth Wellington. Much more.

And Garret wanted her.

Sex. A roll in the hay. What red-blooded male wouldn't want to experience it with a beautiful woman like Beth? And that was all he was interested in. Just having her in his bed and burying himself inside her.

"If we don't want to get wet, Garret, I'd suggest we start down now. We'll try again on Monday."

Jerked from his unchaste thoughts by the reverend's words, Garret responded gruffly, "Yeah, you're probably right. Let's go." He turned his gelding.

Out of nowhere, the grizzly appeared on the trail before him, standing on its hind legs and roaring its fury. Garret's horse reared, nearly tumbling over backward. Unseated, Garret hit the ground hard, the air knocked from him in a rush. He had only an instant to expect to feel giant claws swiping at his flesh. But instead the loose, rocky terrain gave beneath him. He slid down the hillside, rolling out of control, smacking into tree stumps and boulders, then tumbling on, gaining speed as he went.

He thought he heard the crack of rifle fire, hoped Hezekiah had killed the grizzly. If the bear was following Garret's descent, he would be helpless to protect himself.

That was the last conscious thought he had before

a bright light flashed in his eyes and pain exploded in his head. Then everything went black.

"What is it you suggest we do now, Bunny?"

Standing in the stock room with her back to her sister, Bunny smiled to herself as she swept the feather duster across the tops of the canned goods display. "I haven't the foggiest notion, dear sister. Mr. Simpson does seem determined to win the affections of our new schoolmarm, doesn't he?"

"Well, I don't see your Mr. Steele beating down your door, either," Patsy snapped sarcastically.

Bunny gritted her teeth, her good humor instantly forgotten. "Perhaps not yet, but he will."

"Don't be too sure about it. Remember, his daughter is terribly fond of Miss Wellington, and she doesn't like you at all."

Bunny turned around and smiled again, this time for the sake of cruelty. "But if Beth has already married Mr. Simpson, it won't matter what the brat wants. Will it?"

The argument might have continued if the bell above the shop door hadn't alerted the sisters to a customer. Patsy sent an angry glare in Bunny's direction, then went to see who had entered the store. Bunny sighed.

Deep down, she had to admit her sister was right. Garret Steele didn't seem any more inclined to notice her now than he ever had. It was also true that Janie Steele didn't like Bunny much. Oh, the brat tried to hide it, but Bunny could tell. And the feeling was mutual.

She threw the feather duster into a corner, then climbed the stairs to the apartment she and Patsy shared.

Thirty-four. She was thirty-four years old and living with her fat, homely sister. It wasn't fair. Life just wasn't fair.

Her thoughts returned to the new schoolmarm. She was glad, of course, that it was the mayor who seemed predisposed to help Beth Wellington, but Bunny wasn't a fool. She knew there was still plenty of danger of Beth turning other men's heads, including Garret Steele's. She didn't want that to happen. She had to do whatever she could to prevent it.

But what?

She put the kettle on the stove, then took down a cup and saucer and the canister of tea.

She and Patsy had hoped to control things by having Beth live with them. They had hoped to convince Beth not to move out to that dreadful cabin, believing it made her too available to the single men of the community. They had tried to trick her by telling untrue stories about some of the citizens of New Prospects, hoping she would say or do something that would cause her to be rejected by people in this town.

Unfortunately nothing they'd tried had worked. Beth Wellington, in addition to having been born beautiful, appeared to live a charmed life.

But Bunny Homer was nothing if not persistent. She wasn't beat yet. She would find some way to rid her town of that woman.

Beth awakened from her nap, feeling groggy and disoriented. She hadn't expected to fall asleep when she'd lain down on the bed. She'd only meant to close her eyes for a few moments.

Brushing her hair away from her face, she sat up and stretched, then looked around the room. It was deep in shadows, yet she was certain she couldn't have been asleep so long that evening had come. Squinting, she checked her watch. She was right. It was only five o'clock.

She rose from the bed, walked to the door, and opened it. She was greeted by a sky heavy with angry black clouds. The air smelled of rain.

Thank goodness Owen had covered the roof.

A bolt of lightning flashed in the distance. Moments later, thunder rumbled toward her. But it didn't fade when she expected it to. Then she realized what she heard wasn't thunder but the sound of a galloping horse. She stepped outside just as the horse and rider came racing into the schoolyard and up to her cabin.

Something tightened in her chest when she recognized the man on horseback, when she saw the expression he wore. "Mr. Whitaker, what's wrong?"

"It's Garret," Jake answered. "He's been hurt. I'm on my way for the doc, but Janie made me swear I'd stop and ask you t'come out. The little gal's mighty scared. I think she needs you, ma'am."

"I'll go right now."

"Thanks." He spun his horse and galloped away without another word.

Garret's hurt.

Beth ran to the lean-to and grabbed the saddle and bridle, then hurried into the corral. Fortunately Flick was not easily spooked by sudden movements or a panicked rider.

Janie needs me.

In what seemed a lifetime but was, in fact, only a matter of minutes, Beth had the gelding cinched up and ready to go. She'd never ridden astride before, but there was no time to worry about it now. She slipped her foot in the stirrup, hiked up her skirts, and mounted the horse. Clinging to the pommel with one hand, she jabbed her heels into Flick's sides and held tight as he set off in a flat-out run.

The distance between the Steele ranch and the school had never seemed as far as it did today.

Flick had worked up a thick lather by the time he galloped into the Steele yard. Beth half vaulted, half fell from the saddle, barely managing to stay upright when her feet hit the ground. The front door stood open, and as she hurried toward it, she could see several men standing in the front room.

"Where is Janie?" she demanded as she stepped inside. *How is Garret?* her mind screamed.

One of the men—she thought it was Patrick O'Toole—replied, "With her dad." He jerked his head toward the bedroom.

She hurried on, not caring about her disheveled appearance or the way all the men were staring at her. She stopped at the closed door and knocked.

"Come in."

She lifted the latch and pushed open the door.

Garret lay on the bed, still as death. Hezekiah stood over him, cleansing an ugly gash on Garret's forehead with a damp cloth. White-faced, Janie sat on a chair in the corner, hands clenched in her lap.

"Janie," Beth whispered.

The girl looked up, let out a small cry, then darted across the room, burying her face in Beth's skirt as she hugged her around the waist. "Miss Beth, Pa's hurt," she choked out, and then began to cry.

Beth stroked Janie's hair. "I know, but he'll be all right." She met the reverend's gaze, saw his concern, fought the return of her own panic. "Why don't you come outside with me?" she suggested softly. "Mr. Whitaker will be back with the doctor soon. We can watch for them together."

With her hand on Janie's back, she steered the child out of the bedroom, past the other hunters, and out onto the porch. Thunder still rolled across the heavens as the wind brought the storm clouds closer.

"Sit with me on the steps." When they were both seated, Beth put her arms around the girl and drew her close to her side. "It's going to be all right."

Janie looked at her with fear-filled eyes. "You didn't see him when they brought him in, Miss Beth. He's hurt bad. What if he . . . what if he dies?"

"Oh, Janie." Beth pulled her against her breast and stroked her hair once again. "He's not going to die." *Please, God, don't let him die.* "Your father is a strong man. I'm quite certain he'll be up and about in no time at all. You'll see."

"I'm scared. Real scared." Janie began to sob again.

"Shh," she crooned. "Shh. It's all right. Everything is going to be all right. Shh."

"I don't want t'be alone. You'll stay with me, won't you, Miss Beth? Please don't go."

"I'm not going to leave you, Janie. I promise. I'll be right here. It's all right. It's all right."

Beth had no idea how long they sat on the porch—
lightning flashing, thunder roaring, and Janie crying—
before it began to rain. She was thankful for it, for
then she was able to allow her tears to fall, streaking
her cheeks, mingling with the raindrops on her skin.
Silently she repeated again and again, Please, God, let
him be all right. Please, God, don't let him die.

When Dr. Werner arrived in his buggy, followed
by both Jake Whitaker and Owen Simpson, Beth and
Janie rose from the step, still hugging one another.
Beth's heart beat at a fearful pace as she watched the
white-bearded doctor hurry past them, black bag in
hand. Jake followed him inside.

Owen, however, paused beside Beth. "You're
soaking wet," he said as he placed a hand on her
shoulder. "Come inside before you catch your death."

"Janie's frightened," she whispered. She glanced
toward the men from the hunting party who were still
standing about in the living room. "I think they
should leave. It's as if they're waiting for him to die."
She couldn't stop the involuntary shudder.

He nodded. "I'll take care of it. But first I want
both of you inside." He shepherded them through the
doorway and straight through to the kitchen. "Sit
down."

Beth and Janie both did as they were told but never
let loose of each other's hands.

Owen strode back into the living room. "Why
don't you all go on home before it gets dark? Looks
like the rain's starting to let up. We'll let you know
how Garret's doing."

The men mumbled a general sound of agreement,
then moved out the door, Owen and Jake with them.

Janie squeezed Beth's hand, drawing her attention. "The reverend said they got the grizzly," she said in a voice still choked with tears.

"Did they?"

The girl nodded, trying so hard to look brave.

"That's good."

The bedroom door opened and Hezekiah came out. He glanced around, found Beth and Janie in the kitchen, and walked toward them.

Beth's heart was pounding so hard, she was certain he must be able to hear it. Janie's grip tightened until it was almost painful.

"He's beginning to come around," the reverend told them. "God be praised."

"Yes," Beth whispered, and felt the urge to cry once again.

Owen joined them in the kitchen. "What's the word, Hezekiah?"

"His left arm is broken, and he's pretty much banged up and bruised all over. Might have a broken rib or two. The doctor's sewing that cut on his forehead now. But it looks like he'll be none the worse for wear with some time to heal."

"What exactly happened?" Owen asked. "Jake said you were with Garret."

The reverend nodded. "The bear came out of nowhere. Attacked his horse. Garret was thrown free and fell down the mountain. It was pretty rough terrain." He glanced at Janie, then back at Owen. "It could have been much worse."

"You shot the bear?"

"Yes."

"Well, that's good news. Garret doesn't need to

worry about losing any more cattle while he's on the mend." Owen's smile was humorless. "Maybe now we'll be able to keep him down until he's recovered."

Janie rose from her chair. "Can I see my pa now, Reverend Matheson?"

Hezekiah nodded as he gave her a reassuring smile. "Of course, Janie. Go ahead. I'm sure he'll be glad to see you."

The girl hurried away.

Beth wished she could have gone with Janie. She longed to see with her own eyes that Garret was going to recover. But, of course, it wasn't her right to do so. She was nothing to him except his daughter's teacher. She was here for Janie, not for Garret.

"Beth." Owen laid his hand lightly on her shoulder. "I'd better see you home."

"Janie asked me to stay. I can't leave just yet. I have to stay as long as she needs me."

He nodded. "Then I'll wait with you."

"She was so frightened." She paused. "Do you truly believe he'll be all right?"

"Yes. And so will Janie. Jake's here, and the women'll bring food in for them. Folks in these parts always lend a hand when it's needed."

Beth nodded as she stared at the bedroom door. "Of course."

But silently she wished Garret and Janie didn't need the help of friends and neighbors. Silently she wished that she—Beth Wellington—were all they needed.

11

Garret hadn't been so idle since he was a babe in his ma's arms. Nor had the Steele ranch ever seen as many visitors as it did over the next week. Just about every family within an easy riding distance was represented at one time or another, all of them bringing wishes for a speedy recovery and something for them to eat in the meantime. The kitchen overflowed with casseroles, canned vegetables, loaves of bread, cakes, and pies, all of them prepared by the generous women of the valley.

"I'm gonna get fat before I can work again," he told Jake after the Homer sisters left the house, their third visit of the week.

The only person who didn't come calling in the days immediately following his accident was Beth Wellington. Janie had told him Beth was there the day he'd taken his fall, but she hadn't been back since. Garret was surprised at how her absence made him feel.

Not that he didn't know what was going on in her life. What Janie couldn't tell him, Owen did.

Janie'd reported how all the children liked their new teacher and had said things were much better now that Trevor wasn't around to bully the little kids. She said Miss Beth made a game out of many of the lessons, so learning was as much fun as it was work.

Owen told him Beth had moved into her one-room cabin and succeeded in making it quite comfortable and homelike. He'd taken her to supper at the restaurant in town earlier in the week, and he thought they were getting on rather well. He hoped to propose marriage to her before the summer was out.

Garret was oddly disturbed by that piece of news. "So soon?"

"Not soon enough for me," his friend replied with a grin.

"She hasn't even been here a month."

"Some things a man just knows are right. This is one of those things."

Garret was irritated by Owen's cheerful certainty. "That's what I thought with Muriel."

"You can't compare Beth with Muriel, and you know it."

That was true enough. Garret had learned quickly that Beth and Muriel had little in common beyond a unique physical beauty and a background of privilege.

"Besides," Owen continued, "I'm thirty-one. It's time I settled down. Who knows? Maybe we'll even have a family. I never wanted kids much, but I suppose I'd change my mind if Beth was their mother. Heaven knows I'd sure enjoy making them."

Garret's mood grew darker by the minute.

"When the time comes for the wedding, I hope you'll stand up with me."

"Mighty sure of yourself, aren't you? She just might turn you down."

Owen chuckled. "Well, I'm not without some charm, you know? It isn't as if I couldn't have found a willing woman before now. I just wasn't ready to marry. Too busy with the bank and all. But no man in his right mind wouldn't want to marry a girl as beautiful as Beth. I'll make certain she agrees to be my wife. You'll see."

Garret tried to be glad for his friend. Only he kept remembering the moment in the schoolroom when he'd held Beth in his arms and had comforted her. He kept remembering the silkiness of her hair and the warmth of her body and the green of her eyes and the sweet, seductive shape of her mouth. He imagined what it would be like to kiss that mouth, to unclothe that body and hold it close to his own, to pull the pins for that hair and watch it tumble over her shoulders.

But he darn well better *stop* imagining such things if she was going to be married to someone else.

He closed his eyes and slid down in his bed. He feigned a yawn, then muttered, "I'm sorry, Owen. Feelin' a bit tired. I think I need some shut-eye."

"Sure. I'll come back in a day or two."

Garret heard the legs of the chair slide backward on the wooden floor, then listened to the sound of footsteps and the opening and closing of the door as Owen let himself out of the bedroom. When he was alone again, Garret rolled onto his right side, groaning as pain shot through him, sore muscles and cracked ribs complaining.

Some friend he was. Instead of being glad for Owen, he was having lustful thoughts about the

woman Owen wanted to marry. Even when Garret
was battered and bruised, his arm broken, and his
head pounding, his body responded to the images of
Beth he'd conjured up.

*Maybe we'll even have a family. . . . Heaven
knows I'd sure enjoy making them.*

Beth would make a wonderful mother. Garret had
watched her with Janie and known she was meant to
have children of her own. She should be married, and
she should have a half dozen babies, at least. Owen
was willing to make both things happen.

Garret wasn't willing to do either. Not with Beth.
Not with any woman.

That should have settled it.

For some reason, it didn't.

Beth paused in her clothes washing and straightened,
stretching the kink out of her back. Even though she'd
placed the washtub in the shade of a leafy tree, it was
impossible to escape the hot rays of the sun. Tendrils
of hair clung to her forehead and the nape of her neck.
The skin on her hands was rough and cracked, and she
wondered if they would ever stop hurting.

She had learned one important lesson in the week
she'd been living on her own. She would never again
fail to appreciate the work someone might do for her,
whether for pay or as a favor. She'd never realized how
hard Mrs. Crumb and Mary—and, in better days, the
other servants—had worked. She'd never dreamed
how many hours could be consumed by things such as
washing and ironing, mending and dusting, preparing
food and cleaning up afterward.

Of course, it might be easier if she knew what she was doing. She smiled wryly, remembering her recent experiences in the kitchen. If she didn't know better, she'd think the stove was a demon come to earth to torture her, not to mention burn any food she tried to prepare.

But she was improving, she reminded herself. She couldn't expect to master everything the first time she tried. Or even the second and third times. All she needed was patience.

She recalled the past week with her students and felt a spark of pride. Obviously her talent lay more with teaching than in tending a home. She'd quickly come to love all the children in her classroom. She'd found pleasure in discovering their individual talents and weaknesses. She'd awakened every morning eager to see what new and wonderful experiences they would share.

And each night she'd dreamed of having children of her own. And then she'd always dreamed about Garret.

Beth gave her head a firm shake, then began to vigorously rub a dress up and down the washboard. She didn't want to think about Garret. She didn't even want to think about his daughter. But, of course, she did.

All week long she had noticed the look of worry in the child's eyes. Too much worry for one so young. Beth had longed to hug and comfort her. But to do so would have subjected Janie to more taunts of "Teacher's pet!" and she hadn't wanted to be the cause of it.

"How is your father doing?" Beth had asked every day.

And each time Janie had answered, "He's gettin' better."

But Beth could tell the girl was still afraid her father might die, just as her mother had. She wished she'd known how to dispel those fears.

She also wished she could dispel her own. She longed to see Garret for herself, longed to look at him and know he would recover. It didn't matter that Janie said he was getting better. It didn't matter that Owen told her Garret was out of danger. She wanted to see him for herself.

But she'd made herself stay away. She'd told herself it was because she had too much work to do. She wasn't fooling herself, of course. She stayed away because of her increasing feelings for him. If she thought he might ever return those feelings . . .

She shook her head again, then squeezed water from the blue dress, gave it a brisk shake, and hung it on the clothesline. As she reached into the basket and took out a petticoat to wash next, she heard the sound of an approaching horse.

She glanced up, not surprised to see Owen riding into the yard. He'd come to see her every day for a solid week. She supposed she should have ceased her scrubbing and attempted to make herself more presentable.

"Good afternoon, Beth."

"Hello, Owen." She continued to scrub the petticoat.

He dismounted. "That's hard work on a hot day like today."

"It's hard work any day," she replied as she wrung the water from the cotton undergarment, trying to hide it from his view as she draped it over the clothes-line.

"Do you know where I just came from, Beth? I was out to see Garret."

Garret. How is he?

"And I told him I was going to ask you to marry me later this summer."

Her eyes widened and her breath caught in her throat as she spun to face him.

"But I see no reason to wait, Beth. I want to marry you. Say you will."

She felt the blood drain from her head. She stepped backward and braced herself against the tree trunk.

Owen stepped around the washtub. "I know it's soon, but I've waited a long time to find you. I don't want to waste any more time now that I have." He touched her cheek with his fingertips. "Garret's going to stand up with me at our wedding."

Garret would stand up with Owen. Garret didn't want her for himself, would never want her. Why couldn't she seem to grasp that as truth?

"Owen." The word came out in a hoarse whisper. She drew a steady breath, then began again. "Owen, you have been a good and kind friend to me from the day I arrived in New Prospects. And I am fond of you." She dropped her gaze from his. "But I don't love you."

"I think I can love enough for both of us."

She looked up again. *I'm in love with Garret.*

"Beth, you are everything any man could want in a wife. You are beautiful and intelligent, gentle and strong. Say you'll marry me."

She would have given almost anything in the world to hear Garret say those very same words.

"Let me provide for you. Let me take care of you."

Why had she fallen in love with the wrong man? She was a fool not to want Owen Simpson. He could have been her Prince Charming on a white horse. Why wasn't he the one who filled her dreams?

"I will cherish you always. You weren't meant to live alone, Beth."

He was probably right. She wanted to be married, to be cherished, to have babies. But shouldn't she love her husband, too?

"Say you'll marry me."

If only he were someone else. If only he were Garret.

Owen cradled her face between his hands. "Say it. Say you'll marry me. I'll make you happy. You can go on teaching if you want. Or you can stay at home if you want. Whatever pleases you, I'll see that you have it. I swear you'd never regret it. Say you'll marry me."

"I can't."

"All right." He sighed deeply as his hands slipped from her cheeks. He stepped back, watching her with sad eyes. "Maybe I'm still rushing it. But I'm not going to give up. I'll be asking again, Beth."

The lump in her throat was enormous. Tears burned the back of her eyes.

"I'll see you in church tomorrow."

She nodded.

"I'd make you happy, Beth. I promise you I would." With those parting words he turned, walked to his horse, stepped into the saddle, and rode away.

*   *   *

"Pa?" Janie's hand alighted gently on his shoulder.

Garret opened his eyes, rolled his head toward his daughter.

"You up to another caller?"

"More food?" he asked, hoping to tease away the worried look in her eyes.

He was rewarded with a smile. "No food. It's Miss Beth."

"Beth?"

"Uh-huh. Can she come in?"

He pushed himself upright, leaning against the pillows at his back. "It'd be mighty rude if I said no, I suppose."

"It's okay, Miss Beth," Janie called out. "Pa's awake."

A moment later she appeared in the bedroom doorway, looking more beautiful than he'd remembered. She wore a dark gray English riding habit that accentuated her lovely feminine curves. A silk top hat was perched on her head, looking both elegant and enchanting. Strands of her warm-colored hair curled at her nape and near her temples. Even bruised ribs and a broken arm didn't stop his body from responding to the pretty picture she made.

"Hello, Mr. Steele." She entered the room. "How are you feeling?"

"Better."

He reminded himself that Owen wanted to marry this woman. He reminded himself that he, Garret, had no intention of ever marrying again. He told himself next time he was in Bozeman he was due for a visit to Mad Maddie's because what he was feeling, what he was thinking, would go away once he did.

"We were all quite worried about you."

Even you? he wanted to ask.

She touched Janie's head with her fingertips. "Your daughter most of all."

She was wonderful with children. She was meant to be a mother. Owen wanted to make her one.

Beth sat on the spindle-back chair beside the bed, looking at him with those guileless green eyes. He caught a whiff of her lilac cologne, and his body responded to the scent.

"You want some tea, Miss Beth? I can make you some."

His daughter's voice dampened his ardor.

Beth smiled. "I'd like that. Thank you."

Janie hurried out of the bedroom, leaving the two adults alone.

"Mr. Steele . . ." She glanced at her gloved hands, folded in her lap. "I . . . I wasn't able to properly thank you for giving me Flick before you had your accident."

"You thanked me already. The day I brought him to you."

She looked up again. "I needed to thank you for more than the horse. You . . . you have been a friend to me. You listened when I needed to talk. You helped me when I needed help."

He caught a glimpse of something in her eyes, in her expression, a look that made the desire to possess her burn hot again. A look that said she felt a similar desire, although he suspected she didn't understand it in the same way he did. And he knew in that instant he couldn't follow through with those mutual feelings. She deserved better than a passionate night in his bed, followed by a soiled reputation. Beth deserved a husband, a home, a family—and he wasn't the man to give her any of those things.

"Owen's helped you, too," he said a bit gruffly.

She drew back. "Yes, he has."

"He's a good man, our mayor."

"Yes," she whispered.

Verbally he continued to push her away from him. "Funny, how two people can be so different and still be friends. Take Owen, for instance. He'd like to get married, settle down, maybe even have himself a passel of kids. Now me, nothing in the world could ever make me want to marry again. And as for kids, Janie's all I want. Don't need any more."

It was true. He didn't need a woman in his life. Things were just the way he wanted them. Him and Janie. That was all he wanted or needed.

Beth nodded, as if she understood all the words that had gone unspoken. "You must still love your wife very much. I'm sorry you lost her."

Still love Muriel? A bitter laugh nearly strangled him before he could swallow it, choosing instead to allow Beth to believe the lie.

Fortunately Janie chose that moment to return with Beth's tea, drawing his visitor's attention away, leaving him alone with his caustic memories. He closed his eyes and allowed his head to drop back against the wall behind him, surprised by the anger burning in his belly, even after all these years.

* * *

It was in November of 1886 when Muriel returned. It wasn't the first time in their three years of marriage that she'd taken up with another man, but it was the longest she'd ever been gone.

As he'd done in the past, he'd told folks his wife was visiting her parents in California. It was habit to keep up the pretense, even when he hadn't expected her to return.

Hadn't wanted her to return.

Muriel's first lover had been a traveling salesman. She'd returned after only a week on the road with him, swearing she was sorry and would never do it again. Her next liaison had been with the schoolteacher. That affair had lasted only a month, until the school term ended and the teacher hastily left town. After that there'd been a series of cowpokes. Just casual moments of adultery before the men moved on to other jobs, other wives. But this time had been different because she'd stayed away so long. Four months with the actor in the traveling theater troupe.

Not that Garret cared anymore. He'd quit caring several lovers back. That's why he was caught by surprise when she showed up at the ranch, begging him to take her back, promising she would be a good and faithful wife, that she would never leave him again. He didn't believe her. He suspected it was because she had nowhere else to go after the actor tired of her. But he was her husband, for better or worse. What else could he do but let her stay?

Winter had set in with a vengeance before he discovered Muriel was pregnant. She tried to lie to him at first. Tried to tell him the baby was his and that was why she'd returned to him, because he was going to be a father. But he'd long since stopped being a fool about his wife. He knew she wasn't telling the truth. She was carrying the bastard child of that actor. He guessed the man had sent her packing as soon as she'd told him she was going to have his baby.

Garret planned to send her back to her father after that. He didn't want her around, couldn't bear the sight of her. But he had no choice except to let her stay until spring, until after the snow had melted and the roads were passable. Which meant he would also have to wait until after the baby was born. But as soon as she was fit to travel, he was sending her away. And if her father disowned her, threw her out into the streets, so be it. It was no better than she deserved.

Then Janie was born. Garret was the one who delivered her, and the minute he held the infant in his arms, he knew he couldn't ever let her go. No matter what her mother did. No matter if his blood didn't flow in her veins. He wasn't ever going to lose this precious girl. She was his daughter, and for her, he would remain married to her mother.

For Janie, he would do anything.

Beth sipped her tea in silence, knowing she should leave. Garret had closed his eyes long ago, and pain was etched into the lines of his face. She longed to set aside the teacup and smooth those same lines with her fingertips. But she hadn't the right to do so. He'd made that clear enough.

It shouldn't have hurt so much. Nothing had ever happened between them. No words of love. Not even a kiss. She should not have felt so devastated.

But she did.

Glancing at Janie, who was now sitting at the foot of her father's bed, only caused her heartache to intensify. She loved Janie as if she were her own child. She'd loved Janie even before she'd fallen in love with her father. She'd had a secret fantasy about the three of them becoming a family.

Oh, what a fool she'd been! She'd run halfway around the world to escape marriage to a man she didn't love, only to fall in love with a man who would never want marriage. Fate had played a cruel joke on her, to be sure.

She rose from her chair and, placing her fingertip over her mouth for silence, let Janie know she was leaving. The girl slid off the bed and followed her out of the room.

"You goin' so soon, Miss Beth?" she asked as she closed the bedroom door.

"I must." Beth set the teacup on the table. "It's growing late, and I still have ironing to do." *I should have been ironing all this time. I shouldn't have come here. But I wanted to know if there was any hope. There isn't.*

"Miss Beth?"

She leaned down and took hold of the girl's hand. "What's the matter, Janie? You look so solemn."

"I just . . . I just wish you could stay."

So do I.

Tears pooled in Janie's eyes. "I . . . I'm not as scared when you're here."

"But there isn't anything to be frightened of." She knelt on the floor. "Your father is going to be well again soon."

"I . . . I know, but—" She sniffed and shook her head.

Beth remembered how alone she'd sometimes felt when she was a child. She remembered how much she'd missed her mother when things went wrong or when she was frightened. Gathering the girl into her arms, she said, "I understand."

"Miss Beth?" Janie's words were muffled against Beth's shoulder.

"Hmm?"

"I . . . I love you."

Beth fought tears of her own. "I love you, too, Janie," she whispered. "I love you, too."

12

Saturday, July 3, 1897
New Prospects, Montana

My dear Inga,

How truly delighted I was to receive
another letter from you so soon and to
learn all is well with you and your family.
Uppsala sounds quite charming and nearly
as small as New Prospects. Unlike Iowa,
there are only a few farms here. Most men
in this region raise cattle and horses on
their ranches. I am learning, little by little,
about this place I have made my home. It
is certainly quite different from England,
as I told you before.

I have discovered I have a love for
teaching beyond anything I imagined I
might. And I believe I may also have a talent for it as well. The students seem to

respond to me. I had a mishap early on with one of the older boys, but he is no longer in school and the summer session is progressing well.

Janie Steele is, of course, one of my pupils. Her father suffered an accident two weeks ago, and she was very frightened by it. So, too, was I. How tragic it would have been if worse had happened. I have observed how very close these two are and am convinced Mr. Steele is a wonderful father. Yet there is a sadness in their home as well. It is obvious to me Janie misses her mother. Indeed, Mr. Steele still mourns the loss of his wife. I wish I might have known Muriel Steele. She must have been a remarkable woman.

I am settled into my tiny log cabin and am slowly learning the necessary skills to care for my own needs. I had no notion how difficult it would be. I am ashamed of how often I took the Langford House servants for granted. There is always more to do than hours in the day. Washing and ironing and mending clothes. Baking bread. Chopping wood for the stove. Cleaning and sweeping and dusting. It never ends. And Mrs. Crumb would pass dead away were she to see my hands.

The people of New Prospects helped to furnish my house, but the best gift of all came from Mr. Steele. He gave me a fine gelding named Flick. I cannot express how much this horse means to me. I have the freedom to go anywhere I wish now. I shall forever be thankful for the generous gift.

But then, I have come to believe Mr. Steele has a generous heart. When I first arrived I thought him taciturn and unfriendly. But I was wrong. There is much to be admired about him. I have often wished I might come to know him even better, but it seems that is not to be.

Tomorrow, the people of New Prospects are celebrating their day of independence from England. Mr. Simpson has asked me to accompany him, and I have agreed to do so. In truth, Mr. Simpson has asked me a far more important question. He has asked me to marry him. I have told him it is much too soon, but he is a persistent man and has not accepted my refusal. I believe, dear Inga, that I will agree to marry him after all.

I don't suppose that will come as any great surprise to you or Mary. Both of you told me I would one day want to wed and have children, despite my experiences with Lord Altberry. And I would be a fool not to accept the proposal of a man like Mr. Simpson. He will be a good husband to me and a fine father for the children I hope I will have. What more could I ask? Surely love will come with time. I have been told so often enough. Even Mr.

Simpson tells me it is so. I do very much want to believe him.

I still have not heard from Mary Malone and am growing concerned. Do you know if she is still in New York City? Have you received any letters from her?

Please greet your parents for me, and tell your sisters I hope they are behaving and not breaking the hearts of too many young men in Uppsala.

Affectionately,
Beth Wellington

Garret winced with each bump of the wagon as it rolled along the rough road toward New Prospects. Still, it felt good to be going somewhere. Two weeks of inactivity had nearly driven him crazy. Lying in bed left a man's mind free to explore too many thoughts he'd just as soon avoid.

Speakin' of which, he thought as the schoolhouse came into view. And beyond it, the cabin. *Her* cabin.

Beth was never far from his thoughts. Every day he'd remembered how pretty she'd looked in her elegant riding habit when she'd paid him her one and only visit. And then he'd reminded himself he couldn't provide anything as costly as that outfit if he saved up for a whole year. A woman who was used to such finery grew quickly dissatisfied when forced to do without. He'd learned that lesson the hard way.

"Flick's not there," Janie said, intruding on his thoughts. "Miss Beth must've already left for church."

"Guess so."

She sighed. "I was hopin' she could ride in with us."

"Don't you get enough, seein' her at school every day?"

Janie's eyes widened as she looked at him. "I couldn't ever get tired of bein' with her, Pa. She's easy t'talk to."

Wasn't he easy to talk to? Garret wanted to ask, feeling suddenly out of sorts. Wasn't it bad enough he couldn't get Beth out of his head without her stealing his daughter's affections to boot?

He swallowed a curse. What was he getting so worked up over? Janie didn't need anybody but him. Even when Muriel had been alive, it had been Garret the child went to for love and attention. Nothing had changed. Look how she'd fussed over him ever since he'd been hurt.

He had a sudden image of Beth seated at his bedside, running her fingers over his brow, felt a strong and unexpected yearning to feel the tender care of a woman.

No, not just any woman.

Beth.

Following the opening hymn, Hezekiah opened the large black Bible on the altar and read from the Holy Scriptures: "'He that loveth his wife loveth himself. For no man ever yet hated his own flesh; but nourisheth and cherisheth it, even as the Lord the church: For we are members of his body, of his flesh, and of his bones. For this cause shall a man leave his father and mother, and shall be joined unto his wife, and they two shall be one flesh.'"

Beth glanced surreptitiously at Owen, sitting beside her in the third pew from the front. *And they two shall be one flesh.* What was it going to be like, to be as one flesh with Owen Simpson? Would she be frightened when the time came? Would he be gentle with her? Would she learn to covet his kisses? Would her heart skip a beat when she heard his voice? Would she look at him one day and discover she loved him?

Please, let it be so.

Last night she had decided this was the day she would tell Owen she would marry him. She knew he would ask her. He'd asked every day this week. This time she would give her consent.

Hezekiah paused in his reading from the Bible and looked toward the back of the church. A tolerant smile curved the corners of his mouth, and Beth suspected it meant the Steeles had just entered, late as usual. She felt a spark of pleasure, knowing Garret was well enough to come to church. How relieved Janie must be, she thought, while resisting the urge to glance behind her.

"Miss Beth? I . . . I love you."

"I love you, too, Janie."

Dear Janie. Why did it feel as if she were losing her? It needn't feel that way. Just because she planned to marry Owen didn't mean she couldn't love Janie. Even when she had children of her own, she would still love the girl just as much. Marrying Owen wouldn't—couldn't—change that.

But it would mean she could no longer love Janie's

father. She felt a tightness in her belly, an ache in her heart that, for a moment, threatened to overwhelm her.

Then she stiffened her back and lifted her chin, reminding herself she'd faced loss before and survived. She'd faced much worse than loving and not being loved in return. She'd seen both her parents die. She'd lost the only home she'd ever known to a distant relative. She'd left behind her native country and crossed an ocean and a continent to get here.

She'd endured all of that; surely she could get through this, too.

Owen laid his hand over hers and squeezed gently. She turned her head. He smiled.

Her heart ached as she smiled in return.

Three hours later Beth allowed Owen to draw her away from the picnic grounds, the tables laden with food, the games of horseshoes and three-legged races, the old men smoking pipes and old women telling tales, the farmers and ranchers with their talk of the weather and the women with their talk of children and the cost of dry goods. He took her arm and led her to the banks of the meandering creek that cut through the center of Town Park.

She knew why he took her there.

"You're a popular lady, Beth." They strolled arm in arm along a tree-shaded path. "Everyone else has monopolized you from the moment church let out. Now it's my turn. I want to celebrate Independence Day with my girl."

She felt a nervous shiver, hoped to delay what she

knew was coming. "I'm having a wonderful time. I suppose my British sensibilities should be offended at this particular celebration, but I confess I'm enjoying it all tremendously. The village near Langford House was too small and too poor for a country fair, and when we were in London . . ." She paused, smiled, then shrugged. "Well, the English aristocracy has its own perception of what is fun, and I don't believe this is it. Perhaps that is precisely why I find it so."

"Beth." He stopped, causing her to do the same. "Have I told you how beautiful you look today?"

"You tell me I look beautiful much too often."

"Do I? I don't think that's possible."

Her smile faded. "Owen, it is no great accomplishment for one to look as one is born to look."

"I've offended you. I'm sorry."

"No, you have not offended me. It's just that my looks are not all I want to be to—"

"Hey!" He turned so they were standing face-to-face. "I can't help loving how pretty you are, Beth. But I love a whole lot more than that about you. You know that. You know I do."

"I hope so," she whispered, dropping her gaze from his.

He took hold of her upper arms, pulling her close. "I swear it on my heart, Beth."

She didn't pull away when his mouth met hers. In truth, she leaned into it, hoping, waiting.

When Perceval had kissed her, she'd been repulsed. She'd avoided such encounters whenever possible. And when not, she'd sought a means of escape as quickly as she could. It wasn't like that with Owen. It wasn't distasteful. It was simply not . . .

Not exciting, she thought as the kiss ended.

He didn't pull away from her. Speaking low, his breath upon her cheek, he said what she'd known he would say. "Marry me, Beth."

She waited, feeling as if she were standing on the precipice of her future. A wrong step and . . .

"Marry me, Beth," he repeated.

"All right, Owen." She looked into his eyes. "I will marry you."

His expression was one of utter surprise and amazement. That he'd been expecting her to refuse him once again was clear. Suddenly he grinned and let out a whoop so loud, it caused birds to break into flight out of the nearby trees. It was not the usual sort of behavior for the town's mayor.

Beth couldn't help but respond to his joy with a smile of her own.

"I'll make you happy, Beth Wellington. So help me, I will. You'll never have cause to regret it."

He pulled her close and kissed her again, knocking her hat askew. She was just trying to repair the damage when several men came charging through the trees and underbrush.

"What's wrong?" Hezekiah demanded, looking from Owen to Beth and back again.

"Not a thing, Reverend," Owen replied. "Not a thing's wrong. Miss Wellington just now agreed to become my wife."

She caught a glimpse of Garret then, some ways back on the path. She couldn't see his face clearly, but something about him—the way he stood there, unmoving, watching and listening—made her chest tighten and her heart ache.

He turned and walked away.

The crystal vase hit the wall and shattered, sending tiny glass fragments flying in all directions.

"It isn't fair!" Patsy shrieked. "Owen was *my* beau."

Bunny clucked and shook her head at her younger sister. "Don't be foolish, Patsy. Owen Simpson was never your beau." She couldn't help the smug smile she wore. After all, she needn't worry about *her* Mr. Steele any longer.

"You said our plan would work. You said it was brilliant." Patsy picked up a small figurine and threw it in the same direction as the vase. "You said everyone would hate her. That she would make mistakes. But she hasn't. They all *like* her!" She tossed another figurine.

"Sister dear, you must control yourself. Destroying all our possessions won't get Mr. Simpson back."

Her face red, huffing and puffing as if she'd just run a mile, Patsy sank onto the sofa. She dropped her head forward, forming several chins with generous folds of skin against her neck. "It isn't fair," she whimpered one last time.

"Are you finished?" Bunny asked impatiently.

Patsy nodded.

"Good. Then we shall simply have to put our heads together and come up with another plan to send that woman on her way."

"Like what?"

"I honestly don't know." Bunny crossed the room and bent to pick up the larger shards of glass. "But we'll come up with something."

Patsy sniffed. "But she's engaged to Owen."

"Engagements are often broken." She glanced over her shoulder. Her sister was crying, tears streaking her pudgy cheeks. "Do stop that, Patsy. You look positively dreadful. And if you would just try to control that appetite of yours, maybe you wouldn't be so fat and unattractive. Maybe then Mr. Simpson would have wanted you instead of that foreigner."

That only made the crying worse, and Bunny supposed she shouldn't have said what she had. But it was an old habit, jabbing Patsy about her weight. The words just slipped out. Still, Patsy should have known Bunny would find a way to help. She always did. It was a burden she carried, always being the older, more intelligent sister of the two.

And she could afford to be more generous. After all, she needn't worry any longer about Garret becoming enamored with that Wellington woman. In fact, she wondered why she'd ever been concerned. It had been most apparent today that the two were no more than polite acquaintances. If not for Janie—*the little brat*—they would not even have spoken to one another. At least, that was how it had seemed to Bunny.

She straightened and carried the broken glass into the kitchen to discard. Then she went into her bedroom, opened the top drawer of her bureau, retrieved a handkerchief, and took it to her sister.

"Dry your eyes, Patsy," she said, "and cease this caterwauling at once. We must think what we might

do to rescue your Mr. Simpson. Miss Wellington said
they won't be wed until Christmas. That is more than
five months away. It should be plenty of time."

"Plenty of time for what?"

"A teacher's reputation must be above reproach.
There must be some reason Miss Wellington broke
her engagement in England to come to America. And
here it is, scarcely a month since her arrival, and
already she is engaged to another man. A man who is
hardly more than a stranger to her. Does that sound
like a woman of high morals to you?"

Patsy sniffed again. "No." She tipped her head to
one side as her lower lip rolled outward in a fleshy
pout.

"Don't you worry, sister dear. We'll find something to make Miss Wellington tuck her tail and
skedaddle right out of New Prospects."

"Wish you were feelin' better, Pa," Janie said as
Garret climbed up to the wagon seat.

"I'm okay, Janie. Just a bit tired."

"You sure I shouldn't come home with you?"

"I'm sure, pumpkin. Stop worryin' about me. Go
have some fun with your friends."

She hesitated only a moment, then darted off for
more games with the other Fourth of July celebrants.

Garret smiled as he watched her disappear into the
crowd.

"I'll have her home soon as the fireworks are
done," Jake promised.

He looked at the cowboy, standing beside the
wagon. "Thanks, Jake."

"Not a problem. I reckon I enjoy the fireworks as much as any kid." He frowned. "You look a bit the worse for wear, boss. You need me t'ride along with you?"

"What I need is for you and Janie to quit cluckin' over me like a couple of mother hens. I got a few bruises and a broken arm. That's all."

Jake shrugged. "All right. Reckon you know best."

"Darned right I do," he muttered as he took the reins in hand. "Giddup there." He slapped the leather against the rumps of the team and turned the wagon toward the road.

They hadn't made it more than a dozen yards when he saw Beth riding toward him on Flick. She had changed out of the dark green dress she'd worn to church and into her riding habit. Riding sidesaddle, she looked elegant, graceful, almost regal—every inch the English noblewoman that was her birthright.

He considered driving right on past her, but then she stopped and waited for him to reach her. He didn't have any choice but to halt his team. Unless he wanted to be just plain rude, and there was no call for that.

"Hello, Mr. Steele."

"Miss Wellington." He bent his hat brim in greeting.

"You seem much improved over the last time I saw you."

"I'm gettin' along just fine. See you got yourself a sidesaddle. Didn't know there was any of those fancy things around these parts."

"It was a gift from Mr. Crew. He saw how uncomfortable I was riding astride. He took this saddle in trade for work he did but was never able to sell it. So he was kind enough to give it to me. I wanted to pay him, but he refused."

"I never could figure how a woman keeps her seat on one of them." He shrugged, then added, "But it suits you. You look right pretty, sittin' your horse like that."

The air grew heavy around them, the silence pregnant with words unspoken.

Garret cleared his throat. "Guess congratulations are in order. Owen's a lucky man."

"Thank you." Her voice was barely above a whisper. "It's very gallant of you to say so."

"No. I mean it."

"You didn't think I belonged here when I first arrived."

He frowned as he shifted his gaze toward the horizon. "I was wrong, Miss Wellington."

"Thank you," she said again.

"You gonna keep on teaching once you're married?"

"If the school board will allow it."

"Owen will make them allow it." He looked at her again, felt his belly tighten as he was struck afresh by the pure exquisiteness of her appearance. "I think Owen would make the world stand on its head if that's what you wanted." *And who could blame him?*

It was Beth's turn to glance away. "I hope I shall be able to make him happy."

"You will."

"Well." She met his gaze again. "I suppose I shouldn't keep you any longer, Mr. Steele. You must be weary, and Owen is waiting for me. He's going to show me his home before the fireworks begin."

Owen was waiting for her. Owen would always be waiting for her.

And come December, it wouldn't be just Owen's home. It would be their home.

"Yeah. You'd better go. Owen'll be wonderin' what happened." He slapped the reins, and the wagon jerked forward. "So long, Miss Wellington."

"Good-bye, Mr. Steele."

13

For Beth, the days of July flew away, filled from sunrise to late into the night with one task after another. She continued to learn to manage her own household, sometimes even dining on a meal that tasted good—which was always a pleasure as well as a surprise. She stopped scorching her clothes with the iron, and she even coaxed some flowers to bloom along the front of the cabin, making the place appear more cheerful, more like a home.

Owen was as attentive as ever, calling on her daily, often bringing her gifts, both large and small. If she regretted her decision to marry him, she never let on, not even to herself. He was so obviously happy, she knew she would be a fool not to feel the same. So she tried her very best to do so.

Several women—Stella Matheson, Catherine Perkins, and Frances Werner—offered their help with the wedding since Beth had no family of her own. She was warmed by their generosity, touched that they would be so kind while she was as yet a newcomer to New Prospects.

But it was the children who brought her the most pleasure. Every day she saw progress in her young charges. There was a special joy in seeing a child's face light up with sudden understanding, a great sense of satisfaction when one of her students overcame some obstacle to learning.

Each day Beth felt a little more comfortable with her surroundings, a little more a part of her adopted country. Soon, she believed, those who still viewed her as an outsider, a foreigner, would cease to do so. She would simply be the schoolteacher. It was happening already, and she liked that.

Only in the dark of the night, when she lay alone in her narrow bed in her small log cabin, did she sense her heart crying out a warning. Only in her dreams did she imagine a different future from the one she was planning by day. Only in a most secret place did she recognize a love that would never come to fruition.

Not once did she see Garret in those days following the town picnic. Not once did he come to town. Not even to church on Sundays.

And so the days of July passed.

Standing in the stall, Janie held up one of the black-and-white puppies and showed it to her father. "I think we oughta give this one to Miss Beth."

"Has she said she wants a dog?"

"No, but I figure she's gotta be lonely, livin' by herself like she does. One of Pepper and Penguin's pups would keep her good company."

He'd worked danged hard not to think about Beth marrying Owen, not to remember how pretty she'd looked in her riding habit, seated sidesaddle on Flick, the sun reflected in red highlights off her auburn hair. He didn't want to be reminded of how strong the desire had been to hold her, to kiss her, to touch and caress, to possess her body with his own. He'd tried hard to forget the strange sense of desertion he'd felt when he'd heard her say, "Good-bye, Mr. Steele." He wasn't happy to recollect it all now.

"She's not going to be living alone for long," he said, sounding more gruff than he'd intended. "She's getting married. Remember?"

"You should have asked her t'marry you, Pa."

It felt like a fist in his belly, the way those words hit him.

"I'd've liked Miss Beth t'be my ma."

He turned away from the stall and from the look of yearning in his daughter's eyes. "We're doing just fine on our own," he said in a voice that invited no disagreement.

He headed out of the barn into the blistering sunlight, walking as fast as he could, trying to outdistance what he didn't want to face. He didn't like to think Janie wasn't content with things as they were, that she might need something he couldn't give her— or someone. He'd thought they made a family, just the two of them. They didn't need anyone else. He didn't *want* anyone else.

"You like Miss Beth, don't you?"

He stopped and turned, surprised to find his daughter had followed him out of the barn. "Yeah, I like her," he snapped.

Janie, still holding the wriggling puppy, seemed unfazed by his show of temper. "She likes you, too. She was real worried about you when you got hurt."

Was she? He grunted as he looked away. "I'm riding out to check on the water hole. You want to come along?"

"Can we take the puppy to Miss Beth first?"

"Janie—"

"Please, Pa. I know she'd want her. Can't we do this first? Please."

It was a fool thing to do, but he relented. "Okay." He told himself it was because he found it hard to refuse Janie when she pleaded like that. He didn't even consider it might be because he wanted to see Beth.

"I'll saddle Maybelle." Janie grinned. "Won't take me long." She raced back toward the barn, disappearing through the wide doorway into the shadowy interior.

"Fool thing to do," he said to himself, echoing his earlier thought.

He had more than enough work awaiting him without taking valuable time to deliver a puppy to the schoolmarm. He hadn't been doing his share around the ranch since his accident. Jake was handling things the best he could, but the place needed at least two men to manage it all. Especially now with the water holes and streams running low after more than a month of intense heat and no rain. Garret needed to be concentrating on his ranch, his land, his cattle, instead of some blasted female.

True to her word, Janie had her pony saddled and bridled in a hurry. When she rode out of the barn,

Garret saw that she'd stuck the puppy in one of the saddlebags. Head and paws poked out the opening between the pouch and flap.

"We're ready, Pa."

"I need my head examined," he muttered as he walked toward his saddle horse, standing in the shade of a large box elder tree. Grabbing the saddle horn with his good hand and pressing his injured arm, still in a sling, against his torso, he pulled himself into the saddle. He flinched at the residual ache in his ribs.

"Still hurts, huh, Pa?"

"Yeah, still hurts."

Side by side they rode away from the ranch beneath a sweltering sun that had already changed the grasslands from green to brown and covered the road into New Prospects with a fine dust. Janie was uncharacteristically quiet, which allowed Garret silence in which to play over again in his mind what had been said back at the ranch.

And the more he considered it, the more it concerned him. Janie wasn't happy with things the way they were. Janie needed something more. She didn't just *want* a mother. She needed one. A *real* one.

Not someone like Muriel. Someone like Beth.

Not someone like Beth. Beth herself.

And not just Janie. Garret needed her, too.

Was it possible he could feel more for Beth than mere lust? Was it possible, after all these years, he might have given his heart and not recognized what was happening until it was too late? Was it possible he might actually love the woman his good friend was going to marry?

God help him. He was afraid it was possible. More than possible.

He was afraid it could be true.

Wearing her oldest dress and a wide-brimmed straw bonnet, Beth knelt on the hard-packed earth in front of her cabin and pulled weeds from the small flower garden. It amazed her, the way weeds could grow in this heat while her flowers struggled to survive.

Pausing in her work, she glanced up at the pale blue sky and wondered if she would ever see it rain again. And she wasn't alone. The dry heat was on the minds of every farmer and rancher in the valley. It was the sole subject of conversation wherever she went. She heard the schoolchildren talking about it during recess. She heard the women talking about it when she went to the mercantile for supplies. She heard the men talking about it after church as they stood in clusters, frowning up at the cloudless sky and speaking in low, muted tones.

She wondered how Garret was faring. Were his cattle surviving the drought? Was he in danger of losing his ranch, as she'd heard other families might? It wasn't her place to wonder such things, of course, but she did anyway.

Oh, Garret, I should not think of you at all.

As if summoned by her thoughts, she heard the approach of horses, turned, and saw Garret and Janie riding toward her. A rush of pure, unadulterated pleasure sent warmth coursing through her, a warmth unrelated to the sweltering heat of the day. She quickly rose, then stood waiting for them, running her hands over the front of her skirt, hoping to brush away the dirt and wrinkles.

It had been not even a month since she'd seen him, yet it seemed a lifetime. From beneath the shade of her bonnet, she feasted upon him with her eyes, noted the sun-bronzed skin of his ruggedly handsome face, the set of his mouth that spoke of lingering pain, the familiar ease with which he sat his horse. Her heart quickened, and there was an ache inside her that she was unable to define, a wanting unlike anything she'd ever felt before.

Janie nudged her pony into a trot and broke away from her father. "Hi, Miss Beth."

"Hello, Janie." Her stomach felt all aflutter. "Good afternoon, Mr. Steele."

He tugged his hat brim in his familiar sign of greeting.

She cleared her throat, then said, "You're looking much improved from the last time I saw you. Janie has kept me apprised of your progress." The confession slipped out before she realized what she was saying.

Garret raised an eyebrow, as if surprised by her admission, but he made no reply.

"Look, Miss Beth. Look what we brought you."

Reluctantly she tore her gaze from Garret, watching Janie as she dismounted and drew something from her saddlebag.

"Ain't . . . I mean, isn't she cute?" Janie held out a squirming bundle of black-and-white hair. The puppy had large brown eyes and a tail that wagged like a clock pendulum gone crazy. "This is one of Pepper's litter. Penguin's her pa. We—me and Pa, I mean—we thought you'd be less lonely if you had a dog of your own."

Beth wanted to look at Garret again, wanted to see if he cared whether or not she was lonely. Fortunately she was able to deny the urge, instead bending to take the puppy from Janie.

As she straightened, she rubbed the puppy's down-like coat against her cheek. "What a sweet gift. I have never owned a pet before."

"Never?"

"No. Father wouldn't allow animals in the house, and the hounds were only for hunting. They were not to be coddled."

"You hear that, Pa?"

"I heard."

Beth followed the sound of his voice. Her gaze met with his, and her heart missed a beat. It seemed as if he could see straight into her soul with those beautiful blue eyes of his. What did he see there? Did he know she loved him? Did he know and not care?

"You'll need to give her a name, Miss Beth. She hasn't got one yet."

Beth took a deep breath to steady her careening emotions, then held the puppy at arm's length and studied the animal's markings, desperate for something else to occupy her thoughts.

"Pa thinks that white on the top of her head looks like a wishbone. You know. Like from a turkey." Janie stepped closer and touched the marking on the puppy's head. "See? Right here."

Beth's heart caught once again, but she refused to look in Garret's direction. "I believe your pa is right.

It does look like a wishbone. Perhaps that's what we should call her."

"That's a great idea!" Janie grinned brightly. "Hey, Wishbone. What d'ya say? You like that name?"

The puppy wriggled and whined.

"She probably wants down," Garret said.

There went her thudding heart again, responding to the sound of his voice. Beth tried to ignore it as she leaned over and set Wishbone on the ground. The puppy immediately scampered off. Janie followed close behind.

"You'll have to keep a close eye on her at first."

There seemed nothing else for Beth to do but turn her gaze in his direction. He had dismounted and now stood beside his horse, looking far too tall, far too strong, far too handsome.

"She'll probably cry a lot for a night or two. She'll miss her mother and the other pups."

"I'll take good care of her, Mr. Steele."

"I know you will." He paused, then said, "You're doin' a good job at the school, I hear."

"I hope so. I have tried."

"And you like teaching as much as you thought you would?"

"Oh, yes."

The blue of his eyes seemed to soften. "I'm glad it's turned out so good for you, Miss Wellington."

"Thank you," she answered breathlessly.

"I suppose we oughta be on our way. I need to check the water holes."

"This drought . . . It's very serious."

"Yeah, could be if it continues this dry."

She longed to touch his cheek, longed to feel the

afternoon stubble growing there. Would it be soft or coarse? If he were to kiss her, would it scratch her skin? Or would she only be aware of the taste of his lips?

He took a step toward her.

She caught her breath in a tiny gasp.

He frowned.

She nearly reached for him.

"Pa! Miss Beth! Look!"

She turned her back toward him, uncertain if it was relief or disappointment she felt at the interruption. Perhaps it was both.

Wishbone came prancing across the yard, dragging a branch as large as she was in her mouth. Janie followed behind the puppy, giggling at the sight.

"Janie's always loved animals," Garret commented.

"I know. She mentioned them in her letters often." More softly, "She loves you, too."

Beth's chest tightened.

"She told me today she wished you were her ma."

Tears welled up in her eyes, and she had to bite her lower lip to keep them from falling.

"Guess I didn't realize how much a girl needed a woman around."

What about you, Garret? Don't you need a woman around? Do you wish I were Janie's mother?

He cleared his throat, then called out, "Come on, Janie. We gotta be on our way."

The girl grabbed the puppy from the ground and carried her to Beth. "You can bring her out to the ranch t'play with the other pups whenever you want."

"Thank you, Janie. That's a kind invitation."

"Maybe you could come have supper with us some-time?" Janie looked pleadingly toward her father.

After what seemed an eternity, Garret asked, "Would you like to come for supper at the ranch, Beth?"

Her heart tripped at the sound of her name falling from his lips. She turned slowly, met his gaze. "Yes, I would like that." *Garret*, she added silently.

His blue eyes darkened. The urge to step into his arms nearly overwhelmed her. Then he turned away, stepping quickly toward his horse. "Why don't you and Owen come for supper Friday night?" He swung into the saddle.

Owen. Her fiancé. Garret's friend. Of course he would invite Owen, too.

"I shall pass along your invitation." Her response sounded strained to her own ears.

"Good." He turned his horse's head with the reins. "Come on, Janie."

"Bye, Miss Beth."

"Good-bye, Janie."

"Take care of Wishbone."

"I will."

Janie waved as they rode away. Beth held the puppy against her heart and waved in return, wishing for things that could never be.

Owen frowned as he observed Beth across the table. She'd seemed distracted ever since he'd picked her up in his buggy and brought her to Martha's Restaurant half an hour ago. Her expression was strained, and her eyes had a faraway, almost wistful look. For some reason, he was reluctant to ask what was on her mind. He had an odd feeling he didn't want to know the answer.

He patted his suit coat pocket, taking some reassurance from the small box he felt there. The ring had arrived by post today. The jeweler in Denver had followed Owen's instructions to the letter. He was certain Beth would be surprised and pleased by it.

She took a sip of water from her glass, then turned her gaze out the window. "Do you think it will rain soon, Owen?"

Ah, so that's what had been troubling her. "It had better. Folks are starting to hurt."

"Your bank?" She looked at him now. "Will you be forced to foreclose on people we know?"

He shifted on his chair. "I've already had to foreclose on Karl Booth's place. Couldn't be helped."

"How dreadful," she whispered, once again glancing out the window.

"That didn't have anything to do with the drought. The Booths are a pretty worthless lot. Karl was too lazy to work the place like it needed to be worked."

"It's still dreadful."

"The weather has always affected farmers and ranchers, Beth. That's just the way it is. In hard times, they're the folks who seem to suffer most, losing the land they've worked so hard to keep."

"But where will they go if they lose their homes?"

"They'll move on, find a new place to begin again." He leaned forward, covering her hand on the table with his. "Like you did, Beth dear. Although none will have to go as far as you."

"No, none so far as I," she echoed softly.

He would have sworn her eyes looked teary. "Beth, it's hard, but you needn't worry. Your position is secure, even if you lose some students. The school board has approved keeping you on as New Prospects' teacher even after we're married, for as long as you're able to teach."

"As long as I am able?" She met his gaze. "Why would I not be able?"

He grinned, images of the wedding night they would enjoy teasing him. "Well, when the children begin coming, of course."

Heat flowered in her cheeks, but she didn't glance away.

He tightened his fingers, lifted her hand off the table, and drew it to his lips. "Tell me we don't have to wait until Christmas, Beth. Tell me we can marry sooner than that."

"Owen—"

"Wait. Don't say anything yet." He pulled the small box from his pocket and held it out to her. "This is for you."

"Oh, Owen—"

"Open it."

She stared at him for several heartbeats before taking the box from his hand and lifting off the lid.

"Try it on. See if it fits."

Obediently she plucked the diamond-and-emerald ring from the velvet-lined box, then held it between the middle finger and thumb of her right hand. "Owen, it's lovely. Truly it is. But it's terribly costly. You shouldn't have. Really."

"Here. Let me." Gently he took it from her, then

slid the ring onto the third finger of her left hand. "There, now every man in Montana will know you belong to me."

She didn't smile as he'd expected, nor did she blush again as he'd thought she might. Instead she went still, simply staring at the ring on her finger, her face utterly expressionless.

Dread washed over him. "What's wrong, Beth? Don't you like the ring? If you don't, just tell me and I'll exchange it for something else."

"No, Owen. I don't want a different ring." He thought she might have said something more, but the waitress brought their supper to the table just then. Beth gave the young woman a weak smile and a whispered, "Thank you, Elaine."

Owen allowed the silence to continue throughout the meal. It wasn't until they were back in his buggy, driving toward Beth's cabin, that he remembered she'd never answered his question about the wedding date. But his instincts warned him not to pursue it tonight. She was in a strange mood, and he had the feeling he would be sorry if he pressed her to change things now.

They were almost to the school before Beth spoke. "I nearly forgot. Janie Steele and her father invited us to supper on Friday."

"You've forgotten something else as well. I'll be in Denver all next week. I leave first thing tomorrow morning and won't return until Saturday. So I'm afraid we'll have to decline."

Her voice dropped. "Yes, I did forget." She looked at him. "That's a long trip."

Owen pulled on the reins, drawing the horse to a

halt in front of her cabin. Then he turned, took Beth by the shoulders, and drew her into his embrace. "Too long," he answered huskily, then kissed her, slow and deep.

Eyes closed, Beth allowed the kiss to continue, all the while hoping and praying she would feel something more than mere impatience for it to end. It wasn't that she hated Owen's kisses as she had Perceval's. She didn't. She simply felt . . . disinterested and . . . and dispassionate.

Perhaps I want too much. Perhaps no one feels what I want to feel. Perhaps that only happens in storybooks.

He released her mouth but still hovered nearby. He whispered her name, and she felt his breath on her skin. She kept her eyes shut, waiting, hoping, praying.

Praying she would open them and find it was Garret Steele beside her. Just thinking of him made her heart quicken, made her feel warm all over. There *would* be passion if Garret were to touch her, if Garret were to kiss her. She would not be disinterested then. She was certain of it.

"You'll miss me while I'm gone?" Owen queried.

Guilt rushed over her. He didn't deserve this from her. He was a good, decent man. He loved her. He was kind. He would never hurt her. Despite his comment in the restaurant, she knew he didn't see her as a mere possession. He loved her. He wanted to be with her.

She drew back and opened her eyes, forcing herself to meet his gaze without flinching, so he wouldn't know it was a lie. "Of course I shall miss you."

But even as he kissed her again, she knew she would go to Garret's home for supper on Friday, even without Owen.

She would go because her heart demanded it.

14

Friday, August 6, 1897
New Prospects, Montana

My dearest Mary,

I have settled into my small cabin and have found great contentment as a teacher. There is a peculiar thrill which comes when I know I have succeeded in imparting some knowledge to my students. I often wonder what my father or Mrs. Crumb or any of the others who knew me in England would think if they could see me now. Would they believe that satisfaction and serenity can be found without all the trappings of wealth? Would they believe that a simple country picnic can be ever so much more enjoyable than a grand ball? No, they would not believe it. But it is true, nonetheless.

The most difficult part of teaching at present is the heat. We are in the grip of a drought, and the temperature and sun are unrelenting, day after day. I am told this is unusual for Montana, but that does not make it any easier by the knowing of it. The children do not seem to be as affected by the heat as I am. It destroys my concentration, and each night I go to bed praying the next day shall bring cooler weather and the desperately needed rains.

I have now received two letters from Inga Linberg, both filled with glowing words about her little village and the people there. She says her father has been well received by his congregation in Uppsala, Iowa. Her second letter included an invitation for me to join her family there to teach school. She did not know when she wrote to me that I was engaged to be married.

Yes, it is true, Mary. I have accepted a proposal of marriage from Mr. Simpson, the mayor of New Prospects. Only my heart tells me I have made a mistake. It is all quite sad because Mr. Simpson is a truly good man. He would make any woman a fine husband. But I do not love him. He has said he loves me enough for the both of us, and I know many marriages have started with less and become successful unions in the end. Under other circumstances, I might, indeed, have grown to love him.

But the truth is, Mary, I love another. I have fallen in love with Mr. Steele. And as great as the desire has become to have children of my own, it is only Mr. Steele whom I want to be their father. I know I should be ashamed of such thoughts, but I am not. I want desperately to lie in his arms and know the wonder of conceiving his child as you have done with Seamus Maguire.

There. I have confessed it. I think you will understand as no one else could. And seeing those words, written in my own hand, I know what I must do. I must break my engagement immediately. For even if Mr. Steele should never want me, I cannot marry Mr. Simpson with betrayal in my heart.

Oh, how different everything has turned out to be from what I expected when you and I were awaiting the ship in Southampton.

And you, Mary? By now you must surely have found your Mr. Maguire. Perhaps you have moved from New York City and that is why I have not heard from you. I know your confinement is quickly approaching, and I pray you shall have an easy time of it. Quite selfishly, I confess I wish you were here with me now. I am badly in need of a

close friend and confidante to whom I
could pour out my heart, someone who
would not judge me for the things I feel
or say and who would be able to advise
me. You have been such a friend, dear
Mary, and I shall be forever grateful to
you for it.

With great affection,
Beth Wellington

The air was hot and dry. There wasn't even the
slightest of breezes to stir the withering grass alongside the schoolhouse. Even the children, usually so
resilient against all manner of weather, were quiet
today. They sat in small groups in the shade of the
trees and at the side of the schoolhouse, listlessly
eating lunches their mothers had packed for them.
They spoke in soft voices, as if they hadn't the
energy for volume. Games of andy over, snap the
whip, steal the bacon, and kick the can were completely forgotten.

Beth watched them from the top of the schoolhouse steps. She leaned her shoulder against the
doorjamb, dabbing at the perspiration on her forehead with her handkerchief while daydreaming about
cool, rainy days in England. A short while before,
she'd overheard one of the older boys talking about a
water hole on his place that had dried up and how he
wished they could all go swimming, as they'd done
most summers.

Oh, how heavenly it had sounded to Beth.

In truth, she would be content if she could simply remove her shoes and stockings and plunge her feet into a cold running creek. But even that was an impossibility. The nearby creek was nothing but a slow-moving trickle these days.

She checked her watch, then turned back into the school with a sigh of resignation. Before the four o'clock dismissal, there were arithmetic drills to be done, history lessons to read, and spelling classes for all grades.

Lethargically she moved between the rows of desks toward the blackboard. She erased that morning's penmanship work as her thoughts returned to her students. Because she suspected Joseph Frederick needed eyeglasses, she wrote the arithmetic problems in large numbers so they could be seen easily from the back of the room. Joseph insisted upon sitting in the last row of desks, probably because he was her oldest and biggest student. She was convinced he was a bright boy and didn't want him becoming discouraged simply because he couldn't see clearly from a distance.

Suddenly there was a loud crash behind her. She jumped in surprise, then whirled around to see what had caused the sound. She had expected almost anything but what she found.

Trevor Booth stood in the center aisle, weaving slightly. One look in his glazed eyes, and she knew the boy was intoxicated.

"Betch're glad t'hear what happened t'my pa, ain'tcha, Teach?" His words were slurred and ran together. "Betch're glad we gotta move."

"Trevor, you have been imbibing." She spoke

calmly and firmly, despite how she felt inside. "I demand you remove yourself from the school premises this instant."

He staggered forward, his voice rising. "Oh, you demand, d'ya? Well, I ain't gonna do nothin' you tell me. Y'hear?"

"I said, you are to leave this school now." Her voice quavered this time.

"You're gonna be sorry!" he shouted. "'Fore we leave this hellhole, I'm gonna make you sorry."

I will not be afraid of this boy.

"Miss Beth, you okay?"

Beth's eyes darted toward the entrance, where Janie, who had asked the question, and several other students were now standing, watching with wide eyes. Seeing them there, Beth felt her fear drain away.

Trevor looked at the children, too, then he turned back toward her. "This ain't over yet, 'tween you an' me." He staggered slightly but caught himself before he fell.

"But it is over, Trevor." Surprisingly, she felt compassion for the angry youth, and her tone was gentle because of it. "I'm deeply sorry for your family's misfortune. I understand what it's like to lose one's home and be forced to go to a strange place." She paused, then continued in her best schoolteacher's voice. "But sorry or not, I cannot allow you to disrupt my classroom in this manner. Please leave at once."

He let out a string of vile curse words before turning and staggering toward the door. The children parted like the water before the prow of a ship, letting him pass, no one saying a single word to him.

The instant he was gone, Janie rushed forward and hugged Beth around the waist. "You sure you're all right?"

"Yes, Janie, I'm fine." Beth looked into her eyes, then toward the other students, saying, "You must not tell anyone what happened here with Trevor."

"Why not?" Janie asked.

"Because someone might misunderstand. Trevor is moving away. There's no reason to cause him any more trouble."

"I think Pa should know," Janie said.

"No. If he believes I might be in danger or can't maintain order, I might not be able to remain your teacher." Again she moved her gaze from one student to another. "Please, let's keep this our secret. In a few days, Trevor will be gone, and we'll likely never see him again."

After a long moment, the children nodded their agreement.

"Good. Now, would someone please ring the bell? It's time for classes to resume."

Garret stared at the herd, squinting against the sun's glare. "This weather holds, we'll be forced to sell the cattle soon."

Jake tipped back his hat with his knuckles and looked at the sky. "Yup."

"It'll mean a loss. We won't get nearly the price we should."

The cow hand nodded.

Garret removed his hat and wiped his arm across

his forehead. Then he released a deep sigh. "I was countin' on a good year. The barn needs some repairs, and Janie's growin' out of just about everything she owns."

"I reckon we'll do well enough. We've come through harder times, boss."

He suspected Jake was referring to more than just the price of beef on the hoof. And he was right. They'd come through many a bad year. "Yeah, you're right, Jake. Guess we'll do okay."

"How's that arm?"

"Feeling better now that it's out of that blasted sling." He flexed his hand into a fist, relaxed it, then flexed and relaxed it again. "But it sure is weak."

The other man gave him a sharp glance. "Is there somethin' more on your mind, boss? You sure ain't been much like yerself lately."

Garret shook his head in denial, but it was a lie.

Luckily Jake let it be. "I'll be headin' on up to the north range, then. Want me to drive those cows down when I come back?"

"No. Better wait awhile."

"Right." Without another word, the cow hand spurred his horse forward and cantered away.

"Is there somethin' more on your mind, boss?"

Yes, he could have answered. Beth Wellington was on his mind. Dang near all the time. Ever since he'd found out she was coming to supper tonight without Owen. On Sunday after church, when she'd told him about Owen's business trip, Garret should have suggested she wait to come another time when Owen could be with her. But he hadn't.

He'd wanted her to himself.

God help him.

Ever since the day they'd taken her the puppy, ever since that moment Garret had realized his feelings for the schoolmarm were more complicated than mere sexual desire, he hadn't been able to get her out of his thoughts for more than a few minutes at a time. When he looked around the rooms of his house, he imagined what she might do to bring warmth to them. When he sat at the table with Janie, he thought how the child needed a mother. When he crawled into his bed at night, he felt the emptiness and knew he wanted to fill it with Beth.

But Beth was engaged to marry his friend. He had no right to those thoughts. He was going to have to get over these crazy feelings because he would be seeing her for the rest of his life, the wife of another man. He would see her bearing Owen's babies. He would see her loving them the way a mother should love her children.

He cursed as he jerked his horse's head around, then kneed the gelding into a gallop, trying to outrun the images that haunted him.

At the close of school, Beth rode Flick into town. The main street was almost entirely deserted, most folks having the good sense to stay out of the afternoon sun. But Beth's reason for coming into New Prospects couldn't be postponed, heat or no heat.

She stopped her horse in front of the bank, then slipped off the sidesaddle in a graceful, practiced motion. She drew a quick breath as she stared at the lettering painted on the front window. Even knowing

Owen wasn't there, that she was taking the coward's way out, didn't help. She still dreaded going inside. But in all good conscience, she couldn't go to supper at Garret's until she had delivered the note she carried in her pocket.

Holding her shoulders back like a soldier going into battle, she stepped onto the boardwalk and opened the bank's door.

Harry Kaiser, wearing his green visor and spectacles, glanced up from his place behind the counter. "Howdy, Miss Wellington," he greeted her, adding a toothy smile.

"Good afternoon, Mr. Kaiser. Would it be all right if I left something for Mr. Simpson on his desk? I know when he returns tomorrow he'll come to the bank before he goes home, and I . . . I want him to get my message as soon as possible."

"'Course you can go in," Harry answered. "You're going to be his missus, after all."

Flooded by guilt at his words, she went into Owen's office and closed the door behind her. The room was small and crowded with bookshelves and ledgers and the large mahogany desk Owen had had shipped from back east. It even smelled like a banker's office should smell. She'd thought so the very first time she'd come here, asking for a job as New Prospects' schoolteacher.

But now she scarcely noticed those things. Feeling a bit shaken by the reality of what she was about to do, she sank onto the leather chair behind the desk, then drew the envelope from her pocket. She hesitated a moment longer before opening the flap and drawing out the note.

Dear Owen,

This is perhaps the most difficult thing I have ever had to do. I am sure it is quite heartless of me to deliver these words in writing rather than in person. I am sorry for being such a coward, but there is no help for it.

I cannot marry you. As fond as I am of you—and you must believe that I am fond of you—I have come to realize it would be a tragic mistake for both of us were we to marry. I would not make you happy, as you now believe. There are so many reasons, too many to enumerate.

Please believe me when I say I wish it could be otherwise. I hope one day you will find it in your heart to forgive me.

Beth

Post Script
I shall return your beautiful ring when next I see you.

With tears in her eyes, Beth refolded the note and slipped the paper into the envelope. Then she laid it in the center of the tidy desk, the stark white paper glaringly bright against the dark wooden surface. She stared at Owen's name, which was written on the front of the envelope.

I'm sorry, Owen. It was never my intent to hurt you.

With a sigh, she left his office. She bade a quick farewell to Harry Kaiser, then hurried outside, never noticing Bunny Homer, who stood in a corner of the bank, watching.

As soon as the door closed, Bunny walked over to the counter and presented her deposit to the teller. "Miss Wellington appeared somewhat distraught, don't you think, Mr. Kaiser?"

"Did she? Can't say I noticed."

You never notice much of anything, you old goat. "Yes, I believe she did. I hope nothing is wrong."

"Don't think so. She just wanted to leave somethin' for Mr. Simpson. A note, I think. Said she knew he'd come here first, and she wanted him to get it right away." He grinned. "Guess she knows Mr. Simpson pretty well. Whenever he's been outta town, he always comes here 'fore goin' home."

How curious, Bunny thought. What on earth could be the purpose of leaving a note for Owen at the bank rather than waiting to speak to him in person when he returned?

She glanced toward the office, only a few steps away. She could see an envelope in the center of the desk. If she only had a minute or two . . .

She looked back at the clerk, who was busy tallying her deposit. And there, on the counter to his left, mere inches from her reticule, were several stacks of coin. Slowly she slid her purse forward until it nearly touched the first stack. Then she leaned toward Harry, pointing at a figure he'd written on his pad. "Are you quite sure that's correct, Mr. Kaiser?" she asked innocently while giving her reticule a tiny shove.

With a loud clatter, coins fell to the floor, rolling and bouncing every which way.

"Oh, my goodness!" Bunny exclaimed. "Oh, dear me! Mr. Kaiser, did I do that? Oh, here. Let me come around and help you pick them up."

"No. No. That's all right. Bank customers aren't allowed behind the counter. I can get them. No problem." He knelt and began gathering the scattered coins.

Without a second's hesitation, Bunny rushed into Owen's office, opened the envelope, and read the message written there. A knot formed in her belly. Why would Beth break her engagement to Owen?

Instinctively she knew. Garret. It had something to do with Garret Steele.

Well, she wouldn't allow it. She wouldn't. She had to have some time. She had to find a way to stop this from happening. Better Owen marry Beth and Patsy be unhappy than for Garret to have a chance to fall for that woman's charms. Owen mustn't get this message. Not yet, anyway. Bunny had to buy some time.

She shoved the note back into the envelope, looked around the office for somewhere to hide it, then decided to drop it between the wall and the desk, certain it would never be found there. Then she hurried back to the counter just as Harry stood up. She could only hope he would think her high color was due to embarrassment for spilling his coins.

"There. That wasn't so bad," he told her.

"I'm so clumsy, Mr. Kaiser. I don't know what I

should do with myself. All your work, counting them and all. I really must apologize once again."

He handed her a receipt for her deposit. "Not at all, Miss Homer."

She gave him one of her best smiles, then rushed out of the bank, her heart hammering wildly in her chest.

15

Beth nervously studied her reflection in the small mirror on the cabin wall. She'd been tempted to wear one of her best gowns, the deep green one that was so flattering to her coloring. But she'd had the good sense not to give in to the notion. Instead she wore one of her riding habits, albeit one especially and quite carefully washed and pressed for tonight. She allowed herself only one decoration, a gold brooch that had once belonged to her mother. She left Owen's ring in the bottom of her jewelry box.

She pressed her hands flat against her stomach, doing her best to calm the fluttering sensation within. She felt like a schoolgirl awaiting the arrival of her first beau. Not that she'd ever had these feelings before, but she'd heard other girls talking about it all those many years ago. She'd thought it was pure silliness then, but now she realized it was real. And she realized just how wonderful and how terrible it could be.

She'd taken a big risk this day. Bigger, perhaps,

than leaving England and traveling across the Atlantic Ocean. She had turned away from a place of safety, turned away from a man who would have provided well for her, given her a beautiful home, given her children and anything else she might ever desire, and had secretly pledged her heart to a man who might not ever want what she had to offer.

She glanced at Wishbone, who was running around her feet. "What will I do if he never wants me?"

The question caused her heart to constrict. What *would* she do? Would she stay here and love him from afar? No, she wouldn't be able to bear that. She would have to go away if he couldn't return her love. She wouldn't be able to stay here. She could go to Iowa. Inga had said they needed teachers there.

But she wasn't going to give up before she'd even started. Some small voice inside her insisted she and Garret were meant to be together. Surely if she realized it, he would too.

She checked her watch, for perhaps the fifteenth time since she'd returned from town. She didn't want to arrive at the Steele ranch too early, nor did she want to keep them waiting. But at last it was time for her to leave.

Lightly she ran her fingers over her hair, making certain all was in place, then she set her silk hat on her head and secured it with hat pins. Finally she looked down at the puppy a second time, smiling as she remembered the day Garret and Janie had brought her to Beth. "Stay out of mischief while I'm gone," she demanded with a wag of her finger, "and don't chew up everything in sight."

Still smiling, she pulled on her gloves, picked up her crop, and walked outside. Within minutes she was riding Flick—another gift from Garret—in the direction of the Steele ranch.

Although the shadows were lengthening in the early evening hour, relentless August heat still smothered the valley. Beth allowed the gelding to set his own pace while she, in turn, allowed herself to daydream.

She imagined herself at home in Garret's log house. Funny, she'd thought the place small and crude when she'd arrived in New Prospects in May. Somehow, over the succeeding months, it had changed in her memory. Not that it seemed larger or grander. Only that it seemed welcoming, cheerful, a place for a family to call home.

A voice from her past mocked her. *"But you don't believe in happy ever after or a Prince Charming on a white horse, Elizabeth Victoria Louise. Remember?"* She could almost see Perceval's condescending sneer.

"But I *do* believe," she argued aloud. "I've learned to believe."

Her heart swelled with hope. She would tell Garret she'd broken her engagement to Owen. She couldn't tell him she loved him just yet, but she could find ways to show him how she felt. Surely, given time, he might come to love her, too. Surely, he might also be looking for happy ever after.

"I believe he is. I believe he must be."

"Talkin' t'yerself, Teach?"

She let out a startled cry as Trevor Booth stepped out from behind several large trees alongside the road and stood in her path. In a reflex action, she jerked on the reins, stopping her horse.

Trevor pointed at her. "I'm tired o' you makin' folks snicker 'bout me behind my back." He spoke in an angry but clear voice. Any sign of his earlier intoxication had vanished. There was something feral in his gaze, something threatening in his stance.

Beth tried to summon a note of authority as she said, "Trevor, you and I have nothing to say to each other. You are not one of my students. Now you must excuse me. I have an appointment to keep." She nudged Flick with her heels and started forward, turning the horse to circle around the young man in the road.

"Damn you!" he shouted as he leapt in her direction, catching the reins with his fingers and jerking hard.

Frightened, Flick reared straight up, then twisted to one side. Beth tried to keep her seat, but it was impossible. For that split second before she hit the ground, she feared the horse would fall over on top of her. Then the air *whoosh*ed out of her, and pain flashed behind her eyes as she struck her head against a rock. She rolled over, trying to clamber to her feet. She was knocked flat again, this time by Trevor's boot.

But real terror didn't take hold until she heard Flick galloping away, leaving her alone on the deserted road with this angry young man.

"Stop!" she cried, not sure if she meant the horse or Trevor.

He grabbed her by the upper arm and hauled her to her feet. She was quickly reminded of how strong this farmer's boy was. He was built like a brick wall, broad and thick and muscular.

"You think anybody'd care if you just up'n disappeared, Teach? Maybe that fool mayor, but nobody else. They'd say good riddance t'that snooty woman, that's what they'd say. You weren't wanted here, you an' your uppity ways."

His fingers tightened around her arm as he spoke until finally she couldn't hold back a whimper of complaint. The sound made him grin. Then she saw the return of something even more threatening in his eyes. She tried to scream, but the sound caught in her throat, trapped by a fear so thick she could taste it.

With a surprising abruptness, he spun and marched toward the trees, dragging her along with him. At first she did little but stumble along. Then self-preservation flared, and she began to struggle. With her free hand, she yanked loose her hat pin and jabbed him with it. He yelped as he grabbed her wrist and wrenched the weapon from her hand, tossing it into the underbrush. Then he started walking again, taking her deep into the copse where trees grew closely together, forming what should have been a lovely oasis from the blistering sun but instead was a place of shadows and fear.

Suddenly Trevor stopped and shoved her to the ground. "You know what, Teach? It's time you an' me had a different kind o' schoolin'."

"Trevor, don't—"

"I ain't the boy you think I am. You think I'm not old enough t'know what t'do, don'tcha? Well, you're wrong. I been with whores before. I know how they like t'be treated. I don't reckon you're no different than no whore." He grabbed her by the hair and gave it a yank. "Are ya?"

She had thought this sort of cruelty was something learned over a long period of time. A monster should be years in the making. Decades. She'd never have guessed a boy of sixteen could have the same perverse look of anticipation she'd seen in Perceval's eyes.

She began to withdraw into a secret place inside herself, began to view the scene as if from a distance. She'd nearly forgotten this place existed, but here it was.

Flick raced into the yard, a cloud of dust rising behind him, stirrup flapping against his left side, reins trailing in the air like black ribbons behind a bonnet. Garret didn't waste time wondering what might have happened to Beth. He simply told Janie to take care of the frightened horse. He'd be back as soon as he could. Then he was on his own gelding and galloping away from the ranch.

He sent up a silent prayer for Beth's safety, even as he tried to convince himself it was unlikely to be anything more serious than Flick shying at an animal or a bird and Beth falling on her rump. Only he wasn't convinced by his own arguments. That little cow pony didn't spook at picket pins or killdeer. Nor was Beth the sort of rider to be so easily unseated.

Something was wrong. Something was horribly, terribly wrong. And no amount of reassuring words was going to change the sense of foreboding that caused him to demand even more speed from the animal beneath him.

Garret would never know what caused him to rein in as he neared the copse of cottonwoods and box elders growing near the road. There wasn't any sign of Beth. She wasn't standing in the shade of a tree, brushing away dirt after a fall from her horse. There wasn't any sound.

Perhaps that was the reason he'd stopped his horse. Perhaps it was the lack of any sound at all. This time of early evening, just as the heat of day began to give way to the promise of a somewhat cooler night, the birds usually began chirping in celebration. Now they were silent. Too silent.

He narrowed his eyes and swept his gaze over the area. And that's when he saw it. Her hat. Her black silk riding hat. The one that always perched so prettily atop her shiny auburn hair.

His sense of foreboding increased. He subdued the urge to call out her name, instead dismounting and quietly, cautiously, moving into the trees. He would have sworn he could hear his own heart beating.

Then he heard something else. It was faint, too faint to identify, but he followed the sound, his sense of urgency growing with every step as he moved deeper into the copse.

Garret caught a glimpse of Beth through a break in the trees. She was kneeling on the ground, sitting back on her heels. Her hair fell in wild disarray around her shoulders. She was clutching the jacket of her riding habit in one hand. Her white blouse was torn down the front, revealing the soft swell of her breasts above her chemise. Tears streaked her cheeks, but otherwise she didn't move.

He took another step forward, and that's when he saw Trevor Booth, just a split second before he slapped Beth with the back of his hand. "Why don't you say nothin', Teach? Don't you got somethin' t'say now?"

Fury exploded in Garret. He catapulted forward, hitting Trevor's body with his own, knocking them both to the ground. Garret landed several quick, well-placed blows, using his advantage of surprise for all it was worth. The boy was big and strong and tried to fight back, but he was no match for Garret. A left upper cut was the final punch. Trevor's eyes glazed over, then closed as he toppled backward.

Garret spared only a quick glance to make certain his opponent was out cold before turning toward Beth. She hadn't moved, and her complete stillness alarmed him even further.

"Beth." He said her name tenderly as he dropped one knee to the ground. "Beth, look at me. It's Garret." He placed his hand on her shoulder.

She lifted her gaze. At first her eyes were blank. Then, slowly, he saw recognition dawning. He also saw pain, fear, and remnants of things past. He cursed the callous man in England who had caused those old hurts, and he cursed the stupid boy in Montana who had brought fear back into her life.

"Come on," he said in a low, reassuring voice. "Janie will be waiting for us."

"Janie?" she whispered.

"Yes. I told her I would bring you back." He gripped her upper arms lightly, easing her to her feet. "Janie's waiting with Flick at our place. It isn't far."

Beth lifted a hand to her tousled hair. "My hat. I've lost my hat."

"No, it's not lost. It's out by the road."

"By the road." She turned her head, as if to look

for her hat, then froze when she saw Trevor lying unconscious on the ground. "Is he . . . is he all right?"

"Don't worry about him. He'll come to in a bit."

"What did I do to make him hate me so?" She hugged herself. "He's only a boy. He's only sixteen. Why would he want to hurt me?" She paused, then asked, "What's wrong with me?"

Garret couldn't bear it any longer. "There's nothing wrong with you." He swept her off her feet—one arm beneath her knees, the other supporting her back—and strode through the copse.

It surprised him, the way he felt. He'd been angry enough to kill when he'd first seen Trevor strike her. Even now the rage filled him. But overriding the rage was the need to protect the woman in his arms. He needed to comfort her, to make her forget whatever had happened there. He needed to see her smile return and feel the quivering in her body cease.

And those needs stayed with him as he mounted his horse and turned the animal toward home.

Beth hadn't spoken another word since he'd picked her up. She just lay nestled against him, feeling much smaller and more fragile than he'd ever imagined her to be. He remembered the sound of hand against cheek when Trevor had slapped her, and his arms tightened even more. He should have realized the Booth boy wouldn't stay away. He should have known he would ignore Garret's warning to steer clear of the school and the schoolteacher. The elder Booth was no good and shiftless, and the apple hadn't fallen far from the tree when it came to Trevor. Perhaps he was even worse than his old man.

He's only a boy. He's only sixteen.

He heard Beth's confusion as the words played over again in his head. But he could have told her boys became men early in this country. The land demanded it. He should have understood Trevor would still want to cause trouble, to get revenge, if nothing else. When he'd thrown him out of the school, he should have known that wouldn't be the end of it. He should have done something to protect Beth, to warn her what could happen.

But it wasn't my concern, an inner voice insisted. Beth belonged to Owen. It should have been Owen looking out for her best interests. It should have been Owen seeing that she wasn't riding alone on this road, unprotected, where something like this could happen. It should have been Owen, but it hadn't been.

"Garret, stop."

He glanced down as he drew in the reins.

"Put me down, please." Her voice was soft but firm.

"We're almost to the ranch."

She lifted her head from his chest and looked up into his eyes. "We can't let Janie see me like this. She mustn't know what happened."

"But—"

"Put me down."

He did as she asked, holding on to her upper arms as he carefully allowed her to slide from the side of the horse. When he was certain her knees wouldn't buckle beneath her, he released her, then dismounted.

It was somewhat extraordinary, observing how she pulled herself together. Not just the way she gathered

her heavy shank of hair and twisted it into some sem-
blance of order. Not just the way she used a brooch to
pin closed her torn blouse or the way she swept the
dirt from her jacket and the skirt of her riding habit.
Not just the way she stiffened her spine and squared
her shoulders. What was remarkable was what he
knew instinctively was going on inside her, the collection of her thoughts, the drawing in of her emotions,
the way she dispassionately shut off the memory of
what had happened to her a mile back.

When she was finished, she looked up at him, and
if he had not been there, if he had not seen her in that
copse, he never would have guessed anything had
happened at all. Her demeanor was one of quiet, self-
assured elegance. She was every inch an English gen-
tlewoman, a member of the aristocracy, one of the
idle rich with no worries or fears.

"We forgot my hat," she said as she touched her
hair. Something flickered behind her eyes, a brief
remembrance. She turned and looked in the direction
they had come from. Then she said, "You must go
back."

"For your *hat?*"

"No." She shook her head. "To make certain
Trevor isn't hurt."

"You want me to go back and make sure that son
of a—"

"Please." She met his gaze once more.

"After what he did to you?"

"I'm all right now."

"But he was—"

"Garret, please." A glimmer of tears shone in her
eyes. "I was his teacher. I cannot simply leave him

there. What if he were badly hurt? What if something worse should befall him? I could never forgive myself."

He swore beneath his breath. "All right, I'll go back and look. But he deserves whatever he got."

She neither agreed nor disagreed. Her expression revealed none of her thoughts. "I shall walk to the ranch. I shall tell Janie you returned for my hat."

"If that's what you want."

"It would worry Janie if she knew what . . . what really happened. We shall tell her only that I fell from my horse. It is true, after all." Her voice dropped to a whisper. "I did fall."

The urge to strangle Trevor returned as Garret realized how flimsy was the veneer of courage she presented to him. "Sure, we can tell her anything you want."

Beth managed to keep up the pretense of everything being all right through all of Janie's fussing over her. She fabricated a story about how she was thrown from her horse and reassured the child she was none the worse for wear after the experience.

Garret returned without her hat, saying he couldn't find it. When Janie went into the kitchen to get Beth a glass of water at her father's request, he whispered that Trevor had been gone by the time he'd returned. "He couldn't have been hurt bad or he'd still be there."

She should have been relieved by the information, but for some reason her anxiety only increased. Still, she managed to carry on a relatively normal conversation throughout the supper Garret and his daughter had prepared. She did little more than move her food around her plate, but she didn't think Janie noticed. The girl was her usual chatty self and carried on about school and her pets and myriad other topics.

Finally, when the strain to appear strong for Garret and in good spirits for Janie became unbearable, she thanked them for their hospitality and said it was time for her to leave. Garret didn't object. He simply told Janie to clear up the supper dishes while he saw Beth home.

But when they stepped outside into the gathering twilight, Beth envisioned the empty cabin awaiting her. Worse still, she imagined Trevor standing in a dark corner of that cabin. And she began to shake, as if buffeted by a terrible storm.

It *was* a terrible storm. A storm of memories too difficult to be borne. Memories that went back beyond just a few hours ago. The weight of them pressed upon her chest, making it almost impossible to breathe. All her defenses, years in the making, crumbled in that one horrible moment.

"Beth?" Garret's voice seemed to come to her from far away.

She tried to locate him within her sight, but it was already too late. The darkness overwhelmed her.

16

Garret carried Beth into his bedroom and laid her on his bed.

"What's wrong, Pa?" Janie whispered, following him with the lamp. "What's the matter with Miss Beth?"

"She just fainted. She'll be okay."

"She looks awful pale."

"Yeah, she does." He sat on the edge of the bed and brushed tendrils of hair away from her temples, feeling a rush of tenderness, feeling more than he should have felt for a woman engaged to another. "Beth? Can you hear me?"

"Pa, maybe she needs Dr. Werner." Janie sounded scared. "She doesn't look so good. Maybe—"

He turned toward his daughter. "No, she doesn't need a doctor." He gave her a hug with one arm. "I think maybe that fall from her horse frightened her more than she wanted t'let on. That's all."

"You sure?"

"Yeah. Pretty sure." He gave her another squeeze. "Why don't you run get me a damp cloth?"

"Okay."

As soon as Janie was gone, he turned back toward Beth. She lay as still as death and nearly as pallid. His heart tightened at the sight of her. A need to protect and shelter her gripped him like a vise.

Again he ran his fingers over the sides of her face. Again he whispered her name. "Beth?"

She stirred, moaning softly. Her eyelids fluttered.

"Beth, wake up. Look at me."

Confusion darkened her eyes when she opened them.

Garret leaned over her. "How do you feel?"

"What happened?"

"You fainted."

"Fainted?" She tried to sit up, but he held her down with a hand on her shoulder.

"Lie still. Janie's bringing a cloth for your forehead."

"But I'm fine, Garret. Truly I am."

He felt another surge of protectiveness wash over him. He wondered if she realized she had stopped calling him Mr. Steele and tried not to admit how much he liked hearing her say his name. "No, you're not fine or you wouldn't have passed out cold."

"But—" she began, then stopped abruptly.

He could read her face like an open book. He saw the confusion vanish, swept away by remembrance and the return of fear. In that instant he thought he understood her better than he'd ever understood another living soul. "It's okay to be afraid, Beth," he said gently.

She shook her head as she closed her eyes. "No." The word was barely audible.

"Yeah, it is. We're all afraid sometimes." He could have told her he was afraid at this very moment. Afraid of what might happen if he weren't around to protect her. And even more afraid of the way she made him feel. A feeling stronger than mere physical desire. Different from anything he'd felt before.

Janie reentered the bedroom just then. Garret drew back from Beth, removed his hand from her shoulder, and immediately wanted to touch her again. Instead he rose from the side of the bed and motioned for his daughter to take his place.

"You tend to Beth," he told Janie, his voice a bit gruff, "and I'll turn Flick loose in the corral. Miss Beth is staying here tonight. I'll sleep in the loft with you."

"Garret . . ." Beth began, as if she would protest.

But then he glanced at her, and she fell silent. He saw confusion return to her eyes. This time he was the cause of the confusion. He knew it. Knew he needed to do something about it. Knew he should send her back to her cabin just as quick as he could. Knew he should send her away before he did something he would always regret.

"Janie, see if you can't find something for Beth to sleep in." That said, he turned and strode out of the bedroom.

Beth watched Garret disappear through the doorway and wished she could call out to him. She wanted to ask him to stay with her, to never leave her, to tell him she loved him. But she knew it was too soon and this was not the time.

Still, she didn't want to be alone, not even for as long as it would take him to unsaddle Flick and put the horse in the corral. She hadn't been afraid while Garret was with her. As long as he was near, she'd been able to hold at bay the ugly memory of what had happened this afternoon, the ugly memories of what had happened back in England. While he was with her . . .

"Here, Miss Beth. This'll make you feel better." Janie laid a cool cloth on Beth's forehead. "How's that?"

She met the child's gaze. "Much better, Janie. Thank you."

"You sure had us worried. I never saw anybody faint before."

"And I've never fainted before. I feel quite foolish for doing so now."

"You sure you're okay?"

"Yes, dear." She sighed, suddenly overwhelmed by it all. "But I am terribly tired." And it was true. She *was* tired. She was exhausted.

"You stay here. I'll be right back." Janie jumped up and disappeared, just as her father had done not long before.

Beth closed her eyes, wishing for the oblivion of a dead faint. She didn't want to think about anything. She felt all too vulnerable and exposed. Old fears seemed new. New fears seemed too real. She wanted nothing so much as to crawl into Garret's protective embrace and stay there forever.

She rolled onto her side, searching for a memory of someone—anyone—holding her in their arms as Garret had held her a few hours ago. Had anyone ever sheltered her, shielded her, defended her, as he had done?

And in that moment of searching, she had a terrible realization. Her father had known about Perceval's cruel ways. He'd known and it hadn't mattered. He'd known and had turned a blind eye. He had cared more about the money he'd needed than about his own daughter. After the death of his wife, Henry Wellington had been too weak to care for anyone beyond himself.

"Oh, God," Beth whispered. "Why?"

She had left her cabin that afternoon filled with hope for her future, but now hope had shriveled in her heart. What hope had she that Garret could learn to love her when even her own father had failed to do so?

"I found it!" Janie burst into the room, a white article of clothing draped over her arm. "Look. It's one of Ma's nightgowns. It was in the trunk of her things I've been savin' for when I grow up." She stopped and scrutinized Beth with a piercing gaze. "Are you cryin', Miss Beth?"

She shook her head. "No." And it was true. She hadn't been crying. She was too numb to cry.

More subdued now, Janie held out the nightgown. "You'd better put this on."

"Thank you. This is very generous of you, Janie."

"That's okay. I don't mind you usin' anything of mine. You oughta know that."

"I believe I shall go to sleep now. Please close the door on your way out." She knew she sounded stiff and formal, but it was the best she could do.

Janie nodded, her disappointment evident. "Sure, Miss Beth." Then she left.

So Beth was alone, as she had always been, as she was afraid she was always meant to be.

*   *   *

Garret made a bed for himself on the floor of Janie's room in the loft, but he couldn't sleep. He tried blaming it on the warm night. He tried blaming it on the hard wooden floor beneath him. He tried blaming it on the drought and the drying creek beds and the ranch.

But it was thoughts of Beth that kept him awake.

Suppressing a groan, he rose from the makeshift bed and descended to the ground floor. Then he walked to the front door and opened it. He leaned his shoulder against the jamb, staring out at the moonlit night and the blanket of stars that filled the sky.

He remembered the day Beth had arrived at the ranch. He remembered what he'd thought of her— beautiful, spoiled, rich, selfish, without common sense, perhaps even empty-headed. One by one she had dispelled all of his preconceived ideas about who and what she was. Except, of course, she was still beautiful. And she'd become even more so as he'd come to know her, as he'd discovered the beauty within.

It was dangerous for him to think of her the way he did, to allow himself to care even a little. But he did care, and even a little was too much. Beth was going to marry Owen.

He remembered the confusion he'd seen in her eyes as she'd looked up at him. Was there a chance she might . . .

He closed his eyes. No, he answered himself. There wasn't a chance. There couldn't be a chance. Heck, he didn't even want a chance. He and Janie were fine. They didn't need anyone else.

He swore as he looked out at the night once again, admitting the lie he'd been telling himself. He and Janie did need someone else. Janie needed and wanted a mother. Beth had filled that void in a temporary way, but once she married Owen and had children of her own, Janie would be hurt by the loss.

And what about him? Was he going to feel the loss as well?

He turned and stared at the door to his bedroom, knowing Beth lay sleeping on the other side of it. Then, compelled by something stronger than himself, he moved across the room and opened the door.

He'd meant to look in, then leave. But he didn't find her sleeping. She was curled on her side, her back to the window and the moonlight, her body shaking as if from the cold. He heard a soft whimper of despair.

He could no more resist going to her than he could make it rain.

As he sat on the edge of the bed, he whispered her name. She stilled before rolling onto her back. For a long, breathless moment, they simply stared into each other's eyes. Then Garret reached for her, drawing her into his embrace, holding her head against his chest, stroking her silken hair with a callused hand.

He had no right to hold her. He had no right to offer comfort. But it was as if he could feel her broken heart within his own chest, and he couldn't turn away from her now.

Time passed without notice. It could have been minutes. It could have been hours. But finally Beth lifted her head, turned her face upward. Her light green eyes looked black in the night. Her beautiful features were sharpened by moonlight and shadows. Her sensuous mouth promised a sweetness he'd never tasted before, a sweetness he hungered for.

He kissed her, holding her head between his hands. The touch of his mouth on hers was feather light at first. And it was even sweeter than he'd imagined it would be.

Sweet, like Beth.

The small voice of his conscience tried to make itself heard, tried to remind him this woman belonged to another, tried to make him stop what he was doing.

He ignored it.

He traced his tongue along her lips. As a breath of surprise escaped her, he took advantage, his tongue invading her mouth. His body reacted instantly, growing hard with desire. Yet the tenderness he'd felt remained, the need to comfort stronger than the need to possess.

Leaving her mouth, he trailed small kisses across her cheek to her temple, then over to her ear. He nibbled on the sensitive lobe, felt Beth shiver, heard her release a soft groan of delight. The sound caused his blood to course hot in his veins.

And that small voice of his conscience grew ever more distant.

As his mouth claimed hers once more, he eased her back on the bed, stretching out beside her. He braced himself on his side with one arm and traced the fingertips of his other hand down her neck, over her shoulder, and to her breast, only the thin fabric of the cotton nightgown separating skin from skin. He felt her nipple pucker as he ran his thumb over it, felt his erection pulse against her thigh.

At that moment he slammed the door on that pesky, persistent voice of conscience, effectively silencing it for the rest of the night.

The breath caught in Beth's throat as Garret cupped her breast in his large hand. Strange sensations shot through her, sensations both pleasurable and alarming. She'd never felt this way before.

His hand moved from her breast, sliding down her side, not stopping until it rested on her thigh. There, his fingers tugged on the nightgown, inching it upward. The night air whispered over her skin, following the fabric up the length of her legs at a slow, torturous pace.

She was terrified. She was eager.

She knew she should stop him. She didn't want to stop him.

She wanted him to love her. She was afraid he never would.

She wanted forever. She would settle for now.

In the past, when Beth had imagined being naked in front of her future husband, she had known only dread, had known her vulnerability would be greater because of it. But those feelings were forgotten under the magic of Garret's touch. Without hesitation, she allowed him to remove her nightgown.

He paused after tossing aside the garment, and she felt his gaze on her body like an intimate caress. She resisted the urge to hide herself with her hands, lying very still, her heart hammering in her chest, her breath coming in short, ragged bursts.

Why was it she didn't feel vulnerable and afraid with this man? Did love alone make such a great difference?

Again, he cupped one of her breasts, fondling, kneading, teasing. She felt the rough texture of his skin, the hands of a working man. Little shudders of pleasure raced through her, and Beth closed her eyes, not caring what the reason was for the things she felt, simply allowing herself to revel in the sensations for the sake of the sensations alone.

Garret kissed her, and this time it was she who opened her mouth, inviting the invasion of his tongue. She was thirsty for it all, for whatever he wanted to do. Like the drought-parched earth would have done with rain, she soaked up his touch and was greedy for more.

He began to explore her body with his mouth. He kissed her neck, the hollow of her throat, the tip of one breast, then the other. Finally he returned to her mouth, even as his hand took over the exploration. He caressed her skin until it felt on fire. And when he touched that intimate place at the juncture of her thighs, she gasped, held her breath—surprised, alarmed, curious.

Garret whispered her name. Or perhaps it was more of a growl, a primitive sound that made her pulse quicken in response.

Instinctively Beth pressed against his hand, and he began to stroke her with his fingertips. She released the air she'd captured in her lungs, then sucked in another as a great wave of sensations overtook her. Tension began to build. She didn't know whether to move toward him or away from him in order to find release. She did both. She heard a groan, was surprised to realize it had come from her own throat.

"Garret?" With that one word, she was asking many things. What are you doing? What am I feeling? Will you ever love me? Are we wrong to be doing this?

He stopped abruptly. She looked at him, knew he was giving her the opportunity to stop him before it was too late.

She couldn't do it. It was already too late for her. There would be no going back. She loved him too much.

"Garret." This time the word was not a question. It was a promise.

When he heard his name, Garret forgot any lingering thoughts of comforting Beth, of driving away her fears and her nightmares. He was gripped by a passion such as he'd never known, a need to be joined with this woman, a need so strong it overwhelmed him. His nostrils were filled with her scent. She was waiting for him, ready for him.

He rose and jerked his nightshirt over his head, then covered her body with his, supporting his weight on his knees and forearms. It took every ounce of self-control he possessed not to bury himself inside her with one quick thrust. But as hot and furious as the desire burned within him, he was determined this night would be special for them both. He wouldn't allow it to be otherwise. In the morning, he would probably regret what was about to happen, for so many reasons, but he was not about to regret it because it had been a hasty coupling.

Slowly, patiently, with his hands, his mouth, and

the motion of his body against hers, he brought her to the point of urgent need, and only then did he seek entrance. When he met the resistance of her maiden-head, his conscience tried one more time to reason with him.

What are you doing, Steele? She's a virgin.

She wriggled beneath him. He felt her hot breath on his skin. The voice in his head was drowned out by the drumming blood in his ears.

He pushed deeper, heard her sharp gasp, stilled, waiting instinctively for her pain to ease, then began to move. After a moment she joined him in the ancient dance of lovers, following his body with her own. The tempo began to increase, a slow rise at first, then faster and faster and faster until it reached its thunderous crescendo.

He heard Beth's small cry of pleasure mingling with his own as his body shuddered one final time.

And he suspected nothing would ever be the same for him again.

Long after Garret rolled onto his side, still holding Beth close, long after she heard his breathing slow and realized he slept, long after the glistening sweat of slick bodies had cooled and dried on her bare flesh, Beth remained awake. Her desire had been satiated, her curiosity more than satisfied. And although no words of love had been exchanged between them, she felt loved nonetheless.

The dark terror of that afternoon had been abrogated within the circle of his arms. The pain of her father's betrayal had receded. With a caress, a simple kiss, Garret had extinguished the belief that she was unlovable. Hope swelled anew within her heart.

Perhaps he didn't love her tonight. Perhaps he wouldn't love her tomorrow or next week or even next month. She was willing to wait. It was enough for now that he wanted her.

They weren't married. She knew she should be ashamed. But she wasn't. She loved Garret. She was his. It was as simple—and as complex—as that.

With a sigh, she closed her eyes. Tomorrow would no doubt bring problems. She would deal with them when they came. For now, she wanted only to sleep in his arms.

17

There wasn't much about himself that Garret didn't despise in the light of day. There was no good reason for a man to take advantage of a woman the way he had last night. And there was no reason to forgive a man who took the fiancée of his friend into his bed.

Guilt made him angry—with himself, with Beth, with the world at large.

Before sunrise, he was mucking out stalls in the barn. It was a dirty job. Just right for someone like him.

What was he going to do? What was he going to say to Beth when she awakened, when he saw her in the light of day and they both remembered what they had shared in the dark of night? Even now the memory of it gripped him with a sense of awe. Never before had the act of lovemaking been quite the same, quite the beautiful thing it had been last night.

But now it was day, and the questions continued. What if Janie guessed he hadn't slept in the loft?

What excuse would he give her? Would she guess he had been with Beth? Did she have any inkling at her age about what went on between a man and a woman?

And what about Owen?

Lord help me. What about Owen?

He tossed aside the pitchfork, laid his arm on the top board of the stall, then leaned his forehead against his arm. Owen loved Beth. He'd asked her to marry him. Garret had bedded her anyway.

And what did he feel for Beth? A raging passion, to be sure. But it sure as heck wasn't love. He wouldn't let it be. He'd gone down that road once before and had no intention of doing it again. He wanted nothing to do with love or marriage.

He swore as he bounced his forehead against his arm in frustration.

He'd been swept away by passion years before. He'd known seventeen-year-old Muriel two weeks when they'd tumbled into bed for the first time. The only difference was that Muriel had known what to do in that maid's room in her father's San Francisco mansion. Garret had been too green about women and too caught up in the carnal act to realize it at the time.

But Beth was innocent. She had been a virgin.

The rational argument of his conscience only made him more angry, more frustrated. He didn't want her to be innocent. He wanted to despise her as much as he despised himself. At the very least he could point a finger at her and say she'd given herself to him while she was planning her wedding to another man. At the very least he could blame her for that.

He certainly loathed himself for it. Owen was the one friend who knew the whole story about Muriel, who'd stood by him in those early years when Garret had blamed himself for all that had gone wrong in his marriage, who'd known the truth about Janie and had never stood in judgment.

And look how Garret had repaid him.

Whispering a few more choice swear words, he threw himself back into his work with a vengeance, hoping he would discover some answers or at least a way to escape the weight of his own guilt.

He'd mucked out three stalls and had just started on the fourth when he heard his daughter's voice.

"Pa, you in there?"

He stopped and glanced over his shoulder. "Over here, Janie."

She stepped from the morning brightness into the dim light of the barn. "Miss Patsy and Miss Bunny are here t'see you."

It was like being kicked in the gut by a mule. "Where are they?"

"Waitin' in the house."

He swallowed. "And Miss Beth?"

"She's still asleep, I guess. She hasn't come out yet."

He dropped the pitchfork and strode out of the stall and across the barn, his heart hammering a warning gong.

Beth couldn't believe she had slept so late. The sun was fully up, and the bedroom was bright with the light of day. Even as she wondered when Garret had arisen, she was thankful she hadn't awakened to find him still in bed with her. It would have been awkward. She would have been embarrassed this morning even though she wasn't sorry for what had happened.

She smiled as she sat up, sweeping back her tousled hair with her hands. No, she wasn't sorry. She loved him, and she had to believe he cared for her, too. Surely last night wouldn't have been so wonderful if he didn't care for her.

She found a fresh pitcher of water on the dresser, along with a clean washcloth, towel, hairbrush, and hand mirror, and knew Garret had left them there while she'd slept. She was grateful for his thoughtfulness.

She bathed, cleansing away the evidence of the previous night's lovemaking, blushing as she remembered every minute detail. She remembered the touch of his hands, the taste of his kisses, the indescribable pleasure of being joined with him. She didn't even mind the slight discomfort, the ache of sore muscles, she felt this morning. It only served as a reminder of the intimacies they had shared and the delight they had brought her.

She dressed in her riding habit, using her brooch to pin the torn place on her blouse—and refusing to allow the memory of how it had become torn to return. Then she took the brush from the dresser and tried to bring some order to her unruly mane. It was useless. What few hairpins she'd had when she'd arrived at the ranch yesterday seemed to have disappeared. She had no choice but to leave her hair hanging loose about her shoulders.

Through the heavy bedroom door she'd heard Janie's voice just a minute or so before. She knew father and daughter were both up and about. She knew they must both be wondering if she was ever coming out.

Taking a deep breath to bolster her courage, she walked toward the door—and toward Garret and Janie, the two people she hoped would fill her future.

But they weren't the two people she found in the living room of Garret's log house.

Beth froze in the bedroom doorway even as she heard Bunny Homer's horrified gasp. Then the front door burst open and Garret entered, Janie at his heels. The two visitors turned toward him even as his gaze darted between them and Beth and back again, taking in the situation in one breathless instant.

"Mr. Steele, we demand to know what is going on here," Patsy said in a harsh voice.

Garret frowned. "Just what do you mean, Miss Homer?"

"You know very well what I mean. And you with a young child in this house. Have you no shame?"

He glanced over his shoulder. "Janie, go out to the barn and wait for me there."

"But, Pa—"

"Do as I say."

"But I don't—"

"Now, Janie."

Beth wanted to move out of the bedroom doorway, to somehow make the situation appear different from the way she knew it did. But her feet were leaden, her body brittle. If she moved, she thought she might shatter into a thousand pieces.

As Janie headed reluctantly toward the barn, Garret closed the front door and faced the women again. "What brought you here this morning, ladies?"

"I hardly think that matters under the circumstances," Patsy replied indignantly.

Bunny swung around. "Harlot! Jezebel!" She raised a plump fist and shook it at Beth. "I'll see you run out of this town. I'll see that you're never allowed to teach children anywhere again."

Beth cast a frantic gaze toward Garret, but he wasn't looking at her. He was glaring at Patsy.

"This isn't what it looks like," he said in a carefully measured tone.

But Beth knew it was exactly what it looked like.

"Miss Wellington took a bad fall from her horse last evening not far from here," Garret continued. "I insisted she rest here and gave her the use of my bedroom. I made a bed for myself in the loft with Janie."

Patsy sniffed. "Do you actually think anyone will believe that story, Mr. Steele? I, for one, certainly do not. Nor will the other members of the school board." She turned toward Bunny. "Come along, sister. We must call a meeting of the board immediately."

"Owen won't be back until late today," Beth said softly, surprised she'd even found her voice.

That was when Patsy narrowed the distance separating them and slapped her across the cheek. "Don't you dare speak his name. You're not fit to use it." She pointed a finger at Beth. "Mr. Simpson is going to know the truth about you. The whole town will know."

Patsy spun away from Beth, grabbed her sister by the arm, and dragged Bunny toward the door. Wordlessly Garret opened it before them.

But Bunny brought them both to a stop in the doorway. She turned to look back at Beth, her gaze filled with even more outrage than her sister's had been. "The wrath of God is going to fall on your head for what you've done. You'll see. I promise you'll live to regret this day."

Within a couple of minutes, their horse and buggy pulled out of the yard at a fast clip, carrying the sisters back to town so they could tell everyone who would listen what they had seen this morning at the Steele ranch.

Garret closed the door again. His gaze met with Beth's across the living room. The silence was oppressive. After what seemed an eternity, he said, "It seems we have a problem, Beth."

She nearly laughed at the understatement. She was about to lose her teaching position. She would have no place to live, no way to earn her keep after she was sent away under a cloud of scandal. Owen, who might have been able to forgive her for the broken engagement, who might have still been her friend, would never forgive her for this, and Garret would never have the time he needed to learn to love her. She would have to leave New Prospects and everything she had come to care about.

In a voice totally void of emotion, he continued, "I guess we don't have any choice except to get married."

She thought she'd misunderstood him.

"We'll get Janie and go see Hezekiah."

She grasped the doorjamb with her right hand, feeling weak in the knees.

He scowled at her. "Look, I know I'm not the man

you meant to marry and this isn't the sort of house you planned to live in, but I guess there's nothing to be done about it now. At least this place is better than the old Thompson place."

"Not the man you meant to marry. . . ."

He raked his fingers through his hair. "After what happened last night, the least I can do is give you my name. It'll give you a little protection, anyways. Folks are still gonna talk, but maybe it won't be as bad."

"Least I can do is give you my name. . . ." She heard the bitterness in his voice.

Feeling sick to her stomach, she said, "I wasn't going to marry Owen. I . . . I'd already decided I couldn't go through with it."

His eyes narrowed, and she knew he didn't believe her.

"It's true." She took a step toward him. "I . . . I wouldn't have allowed . . . wouldn't have stayed last night if—"

"Don't. Things're bad enough as they are. Let's not pretend we didn't do wrong."

"Did we do wrong?" she whispered. She lifted a hand toward him. "I love you, Garret."

His face seemed to turn to stone. He stared at her but said nothing, and the last glimmer of hope that he might someday love her vanished.

Still, she couldn't stop herself from saying, "I left Owen a note, telling him I couldn't marry him." Her gaze dropped to the floor. "Because I love you."

An agonizing silence gripped the room. Each second seemed an eternity. Beth longed to look at Garret again but didn't dare. She was too afraid of what she might see in his eyes. It was difficult knowing he'd proposed out of duty, knowing he felt obligated to marry her against his will. It would crush her if she looked up and discovered he was going to reject her heart completely.

He turned away. "I'll hitch up the wagon." Then he opened the door and went outside.

Janie sat in the back of the wagon, subdued by the strange mood of the two adults up front. When her pa had said he was going to marry Miss Beth, she'd never been happier. But it seemed she was the only one happy about it. Miss Beth looked like she didn't have a friend in the world, and her pa looked like he'd just lost his ranch.

Janie would have said something, too, about weddings being joyous affairs, like the reverend had talked about in church, only something warned her to keep quiet.

They stopped at the cabin near the school on the way into town so Miss Beth could change her clothes. Wordlessly Garret helped her down from the seat, then stood beside the wagon while she went inside.

Janie wished she knew what was going on in his head, because he was sure acting strange.

It was just as well his daughter couldn't read Garret's mind. She would have found it a dark and dreary place.

Years before, when he'd been too young and foolish to know better, he'd taken a tumble in bed with a beautiful girl from a prosperous family. That time, too, he'd let his desire overrule his head, and that time, too, he'd found himself getting married before he'd hardly known what hit him. Muriel's father had seen to that.

Later, Garret had realized Muriel had ensnared him on purpose. She'd used all her feminine wiles to lure him to that maid's room on the top floor of the mansion, then had made certain they would be discovered. She'd even lied and told him she loved him.

But, of course, she hadn't loved him. She'd just wanted someone to take her away from a father who kept too tight a rein on her. She'd thought, mistakenly, that Garret was a cattle baron with thousands of acres of rangeland. She'd thought she was headed for a life of continuing luxury, only without her father watching over her. She hadn't wanted a husband so much as a playmate. She hadn't wanted a home. She'd wanted travel and excitement and fancy clothes. She'd wanted lots of things her new husband couldn't give her, and she'd despised him because of it.

Now, fourteen years later, it was happening to him all over again. Only this time he should have known better. He was old enough not to have fallen into such a trap. He'd told himself a hundred times to steer clear of Beth Wellington, that she would be trouble.

But he'd let himself believe she was different. He'd listened to her talk about her father and Lord Altberry, and he'd felt compassion for her. He'd seen the Booth boy hurt her, and he'd wanted to protect and comfort her. He'd felt things he'd never felt before as he'd held her in his arms, and he'd allowed himself to believe that maybe . . .

He set his jaw.

She'd lied to him, just like Muriel. Maybe she hadn't set the trap on purpose. Maybe he was the one at fault. But then she'd lied to him. She'd said she loved him. She'd told him it wasn't Owen she'd wanted to marry. As if saying so made everything all right.

Maybe he was being unfair to her. But it didn't change the way he felt. And if he were brutally honest with himself, he'd have to admit it was because he was afraid.

He was afraid that one day, after he'd grown to care too much—and maybe he already did—he would lose Beth. He'd lose her because he wasn't the man she thought he was.

He was certain life had just dealt him another losing hand.

Inside the cabin, Beth sat on her bed, holding Wishbone against her chest. She stared across the room with unseeing eyes, feeling battered and bruised, inside and out. The past twenty-four hours reminded her of a storm on the Atlantic that could toss a huge steamship like a child's toy in a bathtub. One minute she had ridden the crest, the next she'd plummeted to the depths.

How many times would she start to hope, only to have it snatched away from her? How many times would she find inner strength, only to have it dissolve into cowardice?

She shook her head, as if trying to shake loose the confusion. Then she looked down at the puppy. "I ran away from a wedding before. I could do it again."

Only she didn't *want* to run away from Garret. She loved him. She wanted nothing more than to be his wife, share his bed, bear his children. She caught her breath as memories of last night swept through her. She wanted him to make love to her like that again and again and again. For the rest of her life.

But would he want to, resenting her as he did?

She wished she had someone to confide in, a friend who could advise her, but there wasn't anyone. Janie, of course, was too young. And Owen, who had been her friend and had helped her so often since she'd arrived in New Prospects, wasn't likely to remain her friend after today.

If only Mary were there. Beth could have used some of her sound advice.

Sure and you know what I'd say to you if I was there. Wouldn't you now, m'lady?

Beth smiled wistfully. She closed her eyes and imagined the petite Irish girl with the wild mane of ink black hair. She could see her, knuckles on her hips, eyes sparking defiantly.

Will you be givin' up after all you've been through? Did you come so far only to turn tail and run like a hare before the hounds?

"I'm tired. I'm not strong like you, Mary."

Not strong? 'Tis a lie you're tellin' yourself. Sure and I think you know it, too. Didn't I tell you one day you'd give away your heart, just as I did to me Mr. Maguire? Don't run away from the right man, m'lady. Not if you love him. You'll be forever sorry if you do. If you love him, there's still hope.

Beth opened her eyes. She did love Garret.

Loved him as she'd never imagined was possible. Perhaps she would never take the place of his first wife in his heart. Perhaps he was marrying her only out of guilt for last night. But there was still hope they would find happiness together. She had to believe that. She had to cling to that hope for all she was worth.

She set Wishbone on the floor and rose from the bed. Hastily she stripped out of her riding habit. She chose one of her favorite gowns to wear as her wedding dress, praying the cream-colored silk would bring her luck for the future.

The ceremony was brief and solemn. The bride and groom stood before the minister, repeating their vows in subdued voices. Their witnesses—the minister's wife, the three Matheson children, and the groom's daughter—couldn't help but notice Garret and Beth never once looked at each other during the exchange of vows. Not until the very end when Hezekiah said, "You may kiss your bride." Only then did they turn their heads and allow their gazes to meet.

Garret saw the swirl of emotions in his bride's green eyes, recognized the uncertainty, the hope, the fear, and he felt again a now familiar urge to hold and comfort her. Of course, if he'd been able to resist the urge before, he wouldn't be married to her now. What was it about Beth, he wondered, that caused him always to act against his better judgment?

He took hold of her arms as he lowered his head

and kissed her lightly on the lips. Then, before he could allow himself to feel anything, he released her and turned back toward Hezekiah.

Holding out his hand, he said, "Thanks."

The minister took hold of the proffered hand and shook it, his grasp firm. "May God bless you both."

Garret nodded stiffly. Could God bless a union that had begun like this?

"Thank you, Reverend Matheson," Beth said in a soft voice.

Hezekiah smiled at her. "It was my pleasure, Mrs. Steele. Make each other happy."

Even more softly she replied, "I shall do my best."

Garret glanced at Beth—at his wife, at the new Mrs. Steele—and he allowed himself a moment of optimism. What if she had told the truth? What if she really had decided not to marry Owen because she loved him instead?

Maybe . . . just maybe . . .

"Miss Beth?" Janie whispered, interrupting her father's thoughts.

He watched as Beth leaned toward his daughter, who had joined them near the altar. "What is it, Janie?"

"Is it okay if I call you Ma from now on?"

A lump formed in Garret's throat, and his heart constricted.

Beth looked at him above the top of the girl's head, her eyes—glittering with unshed tears—asking him for permission. There wasn't anything he could do but nod.

Beth gave Janie a tight hug. "I would like that very much. Very much indeed."

The moment she was released from Beth's embrace, Janie turned a beaming face toward her father. "Pa, let's take Ma home."

Maybe, he thought. Just maybe it would be all right.

18

Owen was exhausted by the time his horse and buggy pulled up in front of the bank. It had been a long week, and the continuing heat wave did nothing to ease the miserable train ride from Denver to Bozeman, not to mention the hours of travel by buggy up to New Prospects. He was dusty, hungry, and thirsty. He was also eager to see Beth. The sooner he took care of a few pressing matters of business in his office, the sooner he could wash up and go out to see her.

He unlocked the door to the bank, opened it, and went inside. After raising the blinds to let in some daylight, he proceeded into his office. He was relieved to see his desk was clear of files and other papers. Not that he was surprised. Harry Kaiser was more than just a capable bank clerk. He was as indispensable as Owen's own right hand. Rarely was there a problem the man couldn't handle in his boss's absence.

With a sigh, Owen removed his suit coat and rolled up his shirtsleeves. But before he could sit down, the bank door opened again, and the Homer sisters bustled through.

"Mr. Simpson!" Patsy exclaimed as she waddled toward him, the rolls of fat beneath her chin quivering like jelly. "Thank heaven you are back."

Inwardly he groaned. He hadn't the patience to deal with these two busybodies today. But he forced himself to smile and say, "Good day, ladies. What can I do for you?"

"I'm afraid we bring you bad news."

He frowned. "Bad news?" Come to think of it, Bunny Homer wore the look of someone who'd had a death in the family. "What's happened?"

"Well . . ." Patsy waved her silk fan to cool herself, beads of perspiration dotting her forehead and upper lip. "Oh, dear. I don't know how to tell you this. It is utterly horrible. Utterly horrible. Truly it is."

"Oh, for pity's sake!" Bunny snapped. "Stop acting the fool." She stepped around Patsy. "Mr. Simpson, in your absence we were forced to call an emergency meeting of the school board. We have unanimously voted for the immediate dismissal of Beth Wellington as New Prospects' schoolteacher."

"Why? On what grounds?"

Bunny drew her gaunt frame to its full height. "Immoral behavior."

"Immoral behavior? What on earth—"

Patsy elbowed her sister out of the way. "She was caught in a . . . shall we say . . . disheveled state coming out of Mr. Steele's bedroom early this morning. And while they had the gall to try to deny anything was amiss, it was obvious to anyone that *that* was not the case."

Owen gripped his desk, stunned into silence.

"And there was a witness to prior breaches of conduct," Bunny added in an ominous tone.

He sat down, not caring if it was rude or not.

Nodding to affirm her sister's statement, Patsy continued, "Trevor Booth saw Mr. Steele and that woman *cavorting* in the wooded area near the Steele ranch. And they were so . . . well, let's just say she was too engrossed with Mr. Steele to realize she left this behind." She set a silk hat on Owen's desk.

It was Beth's. He recognized it immediately. He'd always liked the way she looked in it. Almost regal. Certainly a lady. Surely incapable of the things these vultures were suggesting.

He picked up the hat, held it between his hands. "I'll return this to her. I'm on my way to see her now."

"You won't find her at the Thompson cabin," Patsy informed him with a sniff. "Oh, mercy. Look how she has repaid you for that kindness."

He glared at her, silently demanding she go on even as he wished he could muzzle her.

"Miss Wellington and Mr. Steele were married by Reverend Matheson earlier this afternoon."

Owen was suffocating. He needed air. "Married?" he croaked.

"Well, it wasn't as if Mr. Steele had much choice." Bunny's eyes flashed with indignation and fury. "She tricked him with her wicked ways, that English harlot."

He stood abruptly. "I'll ask you not to speak of Miss Wellington in that manner."

"She isn't Miss Wellington any longer." Patsy

touched his arm. "Oh, Mr. Simpson, I'm so very sorry
for you. But you must understand you have been
saved from a dreadful fate."

"I think you ladies should leave now."

"But—"

"Now!"

"You've endured a terrible shock, but in time—"

"Shut up and get out!" He bit off each word with
precision.

Patsy's face turned beet red as she shrank back
from him.

"Well, I never," Bunny huffed.

He turned his glare on the older of the two women.
"No, you never. You never did anything but gossip
and try to hurt others. You are both bitter, hateful
women, and everyone in town knows it."

Bunny took hold of her sister's arm. "Come along,
Patsy. We have overstayed our welcome."

Owen wanted to say more, but somehow he managed to hold his tongue until they were out of the
bank and the door had slammed closed behind them.
Then he sank onto his chair a second time, this time
resting his elbows on the desktop and cradling his
head in his hands.

Was it true? Had Beth and Garret married? Had
they . . .

No, he wouldn't believe it. Not until Beth told him
from her own lips.

With Janie's cheerful assistance, Beth began putting
away her things in Garret's bedroom. In *their* bedroom, hers and Garret's. Over and over again, she

had to keep reminding herself she was his wife and this was her home. But it still didn't feel real. Only yesterday afternoon she had ridden toward the ranch, determined to win his love. And now she was married to him.

Married . . . to a man who didn't love her, who didn't want her.

Kneeling on the floor, she stared into her trunk, remembering all that had happened this day. After the marriage ceremony, they had stopped at the cabin near the school and Beth had once again packed her possessions into the trunk she had brought with her from England. Garret had placed it in back of the wagon, then driven silently back to the ranch. Just as silently, he'd carried it into the house and into his bedroom. *Their* bedroom. He'd left it for her to unpack, telling her to take whatever space she needed in the bureau and wardrobe. Then he'd made himself scarce.

Fighting sudden tears, Beth withdrew a nightgown and laid it in the bottom bureau drawer. "Janie, tell me about your mother."

"What wouldja like t'know?"

"Was she pretty? Like you?"

"She was real pretty, but I don't look much like her. Her hair was gold, and she had big brown eyes."

"Do you have a photograph of her?"

"Just a little one in a locket. Pa got rid of all the others."

Beth thought about her father. After Anne's death, Henry Wellington had hidden his heartache in drink and gambling and a series of lovers. Garret Steele, on the other hand, had shut himself off from everything.

He hadn't even been able to bear seeing Muriel's likeness.

How could Beth ever find her way into his heart if he had room only for his first wife?

"My ma hated the ranch."

That surprising statement brought Beth's attention abruptly back to Janie. "She did?"

The girl nodded. "She was always sayin' if it was the last thing she ever did, she was gonna see I didn't have t'be stuck here. She always said she was gonna take me to England when I was older and see me married to some lord or duke or somethin'." Janie grinned. "But I only wanted t'go so I could meet you. I wouldn't've wanted to stay. I love it here."

Beth hugged Janie. "So do I," she whispered as she pressed her cheek against the girl's hair.

And she did. She loved the ranch and Montana and New Prospects and everyone in it. For the first time in her life, she'd felt as though she belonged somewhere.

But did she belong any longer? She wasn't wanted as the schoolteacher. Folks would think the worst of her after the Homer sisters were finished with their gossiping. She hadn't even any defense against them, for everything they would surely say about her was true. As for Garret, he'd married her out of guilt. He resented her intrusion into his life. How was she to overcome those feelings and make him love her?

Beth pushed away the swirling doubts. "I should start supper." She stood and held out her hand. "I'll need your help."

Janie slipped her smaller hand into Beth's. "Sure."

Her heart was hammering as she opened the bedroom door, not knowing what she would say to Garret. But the living room was empty, her bridegroom nowhere to be seen. She wondered when he would return, when she would see him again. Trepidation warred with anticipation at the thought. If only he loved her. If only he didn't resent her.

Again she closed her mind to the doubts. She was Garret's wife, and right now she needed to prepare his supper. She would worry about that first. After all, preparing a meal was something tangible. It involved action, and when it was finished, she would know if she had done her job well or not.

As for her other problems, they would not be so easily tackled or so easily assessed. She could only wait and deal with them as each one arose and pray they would work out in the end.

"You'll have to show me where to find things, Janie, and tell me what your father likes to eat." And please, God, let me manage to not burn our first meal as man and wife.

Janie took Beth outside and showed her where the root cellar was. Together they selected the best bunch of carrots they could find, as well as several large potatoes. Next they went to the smokehouse, where Beth selected what she hoped was a good cut of ham.

After they returned to the house, Janie tied an apron around Beth's waist, then showed her where to find the kettles and frying pans. As they worked together, it became quickly apparent Janie was the teacher and Beth the pupil. But the girl made the lessons enjoyable, and Beth found her mood brightening as the time passed.

The carrots and potatoes were boiling on the stove,

biscuits were baking in the oven, and slices of ham were sizzling in the frying pan when they heard a knock on the door.

Beth felt her heart skitter. Garret wouldn't have knocked. It had to be someone from town, and she wasn't certain she was up to facing them yet.

"I'll see who it is," Janie said, then ran across the room and yanked open the door before Beth could protest.

Owen was waiting on the other side.

As their gazes collided, Beth's heart stopped.

He stared at her for an interminably long time before he held out his hand. "I believe this is yours."

She looked at the silk hat and nodded wordlessly, not even wondering how he'd come by it.

He entered the house and placed the hat on the table. "It's true, then? You're married to Garret?"

"It's true," she whispered.

"Why, Beth?"

She shook her head.

"Why would you do this? Why couldn't you at least talk to me first?"

Her throat felt thick and closed. "I tried to explain in my note. You won't believe this, but I never meant to hurt you, Owen. I thought I could marry you. I thought I could learn to love you, just as you said. But when I realized . . . when I realized I couldn't, I took the coward's way out. I couldn't face you, so I wrote that note, trying to explain."

"What are you talking about? What note?"

"Didn't you go to your office? Did you think I—" She stopped abruptly, then drew a deep breath and began again. "Owen, I left an envelope on the desk in your office. I thought you would go there first. I swear I wouldn't have had you find out this way. I left it there before . . . before any of this happened." She motioned with her hand, as if just being there explained what she meant by "any of this."

Owen took a step toward her. "I've been to the bank, Beth. There was no envelope."

A movement in the doorway alerted her to Garret's presence. She looked, saw him standing there, his broad shoulders filling the opening, his eyes dark and unfathomable.

Owen turned around. His expression hardened. "I never expected this from you of all people, Garret. I never expected you to steal the woman I loved."

Garret met and held Beth's gaze for a breathless moment, then he looked at the man who had been his friend all these years. "I didn't expect it, either. I'm sorry, Owen. More sorry than you'll ever know. I don't reckon you'll forgive me for it now."

"Forgive you? Damn right I won't forgive you."

I did this, Beth thought as she watched the two men. I destroyed their friendship.

"Do you know what they're saying about her in town?" Owen demanded of Garret. "Do you know what sort of gossip those Homer women are spreading?"

"I know."

"She didn't deserve this." Owen glanced over his shoulder at Beth. "And neither did I."

She reached toward him. "Owen, I'm sorry. I never meant—"

"I think I'd better get back to town," he interrupted.

"It's been a long day." He left then, moving past Garret without meeting his friend's gaze again.

Except for the sound of boiling water on the stove, the house was gripped by a painful silence.

After what seemed like an eternity, Garret said, "I'll wash up for supper."

Beth winced as the door swung closed behind him, feeling as if he had slammed it in her face.

Perhaps he had.

It was a long and torturous meal, full of silence. Janie was back to looking hurt and confused. The adults were both grim.

Garret noticed Beth didn't eat more than a couple of bites. He couldn't blame her. His own appetite was gone.

He kept replaying Owen's visit over in his mind. He kept hearing his friend say there'd been no note, no envelope. He kept hearing Beth insisting she'd written one and left it for him. Who was telling the truth? And did it even matter?

No, it didn't matter, he decided. Whatever else had happened, all that really mattered was he'd taken the woman Owen loved into his bed, then he'd married her. He'd betrayed the one person he'd always been able to trust.

He looked at Beth across the table and knew an ache in his heart such as he'd never felt before. In that moment, he ceased to blame her. Guilt had made him want to find fault with someone other than himself. To find fault with her. But the truth was, everything that had happened was his responsibility and his alone. He was the one who had wanted to hold Beth, to comfort and protect her. He was the one who had entered the bedroom last night and had kissed her, undressed her, lain with her, loved her.

Loved her.

He stood up, tipping his chair over backward. Both Janie and Beth jumped, startled by the sudden noise as the chair hit the floor.

It was true, he thought as he stared at Beth. He loved her. He'd loved her last night. He'd loved her this morning. He'd loved her when he married her. He'd been so dad-blasted worried he would come to care for her that he hadn't realized it was already too late. Too danged late.

"Garret?" Her voice was tentative.

"I'm not hungry." He headed for the door. "I'm gonna see to the livestock." He stomped out of the house. But when he reached the barn, he just kept right on walking.

How had he let this happen? How had he let Beth weasel her way into his life, into his heart? Beth with her lush hair and her soft skin and her bright smile and—

"Garret?"

He stopped and spun around, angered that she'd followed him, but glad that she had, too.

"We need to talk."

"I don't feel like talkin'."

"Janie is upset by our behavior."

She was right, and he didn't want her to be right.

"We need to talk," she said again, more softly this time. "Please."

He jammed his fingers into the pockets of his

trousers. "All right. So we'll talk." He jerked his head to one side. "Come on. Let's find some shade."

It was a delaying tactic. He wasn't ready to talk about his feelings yet. Not when he'd only just discovered them. Not when those same feelings scared the living daylights out of him. He'd rather face down a charging bull than face this storm of emotions.

He wondered if she'd guessed he was trying to postpone the inevitable.

He led her away from the road and toward a pair of scraggly cottonwoods that grew beside the creek, a creek now dry from the drought. When they reached the spot, he pointed to a place in the shade. "Might as well sit down."

She drew near to him, touched his arm, forced him to look at her. "Sit beside me."

He'd given her the power to destroy him, he realized as he look down into her eyes. He'd been so careful all these years. He'd let no female in but Janie. When had Beth snuck by his carefully laid defenses?

They sat, side by side, facing the shriveled-up creek bed. Beth folded her legs to one side beneath the cream-colored gown she'd worn for their wedding. He shouldn't have let her keep it on. He should have told her to change out of it. He would never, not even in one of his best years, be able to afford a dress like that. There would always be something they needed more.

"I don't reckon I've ever seen a prettier dress than that one," he said.

She looked down, ran her fingers over the fabric, then glanced up at him. "It's only a dress, Garret."

"You're used to fine clothes and things."

"Yes, but people matter more." Her voice lowered, but her eyes didn't. "*You* matter more. *Janie* matters more."

He turned his head, stared across the range toward the mountains. It was easy for Beth to talk like that. She didn't know what was ahead of her. She'd had only a small taste of what life was like in Montana. She hadn't made it through one of their harsh winters yet. She had yet to learn what it meant to be a rancher's wife. He remembered all too well how poverty and hard work had aged his ma before her time. One day Beth would look at him, and he would know that she—

"Will you tell me about Muriel?"

His gut tightened. "No."

He couldn't tell Beth about his first wife. He couldn't let her know what a failure he'd been. He didn't want her to guess he hadn't been able to satisfy any of Muriel's wants or desires, not even the smallest of them.

"All right, Garret. Then perhaps it's time we talked about us."

He looked at her, wishing she would never have to learn the truth, wishing he could make her happy, wishing he could give her everything she might ever want. "Yeah, I guess so."

Beth heard the reluctance in his voice. She smiled sadly. "I'm not going to get any help from you, am I?"

He lifted an eyebrow, obviously surprised by her tiny stab at wry humor.

She drew a quick breath and forged ahead before she lost both her courage and the opportunity. "Garret, I know you didn't mean for this to happen. I know you didn't want to marry me, that you didn't want another wife. But for whatever reason, here we are. We *are* married."

"That we are."

"I also know you don't want to believe I love you. But I do. And I love Janie, too. I couldn't love her more if she were my own. I swear it to you by all that I am. I promise I shall do everything in my power to be a good mother to her and a good wife to you—" Her voice broke, and her eyes filled with tears.

She blinked furiously. She hadn't meant to cry. It was the last thing she'd wanted to do. She'd wanted to be strong, to speak with conviction, to prove to him she was determined and capable and unafraid.

"We are two very different people, you and me." He said it as if the statement proved something.

"That's true."

"We don't really even know each other."

I know you with my heart. "That's true, too."

"There's going to be plenty of talk. Folks in town won't forget any time soon. And you'll be the one who takes the brunt of it. You'll be the one they blame." His eyes narrowed; his gaze was hard. "If you want to leave New Prospects, I'll understand. I'll get the money somehow, send you wherever you want to go. I won't hold you to those vows we took."

She could scarcely draw a breath, her chest was so tight. "But I want you to hold me to them, Garret." Tears returned, and this time she was unable to keep them from falling, streaking salty tracks down her cheeks. "Please hold me to them."

She was in his arms so quickly that she wasn't sure how it had even happened. His mouth claimed hers in a furious kiss. It was nothing like the tender, passionate ones they had shared before. This was a branding, a claiming, a declaration of possession. It thrilled and it frightened her.

And hope burned a little stronger in her heart as she gave back his kisses in kind.

19

"You're sure you want to do this?" Garret asked as he leaned his shoulder against the doorjamb. "We could wait a few weeks, until the talk dies down."

Morning sunlight streamed through the window, making the room look brighter than he'd ever remembered it being. Or perhaps it was the woman standing in front of the bureau mirror, wearing a dress of lemon yellow, who brightened the room.

Beth set a petite, white straw bonnet, accented with daisies, over her freshly coiffed hair. "I'm quite certain I want to do this."

They had made love again last night—their wedding night—and Garret had discovered a few more things about his bride. Although inexperienced, she wasn't unwilling, and with a little guidance she had made some discoveries of her own.

Now she turned from the bureau and met his gaze across the room. A blush rose in her cheeks. He suspected she knew exactly what he'd been remembering.

He forced his thoughts back to the present, warning, "This isn't going to be pleasant."

"I didn't suppose it would be." She picked up her reticule from the bed, then moved toward him in that graceful way of hers.

Tentatively he reached out, touching her cheek with his fingertips. She turned her face to kiss his palm. The strength of emotions that coursed through him in response took his breath away.

She glanced up again, and he could see how she longed for him to tell her what he felt. To tell her he loved her. But he couldn't. The feelings were too new, too strong—too dangerous—to be shared. Once he gave them away, once he spoke them aloud to her, there would be no going back. Already he knew, if she should leave him, he could be destroyed. Better she not know the power she wielded with that hesitant smile of hers or the beseeching look in her apple green eyes.

"Garret, we cannot stop the gossip," she said in a quiet but steady voice. "What we did . . . what happened between us the night you brought me here . . . it was wrong. It was wrong because we weren't married. We know it as well as anyone else. But we can show the people of New Prospects we are not ashamed to be man and wife now. This is our home. These are our neighbors. Whatever comes, we shall face it together."

He wondered if a man could love a woman more with every passing moment.

Beth smiled, but Garret didn't fail to see the hint of trepidation in her eyes.

"If anyone hurts you, I'll have to break them in two," he said gruffly.

Her expression sobered. "Likewise."

He grabbed her, pulled her close against him. He didn't care that he knocked her pretty bonnet free or mussed her just dressed hair. He closed his eyes and silently prayed, *God, let me make her happy. Help me be a good husband so she won't ever want to leave.*

"Pa, aren't you two ever comin'?" Janie shouted from outside.

Beth drew back, offered him another encouraging smile, then rescued her bonnet and returned to the bureau to tidy her hair a second time. Garret, meanwhile, went to answer his daughter.

He stepped through the doorway, glancing first at the cloudless cerulean sky. Then his gaze moved to the wagon, where Janie was waiting. His eyes widened at the sight of her.

She wore one of the new dresses he'd purchased when they'd gone down to Bozeman two months ago, but that wasn't what surprised him. It was her hair. Normally her long strawberry blond tresses looked in desperate need of a good combing. This morning, however, it had been slicked back into two perfect braids, tied at the ends with satin ribbons.

He couldn't remember Muriel ever fussing with Janie's hair. Not even once. But Beth had been here only one night and already . . .

"Is Ma comin'?"

Garret didn't know if it was just an accident of life or a sign of God's benevolence to an unworthy man, but it seemed Garret had given his daughter what she'd most wanted. A mother.

"Yeah," he answered, his voice breaking slightly.

As if to prove him right, Beth stepped from the

shadows of the house into the Sunday morning light. "I'm here." She looked from Garret to Janie and back again. "I'm ready."

He took her arm, held it close against his side. "Then let's go."

Hezekiah didn't know when, if ever, the Steeles had arrived at church before the service began. He certainly hadn't expected them to be early today. But there they were, pulling up in their wagon, the new Mrs. Garret Steele holding a frilly yellow parasol and looking as pretty as a picture.

Standing at the top of the steps so he could greet his parishioners as they entered the church, Hezekiah heard the surprised gasps of several women, listened as hushed voices began to whisper excitedly. Of course, no one had carried tales to him, but he'd heard the gossip nonetheless. And given the hasty wedding yesterday afternoon, he was forced to conclude there might very well be at least a grain of truth to the rumors that were circulating.

This seemed a most appropriate day for his sermon on not casting the first stone. He suspected his flock would need a reminder of God's forgiving nature.

He smiled broadly as the new family approached the church steps. He would have had to be blind not to notice the difference in Garret and Beth today over yesterday. He'd never performed a wedding for two people who'd looked less happy about the occasion than these two had the day before. But this morning they seemed very much like a young couple in love.

Hezekiah grinned, but before he could speak a

greeting, Bunny Homer, in all her righteous indignation, stepped directly into the path of the Steeles, her
sister in tow.

"How *dare* you come to this house of God after
what you've done?" she demanded in a near shriek.

Beth hesitated only a moment before saying,
"Good day, Miss Homer." She spoke softly but clearly
enough for others to hear. "It's a beautiful Sunday
morning, isn't it?"

Bunny turned to Hezekiah, her face beet red. "Will
you allow this harlot into your church? Surely you
won't let her sit with decent folk. Not after what she's
done."

A hum filled the air as people whispered among
themselves.

Hezekiah tried to keep a firm rein on his temper as
he replied, "Tell me, Miss Homer. Did our Lord ever
turn anyone away who had come to sit at his feet and
worship?"

"Well, *He* isn't here now, and the good people of
this town are."

His anger drained. It seemed he was going to be
forced to deliver his sermon right here from the steps.
"But He *is* here, Miss Homer. He's here in all of us
who are willing to forgive, to judge not lest we be
judged."

"Poppycock!" she snapped. "And you call yourself
a man of the cloth."

His response was to merely continue to meet her
gaze until she looked away.

But Bunny Homer was as tenacious as she was
spiteful, and she wasn't going to be silenced just
yet. She waved her arm in a gesture meant to

encompass all the spectators. "You've all heard what happened. You know the shameful things these two have done. You all know that Booth boy saw them, even before my sister and I stumbled into their den of iniquity."

"The Booth boy?" Garret took a step toward their accuser. "What does he have to do with this?"

For the first time, Patsy joined her voice to that of her sister's. "He saw the two of you. He even had Miss Wellington's hat for proof."

Garret looked angry enough to kill as he took another step toward Bunny. "That lying, no-good—"

"Garret," Beth said softly, laying her hand on his arm. "Don't. It will serve no purpose."

"See!" Bunny exclaimed. "Even she knows she has no defense against the truth." She took hold of her sister's arm. "Come along, Patsy. We won't darken the door of this church again until that woman is driven from it." She looked around at those who had witnessed the altercation. "And you would all do the same if you knew what was good for you." Then off the two women stalked.

Heavenly Father, Hezekiah prayed, *what do I do now?*

Beth Steele looked up to the top of the stairs where he stood, a question in her eyes. Hezekiah understood. She wouldn't enter the church if he didn't want her to. It was also clear to him she was a woman of courage. He didn't know if there was any truth in what he'd heard about Garret and Beth. He did know he had come to New Prospects to shepherd a flock, not to judge them for their mistakes.

He beckoned the Steeles forward. "You'd better

take your seats before Mrs. Matheson starts playing
the organ. My wife does pride herself on being
prompt." Then he addressed the others who were still
standing outside. "Come along, my friends. Come
along."

Halfway through the service, with several pews missing the families who usually filled them—most
notable among them being Owen Simpson—Garret
felt Janie's tug on his arm.

"What's wrong with everybody, Pa?"

He placed his mouth near her ear and replied,
"We'll talk about it later." As he straightened, he
looked over his daughter's head to meet the gaze of
his wife.

It was amazing how she was able to communicate
with him with just a glance, the lift of an eyebrow, the
tilt of her head. He'd never have guessed he could be
this attuned to a woman's thoughts. Take now, for
instance. She was telling him she knew what Janie
had asked. She was agreeing they would have to talk
to her, admitting they should have done it last night,
and commiserating with him because they couldn't
shelter his daughter from the unpleasant talk and
reactions of others.

He wondered if she was able to see what was in his
thoughts just as easily. A part of him hoped so.
Another part feared so.

He turned his gaze back to the pulpit. Hezekiah
was in fine form today, but Garret was having a hard
time concentrating on what the pastor was saying.

And who could have blamed him? Forty-eight

hours ago the last thing he would have expected was to be sitting in church beside Beth Wellington Steele. Twenty-four hours ago he would have said it was impossible he would ever love her—or any other woman—for too many reasons to enumerate. Yet here he was, married and loving her . . . and uncertain whether he should be glad or afraid because of it.

There wasn't much that frightened Garret Steele. He'd survived a fatherless childhood in a South ravaged by war. He'd survived losing his mother at the age of thirteen. He'd made it through floods and droughts and blizzards, broken bones, green-broke horses, grizzly bears, and stampeding cattle. He'd endured a hellish marriage for the daughter it had brought him.

But this feeling he had for the woman seated on the other side of Janie had taken him completely by surprise. It was more than just loving her. It was like finding another part of himself, a part that had always been missing. What if he got used to it being there? What if he got used to being whole, and then she took that part of him away again?

He cast another glance in Beth's direction, gazed upon her beautiful profile, felt his stomach tighten at the mere sight of her.

She'd claimed she loved him. Yet it was also true she'd been engaged to another. Had she ever told Owen she loved him? If Trevor hadn't attacked her, frightened her, left her feeling vulnerable and afraid, and if Garret hadn't rescued her, gone into the bedroom and taken her, would she have married Owen? Was she with Garret only out of circumstance? Because she'd had no other choice?

She turned her head, saw him watching her, smiled gently, and he knew the future was up to him. It teetered on the brink, waiting for him to make the right choice. Trust her or not. Take a chance or not.

Of all the decisions he had ever made or would ever make, this one mattered most. Yet he was trapped by his own uncertainty.

Beth wasn't unaware of the soul-searching going on inside her husband. She felt it like a charge of electricity in the air. She wished she knew how to make him love her, how to convince him her love for him was true and lasting. She found waiting for him to come to a conclusion much harder to bear than the censuring glances of some members of the congregation—which was hard enough.

When the morning's worship service was over and the last hymn sung, Garret took hold of Beth's left arm and escorted her toward the exit. Janie ran on ahead, disappearing through the doorway. Beth wished she could do the same.

"Mr. Steele," Stella Matheson called, causing them to stop and turn. "Mrs. Steele."

The minister's wife—a pleasingly plump woman in her early thirties—approached, wearing a wide smile and holding out her hand. When Beth offered her own, Stella enclosed it in both of hers.

"My dear, I wanted to tell you how lovely you look this morning." Stella spoke in a clear, crisp voice for all to hear. "And I also wanted you to know how extremely sad I was to learn you would no longer be teaching the children of New Prospects. Robbie and

Mike have both progressed so much this summer, and
Theresa claims you are the best teacher in the world."

"That's very kind of you, Mrs. Matheson."

"Not at all. Simply stating facts." Stella looked at
Garret, then back at Beth. "But marriage is a blessed
estate, and we all understand your place is now in
your home with your husband and new daughter.
Perhaps, now that you will no longer be occupied
with the educational welfare of all our children, you
will find time to join our ladies' quilting circle when
we resume meeting in the fall."

Beth wished she could hug the woman. "I'm afraid
I know nothing about quilting, Mrs. Matheson."

"Pish posh." Stella dismissed Beth's comment with
a wave of her hand. "There's nothing to it. And you
must call me Stella. Friends shouldn't be so formal,
and I do wish for us to be friends."

"Then I shall be glad to join you . . . Stella." She
lowered her voice to a near whisper. "If you are certain I should."

Stella pressed Beth's hand in a comforting gesture.
"I know you should, my dear." She turned to Garret.
"Take good care of your wife, Mr. Steele."

"I intend to."

Beth was becoming well acquainted with the tumble of emotions such words could cause in her heart.
And they stayed with her as they began the drive back
to the ranch.

They were all three silent, each lost in thought,
until they passed the schoolhouse. That was when
Janie seemed to remember her earlier question.
"What was wrong with everybody today, Pa?" She
crawled toward the front of the wagon, then rose on

her knees behind the wagon seat. "How come Miss Homer was so mean to Ma?"

Garret stared straight ahead, his forearms resting on his thighs, reins laced through callused fingers. Beth recalled how tenderly those work-roughened hands moved upon her skin even as she waited to hear how he would answer his daughter.

"Well," he began after what seemed a long time, "the truth is, Beth and I, we did some things that were wrong, and folks found out about it."

"What things?"

"Things you're too young to understand."

"You're always sayin' that, Pa. You're always sayin' you'll explain it later. But I wanna know."

Garret turned to meet his daughter's gaze. "Pumpkin, you remember how big and heavy Beth's trunk was when we brought it to the ranch yesterday?"

"'Course, I do. I helped Ma unpack it."

"Well, I didn't ask you to pull it off the wagon and carry it into the house, did I?"

Janie frowned. "'Course not. I couldn't've lifted it. It woulda been too heavy for me."

"Exactly." His expression was patient. "And that's just how it is about what happened today at the church, for why folks are acting angry and strange. Telling you why would be like asking you to carry that trunk. It would be too heavy for you right now. Understand?"

"I don't know. I guess so."

Garret lifted his eyes, meeting Beth's gaze. "Well, I know you can understand this, Janie. No matter what folks say, Beth is my wife and your new ma, and nothing's gonna change that. Some folks aren't gonna be very nice to her for a while 'cause they don't understand why she didn't marry Mr. Simpson. They don't like that she married me instead. Maybe they got cause, maybe they don't. All we can do is let 'em know we won't listen to bad things about her. Can you do that?"

"I'll punch anybody who tries to say anything bad about Ma," Janie declared. "I swear I will."

Uncontainable laughter rose in Beth's throat. She twisted on the seat and gave the child a hug. "You mustn't punch anyone, Janie dear," she said, "no matter what anyone says. But I do adore you for wanting to."

Janie hugged her back. "I love you, Ma. I don't want nobody hurtin' you ever."

Her laughter turned abruptly into an urge to cry. "Oh, Janie, I love you, too," she whispered. "You and your father."

She hoped one day soon he'd learn to return her love. One day very, very soon.

20

Tuesday, August 17, 1897
New Prospects, Montana

Dear Inga,

I was delighted to receive your most recent letter. Your description of the parsonage painted a vivid picture in my mind of each and every room. I can easily envision your father in his chair, glasses resting on the tip of his nose, with his Bible open in his lap. From your letter, it is clear your mother has quickly made it feel like home.

I have some unexpected news to share with you. Since my last correspondence my life has undergone an enormous change. I am married, but not to Mr. Simpson. Indeed, it is Janie's father whose proposal of marriage I accepted. It was all quite sudden and took us both by complete surprise.

It is a quite different turn of events from that I had imagined for myself when I left England. In truth, sometimes my life in England does not even seem real to me anymore. I feel very much a part of this rugged land that has become my home.

Perhaps I should not share this in a letter, but I so desperately need to talk to someone about it, and there is no one here with whom I can do so. You see, my husband still holds his first wife in deep regard, and I fear it will keep him from ever sharing his whole self with me. Please don't mistake my words. Mr. Steele is fond of me, and he shows it in countless ways. But the deep love I long for belongs to the wife he loved first and lost.

I suppose I should not complain. I have more happiness than I have any right to expect. As for Janie, she has called me Ma from the moment the vows were spoken. It makes my heart sing when she says it. She is always a special joy. Secretly, I hope I shall be able to give her many brothers and sisters to play with. When I was growing up, I always wished for a sister with whom I could share my hopes and dreams. You are so fortunate, Ingrid, to have four younger sisters of your own.

Before I close, I must share a bit of news which will surely surprise you. I have been invited by the Methodist minister's wife, Stella Matheson, to join the women's quilting circle. I regret deeply that I did not pay more attention to your wonderful needlework while we were aboard ship. I carry the memory of your lovely quilts in my mind even now. I shall tell Mrs. Matheson about them when I attend the first circle meeting.

Fondly,
Beth Steele

Garret stared at the two dead calves and knew he'd run out of time. Glancing over at Jake, he said, "We'll have to drive the herd down to Bozeman."

"They'll be payin' rock-bottom prices."

"I don't see what other choice I've got."

Jake wiped the sweat from his brow. "No, I don't reckon you got any other choice."

Garret hated the idea of being gone from the ranch right now. Except it wasn't the ranch he hated to leave. It was Beth. With each passing day she'd become more necessary to him, more a part of his daily routine. For the first time in his life, he understood what being a family really meant, and he resented being taken from it—and from her—while the feeling was still so new to him. Not that the drive to Bozeman was a lengthy trip. Less than a week if he pushed hard there and back. But even that would seem too long to him now.

"Didja hear Patrick O'Toole's well ran dry?"

Jake's question brought Garret abruptly out of his private thoughts. "No, I hadn't heard."

"Don't look good for him. I reckon he might like to join us on the drive."

If Garret had to sell his cattle for a low price *and* his well ran dry on top of it, he'd be forced into extending his mortgage at the bank. He'd nearly paid it off. Even just a moderately good year would have—

His mortgage.

The bank.

Owen.

He remembered the last time he'd seen Owen Simpson and some of the last words his longtime friend had said to him. *"Forgive you? Damn right I won't forgive you."*

Garret cursed softly. What if Owen wouldn't extend his loan? What if he called it in like he'd called in Karl Booth's loan?

Of course, Booth hadn't made any attempt to pay what he owed the bank on his mortgage. He'd been a man full of excuses and little else. Garret hadn't been surprised, nor even particularly sympathetic, when he'd heard the Booths were leaving the valley. And after the trouble Trevor had caused—first by what he'd tried to do to Beth, then from the lies he'd told the school board—Garret sure as heck hadn't been sorry to see the last of him or his family.

But was it possible Owen was angry enough at Garret to foreclose on his ranch?

Jake turned his horse around. "Reckon I'll ride on over to the O'Toole place, then. I'll see if he wants t'join us on the drive."

Garret nodded absently.

"Boss?"

"Hmm?"

"Don't go borrowin' trouble. We made it through leaner times than this."

"Yeah, I guess we have."

He watched the cowboy ride off, then glanced again at the two calves lying near the dried-up watering hole. The earth was baked and cracked, and only someone who knew what this spot normally looked like would have believed it had ever been filled with water.

What would he do if he lost the ranch? How would he provide for Beth and Janie then? He didn't know anything but cows and horses. This had been his life for twenty years, first in Texas, then on the trail, and finally here in this valley.

The sound of hoofbeats caused him to look over his shoulder a second time. He'd thought it would be Jake returning for some reason. He hadn't expected to see Beth, looking as elegant as ever in her English riding habit, cantering Flick toward him.

She was a lady, used to the finer things in life. He was a cattle rancher, just getting by. What hope was there that two such people could find lasting happiness? When her dresses got old and threadbare, when she got tired of doing without, what would she do? Could he expect her to stay then?

"Hello," she said as she reined in her horse.

"Is something wrong?"

"No." She smiled. "I found myself missing you, so I came to see you."

She had no idea how her smile and her words affected him. She couldn't possibly know.

Uncertainty entered her eyes. "You don't mind that I came, do you?"

"What about Janie? Why didn't she come with you?"

"She's with Theresa Matheson this afternoon. Remember? She's going to spend the night there. They are working on a play of some sort for church, but Janie won't tell me what it's about. It is to be a surprise."

Garret squinted up at the sun. "Mighty warm for you to be out here in the middle of the day."

"No more so than it is for you."

He couldn't argue with that.

"I'm not a delicate hothouse flower," she scolded gently. "You must stop treating me like one."

He nodded but didn't look at her again.

"Garret, how long will it be before you believe I didn't lie when I said I love you? How long before you tell me you love me, too?"

Those two questions drew his gaze to her at last. So it was just as he'd feared. She *could* read his thoughts.

Beth tapped her heel against Flick's ribs, and the gelding moved closer to Garret's horse. Then Beth reached forward with her gloved hand to touch her husband's arm. "How long?" she asked again.

"I don't know."

She sighed. "I see."

"What do you see?"

"That I shall have to be patient a while longer."

Garret was sorely tempted to tell her what she wanted to hear. Not just because she wanted to hear it, but also because he wanted to say it. Would it really make any difference, when she left him, whether or not he'd told her he loved her? Would he be any less destroyed by her absence?

Besides, couldn't she already see the truth in his eyes? Couldn't she already read his mind and heart?

Indeed, Beth *could* tell what Garret was thinking and feeling. At least partially. She knew he cared for her. She also knew he didn't want to. She wished she had the courage to tell him she understood that he would never get over Muriel. She didn't expect him to ever love her as much as he had Janie's mother.

But she didn't want him to admit he still loved Muriel. As long as his first wife's name went unspoken, Beth could pretend she was his only love. She could also pretend Janie was her own daughter. So she said nothing more.

At long last, Garret broke the silence that had stretched between them. "I've gotta drive the cattle down to Bozeman, try to sell them early."

"What does that mean for the ranch?"

He eyed the cracked earth and the two dead calves lying near the bone-dry watering hole. "It means we'll have a lean year. Money'll be tighter than ever."

She saw the tension in his shoulders and wanted to ease it for him. He was a stubborn man, a proud man. She wished she knew how to reach him with words, how to convince him she was not a woman made useless by the trappings of wealth. What little of that life she had known had never satisfied her. But her new life did. *He* did. How could she make him believe it?

"We could lose the ranch if the drought goes on much longer," he added, almost as an afterthought.

"Oh, Garret! Not your ranch. You've worked so hard to make it a success."

"It's mortgaged to the bank. If I can't get the price I need for the cattle at market . . . "

"But Owen wouldn't take your home and land. He's your friend."

"Beth, he's a banker. This is his business. If he forecloses, it'll be for business reasons. It doesn't have anything to do with whether or not we used t'be friends."

"Used to be friends . . . "

Those words stayed with Beth as she rode in silence beside her husband on their way back to the ranch house.

It was her fault a long-standing friendship had met its demise. If she had never agreed to marry Owen when she already knew she loved Garret, this wouldn't have happened. Or if she hadn't broken her engagement and hadn't made that fateful trip to Garret's ranch. Now, when Garret needed not only his friend, but the goodwill of the town's financier, he had neither. And it was her fault.

She cast a surreptitious glance in his direction. He wore his Stetson low on his forehead, shading his eyes from view, but she could still see the sharp cut of his jaw and the firm set of his mouth. His face was tanned a dark brown after many weeks in the summer sun, as were his forearms below the rolled-up sleeves of his shirt. His body was muscular and lean, whip- cord strong, the sort that thrived on hard work. He sat his horse with the ease of a man used to spending long hours in the saddle.

He belonged here. In many ways he was an exten- sion of this harsh land, a land that demanded so much from those who carved a life from it.

What would he do if he lost the ranch he'd worked all those years to build? What if Owen were so angry with Garret and Beth that he sought revenge by tak- ing Garret's land?

She couldn't allow it to happen. She didn't know what she could do, but she had to do something. She couldn't allow Garret to lose his ranch because of her.

He turned his head, found her watching him. Her heart skittered as it so often did when he looked at her. Perhaps it skittered because she always hoped he was about to say he loved her.

Instead, turning his gaze straight ahead again, he said, "I'll be gone about a week."

"A week."

"Jake'll be with me on the drive. You and Janie will be at the ranch by yourselves. Maybe you should go stay with the Mathesons. I'm sure Hezekiah and Stella could make some room for you two."

She didn't know whether to thank him for his con- cern or to throttle him for thinking she was helpless. "We're the wife and daughter of a cattle rancher. We shall do whatever we must do."

He drew back on the reins, stopping his horse.

Beth did the same.

He spoke her name tenderly.

"Yes?" A staccato heartbeat pounded in her ears.

"Thanks."

"For what?"

"For trying to make things work out. For makin' Janie happy, being the ma she needs."

"It's not so difficult a task," she replied, her voice made husky by strong emotions, "loving you both as I do."

Several moments passed before he said, "Yeah."

Beth wondered how long she would have to wait before he finally believed she had loved him even before that first night of passion.

There were times when Bunny Homer wanted to put her hands around Patsy's fat neck and squeeze until the life went right out of her. Like now, for instance, when her sister was twittering like an idiot.

"Don't worry, Mr. Simpson," Patsy said. "I shall put together your order and deliver it to you myself."

Bunny was still furious with Owen for the horrible things he'd said to them that day in the bank. But her sister seemed to have completely forgotten his insults.

Owen shook his head stiffly. "There's no need for that, Miss Homer. I'll return after the bank closes and pick up my order." He turned and walked toward the door.

"Mr. Simpson, wait!" Patsy scurried after him, her face an unbecoming shade of pink. "There was something I wanted to ask you."

He stopped, turned, waited.

Patsy glanced over her shoulder at Bunny, then faced Owen and said, "I was . . . I mean, *we* were hoping you might accept an invitation to dine with us on Sunday."

In a pig's eye! Bunny thought, glaring at her sister's back.

"That's very kind of you, Miss Homer, but—"

"You see, we know you haven't been attending services. What self-respecting person would after Reverend Matheson allowed that . . . that woman to sit there with the good people of New Prospects?"

"Really, I don't—"

"Did you know my sister and I have refused to attend either?"

"I'd heard."

Bunny could scarcely believe it. Patsy had the audacity to lay her hand on Owen's arm in a most familiar fashion, offering her sympathy in a look that could only be called simpering. Unable to bear watching another moment, Bunny spun around and stalked off into the storage room.

It wasn't fair! What if Owen were to accept Patsy's inept advances? What if he were to turn to her for solace after what that Englishwoman had done to him? Even worse, what if he were to marry her and leave Bunny alone with this wretched store?

She didn't know with whom she was the most angry—her irritating fool of a sister or that scandalous harlot who had stolen Garret right out from under her nose. Or maybe it was Owen Simpson who made her the maddest. After all, he should have done something to stop Garret's marriage. He should have seen to it that Beth Wellington wasn't left free to entice other men into her web—or into her bed.

Bunny felt heat rush to her cheeks at the images in her head. She had heard the whispers of other women concerning a husband's rights, and she could not imagine a worse horror than to have a man touch her in such fashion. To think a woman might actually *invite* such liberties seemed impossible, ludicrous. Therefore there was only one reason for Beth's shameful actions: she had gone to Garret's bed to entrap him. For whatever reason—perhaps because she knew Bunny wanted him—Beth had decided she would rather marry Garret than Owen, and she had tricked him into it.

Nothing had gone right since that woman had come to New Prospects. Bunny had waited for Garret's period of mourning to end. Still, he must have known she was willing to marry him, willing to raise that hellion of a daughter of his. Bunny would have known how to teach the child some good manners, too. What would Beth Wellington be able to teach her except her affected foreign ways?

She trembled as her fury increased. And she had every right to be angry. After all, she had been a leader in this town almost from its founding. She should be respected and listened to. But whom had they followed? The reverend and his wife! Those two had essentially sanctioned immoral behavior, and the people of this community had allowed them to get away with it. She had a good mind to write to the church's judicial council. It would serve Reverend

Matheson right if he were stripped of his ministerial robes.

She heard the small bells above the store doorway tinkling. Either another customer had entered or Owen Simpson had finally departed. She hoped it was the latter.

And good riddance, Bunny thought as she stiffened her back, then walked toward the shop with the full intent of giving Patsy a piece of her mind.

"I don't see why I can't go with you, Pa," Janie said as she climbed the ladder to the loft. "I could help on a cattle drive."

Garret followed his daughter up the rungs. "I need you t'stay here and look after Beth."

"Ma could come, too. She rides as good as anybody, even if it is sidesaddle."

The incongruous image of Beth on a cattle drive, riding herd in that English riding habit of hers, made him smile. "Maybe so, but I need you both to watch out for the place while Jake and I are gone." He stood when he reached the loft and followed Janie to her bed. "In you go," he commanded, and watched as she obeyed, lying on top of the covers, her hands behind her head on the pillow.

"I still don't see why—"

"Janie."

"All right. I won't say anything more."

"Good." He sat on the edge of her bed, then bent forward and kissed her forehead. "We'll be headin' out at dawn. We'll drive the herd down there, sell 'em, and get back just as quick as we can. I hope it won't take more than a week. It'll be your job t'look after Beth. She's still gettin' used to things around here. She'll need your help."

"I'll take care of her."

He patted her shoulder. "I know you will." He felt a rush of fatherly love for this strong-willed child and realized how lucky he was to have her with him. Muriel could easily have decided not to return to the ranch after she'd learned she was pregnant. Or he might have sent Muriel away before the baby was born and then would never have seen Janie.

"Pa?"

"Hmm."

She yawned sleepily. "We're mighty lucky, you'n me," she said, echoing his thoughts.

"Why's that?" His voice was husky with unspoken emotions.

"Well, you know how Reverend Matheson says God's in control? And that God loves us so much that he looks out for us?"

Garret nodded.

"Well, I figure God must've wanted you t'marry Miss Beth so you'd have a wife an' I'd have a ma. He must've wanted it a lot t'make her leave England and go to all the trouble of gettin' here the way she did." Janie closed her eyes. "So I reckon that makes us mighty lucky."

He kissed her forehead again, whispering, "Yeah, I reckon it does, Janie. I reckon it does."

Garret remained seated on the bed, watching as his daughter drifted off to sleep and considering what she'd said. Although his mother had read out of the

Bible to him each night when he was little, Garret wasn't what he'd call overly familiar with what the Good Book had to say. But maybe Janie was right. Maybe this had all been part of some master plan. And if so, Garret reckoned he hadn't made the Almighty any too pleased by the way he'd acted. Not when he'd lain with Beth outside matrimony. Not when he hadn't been honest with her about the way he felt now that she was his wife.

When he descended to the ground floor, the house was silent. The lamps had been extinguished except for the one, turned low, in the bedroom. He followed its faint glow to the open doorway and looked in.

Beth stood in front of the bureau, brushing her long cascade of hair. She was wearing a white cotton nightgown, and he could barely see the dark silhouette of her figure through it. He felt the familiar jolt of desire in his loins, the familiar tug of love in his heart.

Could God have cared so much that He'd brought this woman halfway around the world just for him?

You're a fool, he told himself. Nobody'd ever cared that much for him. Why would God bring him Beth when he hadn't been able to make Muriel love him in all the years they were together?

Then Beth saw him in the mirror. Her hand stilled above her head as she stared at his reflection. He moved toward her, needing to touch her, needing to be near her, needing to believe she might truly love him. He stopped, reached out and swept aside her hair, bent to kiss the delicate curve of her neck. He heard her sigh, felt a shiver run through her.

He turned her around. She tilted her head to look up at him. Her eyes were wide, a deep forest green in the dim lamplight. *I love you, Garret,* they seemed to say to him. *Please love me, too.*

He cupped her face in his hands, lowered his lips to hers, heard the hair brush clatter to the floor. Then he scooped her into his arms and carried her to their bed.

With his kisses, with his caresses, he tried to show her how much he loved her. Late into the night, he showed her his love in the only way he dared.

21

The next week was the longest in all Beth's twenty-three years. Over and over she replayed the memory of Garret's last night at home. She remembered every detail of the physical way he had expressed his feelings for her. She couldn't help but be filled with hope. She began to believe he might truly make a place for her in his heart, might truly learn to love her the way she longed to be loved.

To keep her thoughts otherwise occupied, she cleaned the log house, mopping floors, washing curtains, scouring the wood stove, beating the rag rugs. She mended Garret's socks and his underclothes, his shirts and trousers, then did the same with Janie's clothes. She helped feed the livestock and joined Janie in playing with Penguin, Pepper, Wishbone, and the other puppies. In the early mornings, the coolest part of the day, she and her stepdaughter went riding. In the afternoon she helped Janie—her only pupil now—with her school lessons. At night she prayed for

Garret's safe return, for a good price for the cattle, and for rain.

On Wednesday morning, a full week after Garret, Jake, and Patrick O'Toole took the herd south to Bozeman, Beth and Janie went into New Prospects to buy supplies at the mercantile. Beth had put it off until the last minute, hoping Garret would return before they ran completely out of flour. But such was not her luck.

As the wagon pulled up in front of the general store, Beth looked at Janie and said, "Perhaps you should wait for me in the wagon."

"You afraid of what Miss Patsy and Miss Bunny might say t'you?"

There was no point in trying to lie to the girl. Janie would see right through her. "Yes."

"Then I better come in. Pa told me t'look after you."

Affectionately Beth ruffled Janie's hair. "And you have done a wonderful job of it. But I still think you should wait for me here."

"Naw, I better come along. I ain't afraid of them." Janie hopped down from the wagon seat, skirts flying.

Beth laughed. "You *aren't* afraid of them," she corrected as she descended with a little more decorum.

"Nope, I'm sure not."

"Then I shan't be, either." She took hold of the girl's hand, and together they entered the store.

Frances Werner, wife of the doctor, stood near the bolts of fabric, measuring a piece of lilac calico against an outstretched arm. Ethel Russell, whose husband owned the lumber mill, stood before the cash register, plucking coins from her purse while Bunny Homer, wearing an impatient expression, waited on the opposite side of the counter. Martha Hubert, proprietress of Martha's Restaurant, was pointing toward something on the top shelf of the far wall, and Patsy stood on a stool, trying to reach it.

When they saw Beth, they all seemed to freeze in position. The air became thick enough to slice with a knife. Conversation ceased, and everyone stared at Beth as if she had suddenly sprouted another head. She wanted to leave at once.

Janie's grip tightened. "Come on, Ma. We better get our supplies and get back t'the ranch. We don't wanna be gone when Pa gets home."

"Yes." Beth hated the quaver in her voice. She drew a deep breath, hoping it would steady her. Then she walked toward the counter with her shoulders back and her head held high.

"What do you want here?" Bunny demanded sharply.

"We have come to buy a few supplies."

"We have nothing to sell to the likes of you."

"I wish to buy some flour, cornmeal, and coffee. And perhaps something sweet for Janie."

Patsy hurried over. "You heard my sister, Miss Wellington. We don't want your business."

A soft answer turneth away wrath, she reminded herself, then said calmly, "My name is Mrs. Steele."

"And we know how you came by that name, don't we?" Bunny said in a snide tone.

"By marriage," she answered, pretending to be unruffled and feeling proud she was able to carry it off.

Bunny barked a sharp, mocking laugh.

Janie dropped Beth's hand and stepped toward the two sisters, fists formed at her sides. "Don't you be mean to my ma!"

"She is not your mother," Patsy retorted, glaring at the child. "She is your stepmother, and a poor example of one or you wouldn't sass your elders like that. Thank God Mr. Simpson is safe from her evil, wicked ways. Your father will pay for his. You'll see if he doesn't. And so, no doubt, will you, you little heathen."

Beth drew Janie away from the counter, placing her hands on the girl's shoulders and holding her close to her own body in a protective gesture. "You may say what you wish to me, Miss Homer, but I shall not allow you to abuse Janie."

Bunny smiled spitefully. "Then perhaps you should take your business elsewhere, Miss Wellington, because we have no intention of selling you so much as a peppermint stick."

Beth blanched. There was no other place to buy supplies in New Prospects. A person would have to go all the way to Bozeman, and Bunny Homer knew it.

"If you are through with Mrs. Steele," a woman said from the shop doorway, "perhaps you would be kind enough to wait upon me."

Beth looked behind her and watched as Stella Matheson made her way down the aisle. The minister's wife gave Beth a gentle smile, then turned toward Bunny and Patsy. "I'd like five pounds of flour, two pounds each of cornmeal and coffee, and a half pound of tea. Oh, and four nickel packs of Cracker Jack."

Patsy glanced from Stella to Bunny to Beth and back to Stella. Then she hurried off to gather the requested supplies.

Stella greeted each of the other women in the store by name and asked about their families before looking at Beth again. "Mrs. Perkins, Mrs. O'Toole, and I will resume our quilting circle at the end of August. You haven't forgotten you promised to join us, have you? We meet every Tuesday morning at the parsonage."

Joining a quilting circle was the least of Beth's concerns at the moment, but she was grateful nonetheless for the woman's kindness in front of the others. "I haven't forgotten," she answered. Then she took hold of Janie's hand. "We'd better go, Janie."

"No," Stella said, stopping her. "Please wait a moment." She turned back toward the counter just as Patsy arrived with the supplies she'd ordered. "You'll put those on our account?" she said to Bunny, not really intending it as a question.

"Of course."

"Good." She picked up one pack of Cracker Jack and handed it to Janie. "This is for you, dear. Promise you won't eat them until after you've had your supper."

Janie's eyes widened, her anger forgotten. "Thanks, Mrs. Matheson. I promise."

Gathering the rest of the packages in her arms, the minister's wife said to Beth, "Shall we take these out to your wagon, Mrs. Steele?"

Only then did it dawn on Beth what Stella intended. "But I can't allow you to—"

"Shush now. The reverend would be most

unhappy with me if I didn't do unto others as I would have them do unto me." She looked toward the other women in the store. "Good day, ladies. I hope to see all of you in church on the Lord's day." Then she led the way down the aisle and out of the mercantile.

Beth kept trying to think of some way to appropriately thank her. She knew Stella Matheson had put herself in a terrible position by her actions. Already there were a few families who'd stayed away from church services because of the Steeles. The minister's wife could very well have made it worse for her husband and herself.

When they reached the wagon, Janie scrambled up into the back, the pack of Cracker Jack held firmly in her hands, her eyes bright with anticipation.

"I cannot thank you enough."

"Don't be silly," the woman said as she placed the supplies into the back of the wagon near Janie. "It was little enough for me to do. Your husband has helped Hezekiah many times over the years. Why, just two winters ago, he helped make that beautiful altar at the front of the church."

"But because of me you've made trouble for yourself." Beth glanced over her shoulder at the mercantile, wondering how many of the women were watching them through the window glass.

Stella actually laughed, waving away Beth's warning with a flick of her hand. "Don't give it another thought."

"You've always been kind to me."

"Beth . . . May I call you Beth?"

"Of course."

She lowered her voice, ostensibly so Janie couldn't

hear. "I suppose this is a very un-Christian-like thing to say, but the truth is, Patsy and Bunny Homer excel in causing trouble. Goodness, if you only knew what rumors they spread about me when Hezekiah and I first came to New Prospects."

Beth couldn't help a tiny smile as she remembered. "I think I *have* heard them."

"My scandalous past in a bordello?" Stella shook her head. "I could wish they'd come up with something more believable. I am not exactly the sort that sends men's hearts soaring in heights of great passion."

Beth's eyes widened.

"Oh, dear. I've shocked you."

"No, I—"

Stella chuckled. "It's all right. I shock Hezekiah on a regular basis. It's good for a marriage, I believe, to keep one's husband slightly off-balance. A woman shouldn't be too predictable." She patted Beth's shoulder. "And speaking of husbands, I have always liked and admired yours. I'm delighted he's found a woman who loves him with all her heart. He deserves it after what he's been through. Let the gossips say what they will. Whatever brought you and Garret together, I believe the result will be a blessing for you both."

Beth's heart was warmed by Stella's words. "Thank you. You'll never know how much that means to me."

Stella smiled, then leaned forward and lightly kissed Beth's cheek. "I think I do, dear. Now, I had best get back home before those ruffians I call my children destroy the parsonage completely. Hezekiah thinks he is a stern taskmaster, but in truth, he is far too fond of his own offspring to discipline them as they should be disciplined." She turned toward the wagon. "Good day, Janie. Remember, don't eat those sweets until after you've had supper."

"I won't, Mrs. Matheson. Thanks!"

Across the street from the mercantile, Owen stood at the window of his office, staring at Beth Wellington Steele through the dusty glass. Even after nearly three weeks, he still felt a sharp sense of loss at the sight of her. He wondered if he would always feel it.

Then, resolutely, he admitted the cold, hard truth. Beth had never loved him. She had liked him, probably liked him still. She had considered him her friend. But she had never loved him because she had loved another.

He should have seen it. If he was honest with himself, he'd admit he *had* seen it. That's why he'd pushed so hard for her to agree to marry him. He'd known she cared too much for Garret. He'd been afraid he would lose her to him. In the end he'd lost her to him anyway, and he'd lost his friendship with Garret in the bargain.

And whose fault was it?

Owen turned away from the window, not wanting to watch Beth driving away in Garret's wagon. Driving back to Garret's house.

He looked at his desk, at all the papers and contracts he needed to go over, but the thought only further depressed him. Folks were hurting everywhere. There were notes long past overdue. There were people who stood to lose their homes and farms and ranches because of the drought. He didn't want to think about it. Especially since Garret Steele was among those close to defaulting on their loans.

He grabbed his hat and strode out of his office, telling Harry Kaiser he would be gone for the rest of the day.

He'd thought he was headed for home, but his feet carried him in the opposite direction. He ended up at the church. He stood at the side of the road, staring at the white building.

He'd heard, of course, what had happened there two Sundays before. At the time the word had reached him, he'd been as angry with Hezekiah as he'd been with Garret and Beth. First the minister had performed their wedding ceremony, then he'd stood up for them in front of his congregation— despite what they'd done! Owen had secretly been glad some members of the community had refused to go into the church after that.

Only now he wasn't so sure. Over two weeks of soul-searching had taken away most of the anger, leaving confusion in its place.

"Need to talk, Owen?"

He glanced over his shoulder, not even surprised to find Hezekiah there. He supposed talking was what he'd come for, whether he'd known it or not.

"Come on inside." Hezekiah placed a hand on Owen's back. "Maybe the Lord will have a word of wisdom for us if we spend some time in prayer."

Wisdom was sure as heck something Owen could use right about now. Wisdom and a little peace of mind.

* * *

"Hey, Ma, you gotta come outside! Hurry!"

Beth swept aside stray wisps of hair as she turned from the stove. "What is it, Janie? I'm busy at the moment."

"I can't tell you. You gotta see it for yourself. Come here, quick."

Subduing a sigh, Beth moved the skillet to the back of the stove, then went to see what was causing all the excitement. She knew she shouldn't feel impatient. It wasn't Janie's fault her father and Jake hadn't arrived home today, as Garret had said they might. Nor was it Janie's fault Beth had spent the afternoon thinking about Muriel Steele.

Ever since her conversation with Stella outside the general store, Beth had been thinking about Garret's first wife. It wasn't that the minister's wife had revealed anything new. Still, Stella's words had for some reason disturbed the image Beth had created in her mind.

"I'm delighted he's found a woman who loves him with all her heart. . . ."

Wasn't that a strange thing to say? Hadn't Muriel loved him with all her heart? Of course she had. How could any woman help loving him that way?

"He deserves it after what he's been through. . . ."

Did she mean losing Muriel? Or was there something more, something Beth didn't yet understand?

"Look at that!" Janie exclaimed, drawing Beth's attention back to the present.

Beth followed the direction of Janie's outstretched arm. For a moment, she didn't know what she was supposed to be seeing. And then her eyes widened.

Storm clouds. Black, angry storm clouds, hovering on the western horizon. Storm clouds heavy with rain. She could smell the moisture in the air.

"Oh, Janie," she whispered, her heart churning like the wheels of a freight train.

Janie grabbed hold of her hand. "It's gonna rain, Ma. It's really gonna rain."

"Rain." She spoke the word reverently, remembering cool, cloudy days in England when she would curl up in a window seat and watch raindrops running down the glass. Back then, she had wished for it to stop and the sun to come out. But now nothing seemed as wonderful as the possibility of rain.

Except, perhaps, an end to the drought in Garret's heart. Maybe, if it could rain, Garret could say he loved her. Maybe the blessing Stella had predicted would begin with this storm.

Even as they stood there, the wind rose, whipping dust before it in tiny eddies. Thunder rolled far in the distance.

Hurry home, Garret. Hurry home and see the rain with me.

Then a different sound reached her ears. The sound of a horse cantering, hooves striking hard earth.

Garret! her heart sang as she turned around.

Only it wasn't her husband who rode into the yard. It was Owen Simpson.

Janie's grip tightened. "Ma? Mr. Simpson's not gonna be mean t'you like the others, is he?"

She studied his face as he drew his horse to a halt, dust swirling up from the animal's hooves. She found no anger there, no bitterness. Only sorrow. "No, Janie. He won't."

"Hello, Beth."

"Hello, Owen."

"Is Garret back from Bozeman?"

"Not yet."

"Do you mind if we talk for a bit?"

She shook her head.

"Mind if I get down?"

She shook her head again.

He dismounted, then glanced toward the west. "Storm's brewing. Looks like we might get some rain at last."

Beth could see he was struggling for a way to begin. Whatever had brought him here, he was working hard to find the right words. She wished for a way to put him at ease. "It would be a godsend if it rained," was all she could think to say.

"Yes, it would."

Owen Simpson had been kind to her from that first day in his office. He had been her friend. He had been Garret's friend even longer. She wanted them all to be friends again, if it were possible.

"Janie and I were about to have some supper," she told him. "You're welcome to join us if you'd like." Then she waited a bit breathlessly to see if he would accept the olive branch she was offering.

"You sure?"

"Garret's friends are always welcome in our home." She glanced at Janie. "Isn't that right?"

Janie grinned. "It sure is. Pa and me always liked havin' you over for supper, Mr. Simpson. You know that. Here." She reached out her hand. "I'll put your horse in the barn and give him some hay and water." She took the reins and led the sweaty animal away.

As soon as Janie was out of earshot, Owen said, "There's something I'd better get off my conscience before anything else gets said. I came to ask you to forgive me."

"Oh, Owen, there is nothing to forgive you for." She said the words softly, sadly. "I'm the one who should ask for your forgiveness."

"No, you're wrong." He glanced toward the approaching storm. "This was my fault. I knew you didn't love me. You were honest enough to tell me so, right from the very start. I even suspected, somewhere deep down, how you felt about Garret. I just didn't think he'd ever want to marry you or anybody else. Not after Muriel. So I hoped you'd marry me and learn to love me instead, given enough time." His gaze returned, eyes filled with remorse and self-recrimination. "I was the one who pressured you and kept on pressuring you. If I hadn't, maybe things wouldn't have happened the way they did. Maybe folks wouldn't be judging you now. Maybe they wouldn't be saying the things they're saying or treating you the way they are."

Tears sprang to her eyes as she remembered the scene in the mercantile earlier that afternoon. "It's not so very bad," she said, though it was a lie.

Owen was silent for a lengthy spell before saying softly, "You did leave me that note, breaking our engagement. Didn't you?"

"Yes, I did. You've read it?"

"No, I never found it. But I should have believed you when you told me. I believe you now, if that's any consolation."

It was her turn to gaze off at the approaching storm. "I wish Garret believed me."

Owen released a deep sigh. "That's my fault, too. If I hadn't barged in here—"

She lifted a hand to silence him. "No." She turned again. "No more blame. Whatever is between Garret and me is of our doing, our making." She smiled, albeit sadly. "Now I'd better see to our supper before it is burned beyond recognition."

The rains hit the valley with force, as if Mother Nature were trying to make up in a few hours for the many weeks of cloudless skies, scorching sun, and earth-parching drought. The wind whistled out of the mountains to batter everything in its path, bending trees, breaking branches, scattering livestock, destroying the few crops hardy enough to survive this long. Even before nightfall, the sky had been dark with clouds. Now everything was black as ink.

Stung by raindrops driven sideways by savage winds, Garret leaned into the storm and pressed on, determined to reach home tonight. He was too close now to give up, even when common sense told him he should find shelter until this blew over. He was too close to home and to Beth. He wanted to see her. He needed to see her.

A cattle drive was a good time for a man to ponder his life, and Garret had done his share of pondering over the last seven days. He'd remembered how he'd felt when he'd first met Muriel, young and lusty and all full of himself. And hopeful, too. Hopeful he could make a life better than the one he'd had when he was a boy, growing up on land not fit to raise anything more than a crop of rocks. He'd remembered how he'd felt when Muriel first betrayed him, the way his hope had shattered.

Then it had occurred to him, sometime just before they'd reached Bozeman, that maybe it was time he stopped waiting for Muriel to betray him again. She'd been dead and buried over a year now. It was time he stopped looking for her in everything Beth did or said.

By the time he'd started back toward New Prospects—leaving Bozeman a day ahead of Jake and O'Toole—Garret's thoughts had centered only on his family, on Janie and Beth. He had enough money in his saddlebag to pay off the mortgage and some left over to see them through the next year. Janie was happy, happier than he could ever remember her being, and that was all because of Beth. Who was he kidding? *He* was happier than he'd ever been. Or he could be if he'd just go ahead and let himself love his wife.

And that was why he was so determined to make it home tonight. Because he couldn't wait any longer to tell her he loved her.

A sudden gust of wind nearly knocked him from the saddle. His horse stumbled, then dropped to its knees in the muddy road. Garret shouted words of encouragement above the roar of the storm, drawing back on the reins until the animal struggled to its feet again. The rain felt like tiny shards of glass, piercing his slicker.

It seemed like hell itself was trying to stop Garret from reaching the ranch, but he wasn't going to give up now.

*   *   *

"I'd better head back to town," Owen said as he set his glass on the table. "It doesn't look like this rain is ever going to let up. I might as well get wet sooner as later."

Beth was sorry the evening was at an end. The three of them had shared one of Beth's better cooking attempts, then had celebrated the start of the rainstorm with loud cheers and raised glasses. As temperatures dropped, Owen had built a fire in the fireplace to take away the evening's sudden chill. After the fire was going, Janie had lain on the floor with her book while Beth and Owen sat in nearby chairs and talked of many things. Mostly Owen had shared about his friendship with Garret, the things they'd been through together over the years. Owen had made Beth forget the earlier unpleasantness of that day, entertaining her with little anecdotes about other members of the community.

She was warmed by the renewed offer of his friendship and believed the wrong she and Garret had done him had truly been forgiven.

Perhaps that was why she had the courage to ask him one more thing before he could leave. "Owen, what was Muriel like? Why can't Garret seem to let go of her memory?"

He frowned. "What did Garret tell you?"

"Nothing," she admitted. "He refuses to talk about her."

"Then I must do the same, Beth. It isn't my place. When the time is right, he should be the one to tell you."

"But—"

"Ask Garret." He rose from his chair, then motioned with his head toward the fireplace. "Look. She's asleep."

Janie lay on the floor, the open book mere inches from her face. One braid snaked over her shoulder and curled near her chin.

Beth smiled as she stood. "I hadn't realized it was so late. I'd better wake her and get her up to bed."

"No, don't wake her. I can carry her to the loft."

"Are you certain?"

"I'm certain." He scooped Janie up from the floor. "Here we go, little one. Let's get you to bed."

Beth watched him carry her stepdaughter up the ladder, then she turned and walked to the window, suddenly not sorry Owen would be leaving soon. She needed some time to herself. She needed to think about what had gone unsaid tonight even more than what had been said.

A part of her wanted to stay ignorant of the truth, she realized as she stared out at the stormy night. A part of her wanted to pretend Garret had never been married before. A part of her was so afraid she would always fall short in comparison with Muriel Steele. But she knew in her heart the woman would continue to stand between them, like some invisible wall, until Garret was able to talk about her and the love they had shared.

"She didn't move a muscle," Owen said as he descended from the loft. "It's always amazed me, the way kids can sleep through just about anything."

It wasn't until she heard him that she realized her eyes were blurred with unshed tears while others streaked down her cheeks. She swiped at them quickly, not wanting him to see.

But it was too late.

"Hey, what's this?" Hat in hand, he stood beside her. "Is this any way to end an evening?"

"It's nothing. Really."

"Was my company so unbearable?" he teased.

She shook her head.

He sobered. "You miss him, don't you?"

This time she nodded, feeling a fresh flood of tears.

"Hey. Hey there. Don't cry." Owen put his arms around her and patted her back while she pressed her face against his chest. "There's no call for tears."

And that was how Garret found them.

22

Garret stood in the open doorway, windblown rain pelting his back. He watched as Beth stepped from Owen's embrace, surprise in her eyes. She hadn't expected him. She hadn't thought he would return on this stormy night, so she'd invited Owen to be here in his stead.

It was a terrible coldness that possessed him, an unbearable emptiness and sense of loss.

He'd been ready to believe in her. He'd been ready to love her and tell her so. But Beth had betrayed him in a way more abhorrent than anything Muriel had done. Even Muriel hadn't betrayed him with his own friend.

"This isn't what it looks like," Owen said as he met Garret's eyes.

Had the situation been different, he might have laughed. After all, he'd used those exact same words when the Homer sisters had found Beth in his house the morning after he'd made love to her.

And it had been *exactly* what it had looked like.

"Get out," he said, his voice flat and emotionless.

"If you'd let me explain—"

"Don't bother. Just go."

"Listen, Garret, we only—"

"Go."

Beth looked at the man beside her. "He's right, Owen. You should leave."

Garret stepped to one side of the door. With a concerned glance, first at Garret, then at Beth, Owen set his hat firmly over his head, then walked out into the night. Garret pushed the door closed, shutting out the wind and the rain, closing himself in with Beth.

He turned toward her. "Maybe you should have gone with him."

"Why?"

"Wasn't it obvious?"

"No."

"I almost believed you, Beth. I almost believed you were different."

She took a step toward him. "Different from whom?"

If he let her touch him, he'd be lost. He would feel things he didn't want to feel. But it was too late. He already felt them, and it was worse than he'd suspected it would be. If he'd never loved her . . . if he'd never let himself hope . . .

He turned his back toward her again, shucking off his slicker and hanging it on a peg near the door.

"Garret, we can't go on like this," Beth whispered. "Owen is your friend. Neither of us would do anything to hurt you. If you would only listen to me. You know that I love you."

"Do I?"

He heard her sharp intake of breath. He wanted to be glad if he caused her even a moment of pain. He wasn't.

He kept his back to her. He couldn't bear to look into that face, into those eyes.

"Listen, Beth, I know all about women like you. When passion flares, you lose your head. Common sense, loyalty, right and wrong. You forget them all, and the next thing you know you're in bed with a man. Any man."

He remembered the first night he'd made love to Beth. He remembered the way she'd felt in his arms, the ecstasy of her touch, the rightness of their joining.

"And then you get caught, and so you end up married to someone who's never gonna have more than a simple log house outside a small Montana town. You think you can make it all right by telling the fool you love him. After all, those words are supposed to make everything in life better."

He remembered the sweet sound of her voice. No matter what she was saying, it was almost like a song.

"But it doesn't take you long to realize you're never gonna have much more than what you already have. You're not gonna have any more fancy dresses or go to any more fancy dress-up dinners with society folk or travel to exciting cities like New York City or Paris or London or San Francisco or wherever. You realize just how dull your life is gonna be from here on out and that this husband you've got isn't someone you want to settle for."

He remembered the weary expression she'd worn the first time she'd been in this house, the way she'd looked around her, the disappointment he'd guessed she felt.

"So you take up a flirtation with somebody else, just to add some spice to your life. And the next thing you know, you've got a lover, and you think maybe he'll buy you nice things and take you places. Maybe you even go off with him for a while. Only lovers can't really be counted on for long, and suddenly you find yourself with nothing else to do but go back to that miserable log house in Montana and that man you despise because he can't give you what you want, in bed or out of it."

He wanted to stop himself from saying anything more, wanted to make himself leave now, but it was too late. The words kept pouring out of him.

"Your husband can't even give you a baby. But then, you don't want one anyway. It would ruin your pretty figure, and then you wouldn't have every man within a hundred miles panting after you, the way you like most. But you know what? One of your lovers can give you that baby you don't want. He can plant that seed inside you, then send you back to the fool you're married to and let him watch the baby growing inside you."

He imagined Beth large with child.

"Let your husband be the one with you when you give birth."

He imagined Beth in labor.

"Let him be the one who loves that baby like his own even while you are so indifferent."

"Garret?" Her hand alighted on his back.

He turned, stared down at her. Her face was pale, her eyes wide and horrified.

"Dear God," she whispered, sounding anguished. "You're talking about Muriel."

He shook his head. No, it wasn't Muriel. Muriel hadn't had the power to hurt him the way Beth could. Because he'd never had the chance to love his first wife. But Beth? She could destroy him if he let her.

He wasn't going to let her.

"I know who you are, Beth." He backed away from her. "I know *what* you are. You're just the same."

"But I'm not, Garret. I'm not like that. In your heart, you know I'm not."

"I think you should go to Iowa, to your friend. What's her name? To Inga. Or you could go back to New York City. I've got the money from the sale of the herd. There's enough for train fare and to get you by until you can get another teaching position."

She was crying again. He'd forgotten how a woman could turn the tears on and off at will. There were a lot of things Beth had made him forget, for just a little while. Not long enough. Just a little while.

"I think you should leave as soon as you can get your things together. Tomorrow if the weather clears enough. I'm sure Owen would be glad to take you down to Bozeman."

Beth had never known a worse moment in her life than the one in which she'd understood the truth about Garret and Muriel. Not Perceval's cruelty, not her father's indifference, not even Trevor Booth's assault, had been as bad as this.

"If you don't want to go to Iowa or New York," he continued in that same horrible monotone, a voice devoid of feelings, "then you can buy a ticket for somewhere else. Maybe there's even enough money to send you back to England if that's what you want. I don't care where you go as long as you leave New Prospects and never come back."

Her heart was breaking for him. She was filled with pity and empathy. She longed to comfort him, to heal the wounds Muriel had left behind.

His voice cracked. "I won't let you hurt Janie. I want you gone before . . . before she's old enough to understand."

Pity and empathy vanished in an instant, replaced by anger, by a rage so furious that it made her shake. Before she realized what she was about to do, she slapped him across the face as hard as she could.

"Janie is my daughter, too. I love her. I would never do anything to hurt her. You know I wouldn't. You know it!"

The urge to pummel him was nearly overwhelming. She clenched her hands into fists, her fingernails cutting into the palms of her hands.

"You compare me with Muriel without even knowing who I am. You think me spoiled and vain because of my background and my looks. When have you cared who I am deep down inside? When have you looked beneath the surface into my heart? I would never be unfaithful to you. I don't need lovers or wealth or fancy clothes. I'm not like Muriel, and I won't let you say that I am."

She spun around and stalked over to the fireplace. She gripped the board plank that served as a mantel, trying to calm herself. Only she didn't really want to be calm. She wanted to scream and shout and rage, so she whirled to face him again.

"I have loved you. I have loved you with everything

within me. I trusted you. I believed in you. I put my hope and my faith in you. Do you think me so shallow that I'm unable to be happy with simple things? Do you think I don't know the joys of watching a sunrise or seeing the first flowers of summer? Haven't I learned how to make a home for myself? And for you? Haven't I tried my very best? Have you ever heard me complain?"

She longed to strike him again, to knock some sense into his head.

"Do you know why Owen was here tonight? Because he came to apologize. *He* was apologizing to *us.*" She let out a humorless laugh. "Is your mind so filled with distrust that you can't listen to the truth? Don't you care whom you're hurting? Do you think you're the only person in the world who has ever suffered, who has ever been let down by another? Are you going to let that hurt rule your life?"

Garret just stood there, expressionless, and took it. Never uttering a word in defense. And his silence only fueled her rage.

She picked up a small vase from the mantel and hurled it at him, missing his head by mere inches. "You selfish bastard!"

The instant the words were out of her mouth, anger turned to a wretched sorrow. She choked on a flood of tears, and with a cry of despair, she raced into the bedroom and slammed the door closed, then threw herself onto the bed. A moment later she heard the front door close, and she knew Garret had left the house.

Good riddance, she thought. I don't care. I don't care. He can go to the devil, and it won't matter to me.

Then she pressed her face into the pillow and wept.

Garret took refuge in the empty bunkhouse. He found a bottle of Jake's whiskey and helped himself. He wasn't usually a drinking man. He'd discovered many years before that booze didn't solve any of his problems. But right now he wasn't trying to solve anything. He just wanted to drown out the sound of Beth's voice, still ringing in his head. If he thought about what she'd said, if he replayed the words in his mind, he just might give her another chance. He didn't want to do that. He'd tried that with Muriel. Better to be rid of her now.

He took several generous swigs from the bottle, letting the liquor send a flood of warmth through his veins.

He was still drenched from the storm and could use a change of clothes, but he'd be hanged before he'd go back in the house to get them. Instead he built a fire, then stripped down to his underwear, and sat in a chair near the wood stove.

"I have loved you. . . ."

He'd never seen her angry like that before.

He took another drink of whiskey.

"Haven't I tried my very best? Have you ever heard me complain?. . . "

No, he'd never heard her complain. In fact, it was quite the opposite.

"You compare me with Muriel without even knowing who I am. You think me spoiled and vain because of my background and my looks. When have you cared who I am deep down inside?. . . "

He winced, let more whiskey burn its way down his throat and into his belly.

"I would never be unfaithful to you. I don't need lovers or wealth or fancy clothes. I'm not like Muriel, and I won't let you say that I am . . . ."

But if she wasn't like Muriel . . . If he was wrong . . .

He tipped up the bottle and took several more swigs.

"Is your mind so filled with distrust that you can't listen to the truth? . . . "

The truth . . . What was the truth?

"Don't you care whom you're hurting? . . . "

Could it have been as innocent as she said? Could he have been wrong?

"I have loved you with everything within me. . . . "

He wanted to believe her. He'd been ready to believe her before he'd arrived home tonight. He wanted to believe her now. If he could only forget what he'd seen when he'd walked in the door. . . .

Tipping back his head, he drained the whiskey bottle dry.

23

Dear Pa,

I heard you sayin you want ma to leave cause of me so I aint gonna stay neither. Maybe then you and ma won't fight and she can stay cause I know yer better with her here. Don't worry bout Penguin. I'm taken him with me. The two of us will get along alright on our own.

Janie

Beth found the note before dawn the next morning. She had come out of the bedroom, already dressed for travel, her trunk packed and ready to leave. She didn't know where Garret had slept during the night. She'd tried to tell herself she didn't care where, as long as it hadn't been with her.

Then she found Janie's note on the table, and suddenly she cared a great deal about where Garret was.

With the slip of paper clutched in her hand, she hurried to the front door and yanked it open. A cold drizzle continued to fall from leaden skies.

"Garret!" she shouted as she rushed outside and headed for the barn. "Garret!"

The barn was empty.

Hiking up her skirt, panic welling in her chest, she ran to the bunkhouse. "Jake, are you in there?" She knocked, but no one answered. She opened the door. "Jake?"

The ranch hand wasn't there, but Garret was. He was sprawled on one of the bunks, wearing only his underwear, an empty whiskey bottle lying on the floor nearby.

"Garret, wake up!" she said loudly as she crossed the narrow room.

He sat up quickly, groaned as he grabbed his head with both hands, then opened bleary, uncomprehending eyes.

"It's Janie." She held out the note. "She's run away. She heard us arguing, and she's run away."

In an instant his muddled demeanor vanished. If his head ached when he stood up, he gave no sign of it. He took the note and read it. Then his gaze met hers. She saw her own worry mirrored in his eyes.

"Is Maybelle gone?" he asked.

She shook her head. "I don't know. I didn't look. I came to find you as soon as I read it. Garret, she . . . she must have left in the middle of the night." She touched his arm. "The sun isn't even up yet. Where could she have gone in the middle of the night?"

"Wherever Maybelle and Penguin took her, I guess."

He went for his clothes and quickly yanked on his trousers. As he slipped on his shirt, he said, "She wouldn't go into town. She'd know she would just be sent back home by whoever found her first."

This is my fault, Beth thought as she watched Garret pull on first one boot, then the other. If she hadn't started shouting, Janie wouldn't have awakened and overheard them. If she hadn't slapped Garret, thrown a vase at his head, slammed the bedroom door . . . If anything were to happen to Janie because of her display of anger . . .

"I'll saddle up and go look for her," Garret said as he started for the door.

"I'm going with you."

He stopped, looked over his shoulder, frowned.

"Don't argue with me, Garret. I'm going with you. I have to. I can't just sit and wait, not knowing."

After a moment's hesitation he said, "All right. I'll saddle Flick. You put a few things together for when we find her. She's sure to need some dry clothes, and we probably ought to have a blanket, maybe a bit of food, too. I've got a spare slicker in the house. You'd better bring it along in case we get caught in another downpour."

She wanted to tell him she was sorry for what she'd said last night. She wanted to put her arms around him and tell him she loved him and that she wasn't ever going to leave, no matter what he said to her, that she understood why he was bitter and angry, that she wanted to help heal his wounded heart. She wanted to tell him nothing he did would ever send her away, that she was steadfast in her love.

"We'd better hurry, Beth."

She nodded, hoping for the chance to say all those things and more once they'd found Janie.

God, Garret prayed as the horses galloped across the open range, *I haven't ever talked to you much, and maybe you're fed up with the likes of me. I've made a regular mess of things with Beth. I know I was wrong last night. I can be a hardheaded fool, but I expect you know that. I hope you'll give me another chance. I hope she'll give me another chance. Only this isn't about me or Beth, Lord. It's about Janie. She could be most anywhere, and I don't know if we're headed in the right direction. So I'm askin' you to guide me. You don't have t'do it for me 'cause I know I don't deserve it. But for Janie's sake, let me find her. I'd be much obliged.*

They rode hard, keeping their eyes peeled for any sign of Janie. They saw nothing.

At regular intervals they shouted her name, hoping to hear her calling back to them. They heard nothing.

As morning progressed, the skies grew darker instead of lighter. By noon it had started to rain hard again. By late afternoon they were both losing hope, although neither of them voiced their concerns aloud. In fact, they'd shared no more than a dozen or two words between them all day.

Had they gone in the wrong direction? Garret wondered. Had they overlooked some obvious sign? Had Janie realized her mistake and gone back to an empty house?

Oh, God, don't let me lose my daughter just 'cause I'm a fool.

He and Beth had been riding along the base of the eastern mountain range for more than an hour. They were nowhere close to a line shack where they could take shelter for the night. Both of them were soaked through to the skin, despite their rain slickers. In a few hours the black of night would make it impossible to continue the search. If they didn't find Janie soon . . .

"Garret, look!"

He reined in, followed the direction of Beth's outstretched arm with his gaze. And there, amid the trees, was Maybelle, the pony's reins trailing on the ground as she grazed quietly. Garret was out of the saddle in an instant and running toward the small bay mare. As he came charging through the trees, Maybelle shied away, startled by his sudden appearance.

"Janie!" Beth shouted, following right on his heels. "Janie, where are you?"

Garret joined his voice with Beth's. "Janie! Janie!" But he couldn't hear anything above his own thundering heart.

"She can't be too far away." Beth hiked her rain-soaked riding skirt and headed higher up the forested mountainside. "Janie, please answer us."

Garret went in the opposite direction. "Janie, we've come to take you home. Beth and I are here, and we want you to come home with us. Answer me." *Please, God, make her answer me.*

But it wasn't Janie's voice that came to him in answer to his prayer. It was a dog's barking. Persistent, nonstop barking. Penguin! It had to be Penguin.

Garret stopped still and listened, then moved quickly in the direction from which he thought the sound was coming. There was a sudden break in the trees, and there, on a shale-covered incline, stood Penguin. The moment the dog saw his master, he ran to him, still barking, then raced back to where he'd been.

Garret felt cold fingers of dread trace along his spine. "Janie?" He hurried forward, in a moment his worst fears realized.

"Pa?" Her faint voice, almost indiscernible, drifted up through the narrow hole in the earth.

Garret dropped to his knees beside what appeared to be an old mine shaft. "Janie, we're here."

Penguin stopped his barking, and in the sudden silence Garret could hear his daughter sobbing softly.

"Can you move, pumpkin? Did anything fall on you?"

"No."

"Are you hurt?"

"M-my arm. I think m-maybe it's broke like yours was." Her sobs grew louder.

"Try not to cry, sweetheart. We're gonna get you out. But you've got to be brave and listen to what I tell you to do. Okay?"

"I-it's awful dark d-down here. I-I'm scared."

"I know, hon." *So am I.* "But it's gonna be all right."

"It's cold, too. I . . . I wanna go home."

"Me too. We'll just have to get you out real quick. Okay?"

"O-okay."

The opening in the ground was narrow, about

three-fourths the width of his shoulders. It couldn't be the main shaft of the old mine. It had to be an air vent. He had no idea where the original opening was. Chances were good it didn't even exist anymore. These mountains had never held any gold, but for a while, when the Gold Rush was on in earnest, there'd been plenty of men who'd carved their tunnels into the earth, searching for the elusive yellow rocks. In the years since, most of the old mines had caved in upon themselves.

God, don't let it cave in. Don't let Janie get hurt.

He leaned forward. He couldn't see anything beyond a few feet. After that, it was just utter darkness. He reached down into the opening, laying his chest tight against the ground, stretching his arm as far as it would go. "Reach up, Janie. Can you touch my hand?"

Silence, then, "N-no."

He drew back a bit. "Can you see me?"

"N-no. It's too dark."

He straightened and looked around. Think, he told himself. Think of something.

"Pa . . . I—I'm sorry I ran away."

Before Garret could answer, Beth arrived in the clearing. He heard her gasp and knew she understood. A moment later she was on her knees beside him.

"Janie, honey, it's Beth. I'm here with your father."

His daughter's crying was more audible now. "I—I th-thought you were go-going away."

"I couldn't go and leave you, Janie." As Garret had done moments before her, she leaned close to the opening. "Don't be frightened, darling. We're going to get you out."

"She thinks her arm is broken," Garret said softly.

Beth sat back on her heels and looked at him. "What are we going to do?"

"We could try dropping a rope down to her, but if her arm's hurt, she probably couldn't hang on while we pulled her up." He shook his head. "We'll have to find the main mine shaft and try to get to her that way. We'll need help. You ride back to town and get some men and shovels and rope. I'll start looking—"

"That would take too long, Garret. We cannot leave her down there. It will be completely dark soon. She's frightened and hurt. She needs us." She paused, then said, "You must lower me down to her."

"What?" He stared at her, not sure he'd heard right.

"I'm small enough to get through that opening. You could lower me down on the rope, and then I could tie it around her waist and you could pull her up. Unless the hole narrows as it gets deeper, I think I could reach her that way."

Beth looked as weary, as cold, and as frightened as Garret felt. Locks of damp hair clung to her cheeks and her neck. Her complexion seemed gray, like everything else in the dim light. She also looked determined.

"It's too dangerous," he answered. "What if the walls collapsed?" He could lose them both. God help him, if they tried this and the shaft collapsed, he could lose them both. And then what—

"If that danger exists, then it's all the more urgent she not be down there alone."

"Beth, I can't ask you to—"

"You aren't asking, Garret. You would do it if you were small enough. Wouldn't you?"

"Well, I—"

"She's my daughter, too," Beth said with quiet finality, "and I'm going down after her."

She had never been like Muriel. Never. Not once. Yet he had always tried to believe the worst about her in order to cling to his bitterness. Would his anger and stubborn pride cost him the two people he loved?

"Beth—"

"Get the rope, Garret." She placed her hand on his arm. "Please. Janie needs us."

Beth had never been more terrified in her life. The idea of being lowered into that black hole, not knowing what creatures might be hidden there, not knowing if the ground itself might start crumbling in upon itself, left her sick with dread. But if it was bad for her, she knew it was much worse for a child of ten.

While she waited for Garret's return, she talked to Janie, hoping it would help alleviate some of the girl's fears, as well as her own. "Your father has gone to get a rope, darling. He's going to lower me down to you. I'll tie the rope around your waist and he'll pull you up to safety. You'll be out of there in no time." She prayed to God she was telling the truth.

Although she was certain no more than a few minutes had passed, it seemed forever before Garret reappeared through the trees, leading all three of the horses. He left Flick and Maybelle on the edge of the clearing, then brought his big buckskin gelding with him. Each footstep he took caused tiny avalanches of pebbles to roll down the hillside.

Beth stood as he approached, trying to hide her terror, not wanting him to see it. But it was too late. He already had.

"Are you sure you want to do this?"

She nodded.

He brushed her cheek with his knuckles. "Beth, I—" He swallowed hard.

"We'll get her out, Garret," she whispered. She stepped back from him and removed the skirt and jacket of her riding habit, then said, "I'm ready," even though she felt anything *but* ready.

He wound the hemp rope around her waist and showed her how to tie the knot, then he looped the opposite end around the saddle horn. When he looked at her again, he said, "Be careful."

She nodded and sat on the edge of the hole, lowering her feet in before her. With her hands she grasped the rope tightly, her knuckles turning white.

"Beth . . ."

A false twilight shadowed his face as she looked up at him.

"I love you."

It was strange, the power those three little words held. They wrapped around her, warmed her, gave her a strength and courage she hadn't felt before. She'd waited a long time to hear them, and these were not the circumstances under which she'd expected them to be uttered. Yet these seemed to be exactly the right circumstances, this moment exactly the right moment, for her to hear them.

"Not because of what you're about to do, Beth. Because of who you are."

Somehow, she'd already known that.

He touched her cheek again, letting his fingertips linger for only a heartbeat. "You'll both be out in no time."

"Of course we will."

Softly, "I love you, Beth."

Softer still, "I know, Garret. And I love you."

Without another word, he led his gelding down the hillside until the rope was taut. "All right," he called to her. "Whenever you're ready."

Beth drew a deep breath and tightened her grasp on the rope. "Janie, I'm starting down now. Cover your head just in case I knock some dirt and rocks loose." She inched forward and began her descent.

Even steerage in the midst of the worst storm hadn't been as bad as this, Beth decided as she was swallowed by the blackness of the earth. Her shoulders rubbed against the sides of the narrow shaft. The passage was cold and dank, and she felt as if the air were being squeezed slowly out of her lungs, never to return.

"Janie, you had better talk to me so I can tell how near I am to you."

"Wh-what should I say?"

"Why don't you tell me how you fell down here?"

"It was when it was rainin' so hard. I was leadin' Maybelle up the hill, and I th-thought I heard somethin'. I remembered how Pa got hurt up here, and I thought maybe it was another grizzly, so I started runnin' and I dropped right into the hole."

Janie sounded much closer. Beth hoped the tunnel wasn't deceiving her.

"Darling, I want you to reach up with your good arm. I'm coming down feet first and don't want to step on you. The minute you touch my shoe, you tell me."

Tiny showers of loosened earth, disturbed by the rope as it slid over the edge of the shaft's opening, spattered Beth's head and shoulders. She imagined being buried alive, a few pebbles at a time.

Panic began to choke her.

"Beth . . . I love you. . . ."

Remembering his declaration restored calm and increased her determination. She was going to reach Janie and get them both out of here. It had taken Garret a long time to say those words to her, and she was determined to get back to the surface as quickly as possible so she could hear them again.

"Janie, dearest, how are you doing?"

"O-okay."

"You sound close. I must nearly be to you. Try to find my shoe. Reach up as high as you can."

"I'm tryin'."

"Good. Just keep trying."

A few moments of silence, then, "You're here, Ma. I can touch you."

A rush of relief swept through her. "Make room for me. Slide to one side."

The moment Beth was able to, she gathered Janie against her, careful not to squeeze too tightly for fear of hurting her injured arm. "I'm here, darling," she crooned softly, tears streaking her cheeks. "Your mother is here."

*   *   *

It seemed an eternity to Garret before the rope went slack and Beth called out to him she was with Janie. It seemed even longer before he brought them to the surface, first Janie, then Beth.

Only when Beth was aboveground and Garret was able to embrace them both did he begin to breathe normally. And if he lived to be a hundred, he didn't think he would ever feel again such a storm of emotions—relief, fear, love, joy—as he felt right then.

"Are you all right?" he asked. And no matter how often they each answered in the affirmative, he kept asking, "Are you sure you're all right?"

Finally, after about the tenth time, Beth smiled at him as she cradled his face between her hands. "We'll be fine, Garret. I promise you. Now take us home."

Home.

Their home.

His and Janie's and Beth's.

"Yeah," he replied huskily, "let's go home."

24

The first promise of dawn slipped into the bedroom, a soft glow removing the night shadows.

From a chair beside the bed, Garret watched as light fell upon his wife's face. A surge of emotions caused his heart to constrict. He could have lost Beth. He could have lost both her and Janie. He had come so close to driving away those he loved, those who loved him in return. He'd come so close to losing everything that truly mattered to him.

He hadn't slept all night. After getting Janie home, he'd gone into town, awakening Dr. Werner from a sound sleep. By the time the doctor had set Janie's arm and left the ranch, it had been after three o'clock in the morning. Around four o'clock, Beth had finally fallen into an exhausted slumber while sitting at the foot of Janie's bed. Garret had awakened her just enough to help her down the ladder, get her undressed, and into bed. He'd spent the remaining hours before dawn going back and forth between the loft and the bedroom, checking on them both, reassuring himself they hadn't suddenly disappeared, that he hadn't lost them after all.

As more light crept into the bedroom, Beth stirred, a tiny moan slipping through slightly parted lips.

Garret eased off the chair and onto his knees beside the bed. With gentle fingertips he stroked the wisps of hair that had fallen across her forehead. His heart ached with love. It was an emotion so strong it overwhelmed him, left him breathless with wonder.

Her eyes fluttered open. For a moment they were glazed with traces of slumber. Then she saw him, seemed to realize she was awake and not dreaming. A tiny smile appeared. "It's morning already?" Her voice was husky with sleep.

"Almost."

"How is Janie?"

"She's fine. Still sleeping. So should you be."

"Mmm." She closed her eyes.

He loved this woman. Loved her more than his own life. And she had risked hers for Janie. Despite her fears, she hadn't hesitated because she loved the daughter he called his own as much as he did.

What, he wondered now, had he ever done to deserve her? He who had allowed anger and bitterness to wall up his heart for so many years.

She opened her eyes, met his gaze, asked, "Have you slept?"

He shook his head.

"You should."

"Later."

She touched his face, traced her fingertips over the rough stubble of his beard, along his jawline to his chin. Then she brushed them across his lips.

His body should have been too tired to react. It wasn't.

There was something both innocent and seductive about the smile slowly curving the corners of her mouth. "Come to bed, Garret."

She needed her rest. She'd been out in the cold and rain for an entire day and into the night. She'd risked her life. She should be sleeping.

"Come to bed and love me," she added in a whisper.

He pulled her into his arms, pressing her cheek against his shoulder, rubbing his own cheek against her hair. "I do love you, Beth. I've been such a fool. I nearly—"

"Garret." She lifted her head. "Don't. Not now. It doesn't matter. Not any of it. Not anymore." Her tender gaze seemed to caress him, bless him. "You are my husband. I am your wife. Just love me."

With a lump in his throat and his heart pounding in his chest, he shed his clothes and joined her in the bed. He gathered her to him, only the thin fabric of her nightgown separating their bodies. His member was hard with desire, but the desire in his heart was greater than the physical wanting. He wanted—*needed*—her to understand all she was to him, all she would forever be to him. But words failed him. He didn't know how to express these strange new emotions.

As if she'd read his mind, she said, "I know, Garret. I know."

For some reason, he thought of those letters Janie had written to England, letters that had always begun, "Dear Lady . . . " He had resented each and every one as they'd been written, as they'd been posted, and he'd resented every reply as they'd arrived.

It occurred to him then that he was looking into the eyes of a miracle. It was a miracle they had found each other, two strangers from different worlds. Beth had had to cross an ocean and over half a continent for it to happen. She had come to this country because of those letters he'd resented. She had come to America, to Montana, to this ranch, and she had made a place in his desolate heart, loving him even when he'd been the most unlovable.

How could it be anything less than a miracle that she was now his wife?

One day, he promised himself, he would find the words with which to tell her all she meant to him. Until then, he would try to find a thousand ways to show her what he felt, a million ways to prove his love.

If he hadn't cupped her breast with his hand at just that moment, stealing her breath away, Beth might have told him he didn't need words, that she could hear him with her heart. She might have told him she, too, was aware of the miracle of this moment. She might have told him he had taught her to watch for tiny miracles in his smile and in his eyes, to listen for them in his voice, to feel them in his hands and in his kisses.

But his caresses would not be ignored, and telling him about miracles would have to wait until another time.

"Beth," he whispered as he brought his mouth close to hers, then spoke the only words she would ever need to hear, "I love you."

"And I you," she returned breathlessly. "And I you."

"Dear lady. My dear, dear lady."

And as they shared their love with one another, the soft light of morning caressing their skin, another miracle was begun.

Epilogue

Monday, November 1, 1897
New Prospects, Montana

Dearest Inga,

My life continues to take many unexpected twists and turns. Cattle ranching, I have quickly discovered, is not an easy life. There is always more to do than hours in a day allow. Yet I am much more than merely content.

Every morning I awaken with a sense of great expectation. I watch my husband and wonder how I could ever have believed I would be content living alone. I look at Janie, see her growing and changing almost before my eyes, and realize how blessed I am to have been gifted with such a daughter.

We had our first snowfall a week ago.

The entire world seemed to turn white, heaven and earth and everything in between. It was indescribably beautiful. Never in my life have I seen snow such as this, although I am told it shall become a common sight to me, one to be expected every winter. But for now, the magic of it still remains.

When the sky cleared, turning such a brilliant shade of blue that it hurt my eyes, Janie and Garret showed me how to make a man of snow, and then we threw snowballs at one another. By the time we came inside, our faces were bright red with the cold, and my stomach ached from laughing so hard.

A new schoolteacher has been hired at last. I have met her and think Miss Applebaum is ever so much more capable than I was. Although I shall always miss my students, I do not regret the reason I am no longer teaching. Love has a way of filling up all the gaps in one's life.

The most surprising news from New Prospects has to do with the Homer sisters, with whom I stayed upon my arrival here. As I have shared with you in a previous letter, Bunny and Patsy Homer became most disagreeable after my marriage. I suppose it should not have come as any surprise. Everyone tells me Miss Bunny had set her cap for Garret long before I arrived in Montana. And Miss

Patsy, unfortunately, had a fondness for Mr. Simpson which was not reciprocated.

Given the years the Homer family was in New Prospects, the prosperous enterprise of their general store, and the sisters' status as members of the school board and town council, you can understand that these two women had much influence among the citizens here. Therefore, it came as a shock to all when it was learned poor business investments had caused them to lose ownership of the mercantile. Almost before the news could spread, they left town. No one seems to know where they have gone.

The new owner of the general store, Emmett Haskins, is quite a genial man who, much to my surprise, was raised in Buckinghamshire in a village not far from Langford House. His daughter, Emma, who is the same age as I, was born here in America and is as sweet a woman as I have ever met. I think we shall become good friends. More important, I think she and Owen Simpson shall become more than good friends. Perhaps it is because I am so happy and so very much in love that I am able to recognize the early signs of affection between them. I predict it shall not be long before our mayor is married to a woman who will give him the happiness he deserves.

Now I must share the best news of all. I

have been to see Dr. Werner and learned there will be another member of the Steele family arriving next May. How could I have known, all those months ago, that I was not running away from home but running to it? Never shall I run again, for I have found where I belong.

I pray you shall find the same one day, my dearest Inga.

Your friend,
Beth Steele

Read Inga Linberg's story in

Patterns of Love

BY ROBIN LEE HATCHER

coming from HarperPaperbacks
in 1998.

1

December 1897
Uppsala, Iowa

Dirk Bridger drew the wool collar up around his ears, but the wind was bitter cold and his coat was too thin. He slapped the reins against the horses' rumps, hoping to hurry the ancient animals along, even though he knew the gesture was useless. Sunset and Robber had no more speed to give. They were worn out and used up, like far too many things on the Bridger dairy farm.

He frowned, remembering how his ma had used similar words about herself yesterday. "I'm no spring chicken, Dirk," she'd said. "I'm wore out. But if I could just get me some rest, I'd be right as rain in no time."

Only Dr. Swenson didn't seem to think so. He thought Hattie Bridger's illness was much more serious than that.

And so this morning, Dirk had decided to put pride behind him and seek some much needed help.

"You go see that Reverend Linberg," Ma had told him this morning. "He'll know who we can hire to mind the girls."

But who would want to work for what little Dirk could afford to pay? And what would happen if he couldn't find someone willing to help out? His ma was ailing—perhaps dying, if the doctor knew what he was talking about—and Dirk couldn't take care of Ma, his orphaned nieces, and the farm all by himself.

An icy wind buffeted him from behind. He closed his eyes, and for just a moment, allowed himself to remember those last few weeks he'd spent out West. Summer. Hot and dusty. Saloons and pretty, scantily dressed barmaids. Cowboys with fast horses and shiny guns strapped to their thighs.

He gave his head a shake and returned his gaze to the road before him. Daydreams were for young boys and men with no responsibilities. They weren't for him. Not anymore. Not for a long time.

The *Prärieblomman* Lutheran Church came into view, its tall white steeple piercing the cloudless blue of the sky. Beside the church was the two-story parsonage where the Linbergs lived. Dirk hadn't met the minister or his family, even though they'd arrived in Uppsala last May. The Bridger dairy farm was more than an hour's ride outside of Uppsala, and Dirk limited his trips into town to once or twice a month. As for Sundays, Dirk Bridger hadn't darkened the door of a church—*any* church—in many years.

He didn't figure God had missed him.

Dirk drew back on the reins, stopping the team in front of the clapboard parsonage. He dropped the lap robe onto the floor of the wagon, then hopped to the ground. With a few long strides, he crossed the yard and climbed the steps to the porch. Quickly, he rapped his glove-covered knuckles against the door.

Within moments, the door opened, revealing a pretty teenaged girl with golden hair and dark blue eyes.

"Hello. Is the reverend in?"

She smiled shyly. "*Ja*. Come in, please."

Dirk whipped off his wool cap as he stepped into the warmth of the house. The girl motioned toward the parlor, and he followed her into the room.

"I will get Pappa," she said, a flush coloring her cheeks.

Dirk waited until she'd disappeared before allowing his gaze to roam. Although sparsely furnished, the room had a warm, welcoming feel to it. Lace doilies covered a small round table, a lamp set on top of it. A colorful quilt was draped over the back of the couch, another over the arm of a chair. Framed photographs lined the mantel, women with hair worn tight to their heads, their mouths set in grim lines, men with long mustaches and half-smiles.

"Those are members of our family in Sweden," a man said from behind Dirk. His voice was heavily accented with the singsong rhythm peculiar to the Swedes.

Dirk turned.

"I am Olaf Linberg." The reverend held out his hand. "Welcome to our home."

"I'm Dirk Bridger," he said, relieved the man obviously spoke and understood English. "I run a dairy farm west of here."

Dirk guessed the reverend was about sixty years

old. His hair and long beard were completely white, but his stance was unbent, and his face only slightly lined. When they shook hands, he discovered the reverend's grip was firm.

"I believe I know the farm, Mr. Bridger. Sven Gerhard is your neighbor." Olaf released Dirk's hand and motioned toward the sofa. "Please, sit down."

As he accepted the reverend's invitation, Dirk sought the right words to say next. It wasn't easy, asking for help. He'd been taking care of his own for most of his life.

Olaf's smile was both kind and patient. "Whatever has brought you here, young man, I will do my best to be of service."

"I feel a bit strange coming to you, the Bridgers not being members of your church and all. My ma's a Methodist."

"We are all members of God's family." The reverend chuckled softly. "Even Methodists."

Dirk shrugged. Then he raked the fingers of one hand through his hair and said, "Reverend, I guess there's nothin' else for me to do but come right out with it. I need to hire a woman to take care of my ailin' ma and watch after my nieces while I work the farm."

"You are not married, Mr. Bridger?"

"No. The dairy used to belong to my brother John. He and his wife, Margaret, died nigh on two years ago now. That's when I came here to run the place while Ma took care of John's little girls. But now she's sick and the doctor says she's got to stay in bed if she's gonna get well. We thought you might know of someone who'd be willing to work for us. I can't pay much. We barely get by as it is."

Olaf Linberg steepled his hands in front of his chin. "I see."

"Whoever we find's got to be willin' to live in. The house is fair-sized, and she'd have a room of her own. Wouldn't have to share with the girls or Ma. We'd need her to cook and clean, as well as mindin' to Ma and the little ones. It's not gonna be an easy job." He looked down at his hands, now clasped together, his forearms resting on his thighs. "It was Ma's idea I come to see you, Reverend Linberg. She figured you'd know most everyone around Uppsala, most of 'em goin' to your church and all."

"How old are your nieces, Mr. Bridger?"

"Martha's five. Suzanne's three."

The reverend shook his head. "So young to have lost their parents."

"Yeah."

Olaf rose from his chair and strode to the window where he gazed out at the lead gray sky. "I have five daughters of my own." After a few moments of silence, he glanced over his shoulder. "Your nieces are fortunate they have you to care for them."

Dirk felt a stab of guilt. He was fond of Martha and Suzanne, in his own way, but there were times he resented them, too. Sometimes he was even angry at John and Margaret for dying. As if they'd had any choice in the matter. But Dirk had wanted other things for his life than to be stuck on a farm in Iowa, milking cows and mucking manure, and he couldn't seem to rid himself of the bitterness. From the time he'd learned to read, he'd been planning and plotting to see the world, to sail the seven seas, to go to the Orient and Africa and South America. Shoot, if it

weren't for his family and the farm, he could've been
part of the rush to the Klondike goldfields. Maybe
he'd have already struck it rich if he weren't stuck
here, raising his orphaned nieces.

Drawing a deep breath while suppressing those
dark emotions, he stood. "There's one more thing,
reverend. Ma and I don't know but a few words of
Swedish. Whoever we find has to understand
English."

Olaf nodded. "I encourage all members of my congregation to speak English, Mr. Bridger. Language
will not be a problem in finding someone to work for
you."

"He is the most handsome man I have ever seen,"
fourteen-year-old Kirsten repeated for the fourth
time. "When I opened the door and saw him, I forgot to breathe." She flopped backward on the bed,
her arms spread out at her sides as she stared up at
the ceiling. "Dirk Bridger." She said his name on a
sigh. "Have you ever heard such a wonderful
name?"

"Is Pappa still with him?" sixteen-year-old Gunda
asked.

"*Ja*, I think so."

Thea, seventeen and the prettiest of all the Linberg
sisters, shook her head. "He could not possibly be
more handsome than Karl." Immediately, her eyes
filled with tears and her expression turned forlorn. "I
should have refused to leave Jönköping. I should have
told Pappa I would not go."

Inga laid a comforting hand on her sister's shoulder.

"I am sure Karl will find a way to come to America, Thea," she whispered. "You will see."

"Of course he will," Thea said with a sniff. "He loves me."

Ignoring Thea, fifteen-year-old Astrid asked Kirsten, "Are you certain you overheard his name right? Are you certain he has never been to Pappa's church?"

Seated on the end of the bed, Gunda nudged Kirsten's foot. "Why did you not talk to him *before* you went for Pappa? What a goose you are."

Inga had had enough. "Listen to all of you," she said as she rose from her bed. "Gunda is right. You are like a gaggle of geese, clucking and waving your feathers. And you, too, Gunda. Have none of you ever seen a handsome man before? With Mamma out paying calls, did any of you remember Pappa would need someone to serve coffee to his guest?"

Gunda and Astrid jumped to their feet, simultaneously saying, "I will do it."

"No." Inga headed for the door. "You would only embarrass Pappa. You would spend all your time staring at his visitor instead of minding your duty. I will see to it."

There was no further argument. Inga hadn't expected there would be. After all, everyone knew it was her responsibility to act as Pappa's hostess in the absence of their mamma. Everyone knew Inga, the oldest and most levelheaded sister, would always live at home, helping their pappa in his Christian work. It had long been understood by the entire family that she would never marry.

As she descended the narrow staircase, Inga tried

to ignore the sudden tightness in her chest. She knew she should gracefully accept her destiny. She was his right hand, Pappa would say. He would be lost without her. She was more sensible than any of her flighty, flirtatious sisters, he often added, and her intelligence should not be wasted. When Pappa said such things, it made Inga ashamed of the secret fears she harbored in her heart: a fear that nothing exciting or unexpected would ever happen to her and a fear that she was unlovable as a woman.

Such fears made her feel guilty, for they were so contrary to the faith she professed. So she pretended they didn't exist. She pretended to be happy and content with who and what she was.

Still, when she looked at Thea or Gunda or Astrid or Kirsten—all of them golden girls, bubbling over with feminine charm, small and petite and oh so pretty—Inga couldn't help wondering why she had been born so plain, so tall, so thin. She couldn't help wondering what it might have been like to giggle and whisper and flirt, to fuss with her hair and her clothes, to have a young man—like Thea's Karl—try to steal a kiss and proclaim her too pretty to resist.

"Now who is being the goose?" she scolded herself.

And then she stepped into the parlor doorway and saw him, the stranger visiting her father. In that instant before Pappa knew she was there, Inga realized Kirsten had been right. Dirk Bridger was undoubtedly a most handsome man, and her longing to be different became almost tangible.

Perhaps she made a sound, for he looked up. His eyes were dark brown, the darkest brown eyes she had ever seen. The color of Mamma's strong coffee.

"Ah, here is Inga," Pappa said. "Inga is my eldest daughter."

She knew she shouldn't stare. She was acting as silly as Kirsten. But she seemed unable to wrest her gaze from him.

Dirk Bridger stood, and once again, her heart skittered. He was tall, so tall she had to look up at him to maintain eye contact. She couldn't remember the last time that had happened.

Pappa continued, "This is Mr. Bridger. He has come to us for help."

"Help?" she echoed inanely.

Dirk Bridger nodded. "I need a woman to stay at our farm and tend to two little girls and my mother."

"Your mother is ill?" *And what of your wife?*

"Yes."

She wished to comfort him, this stranger. Instead, she asked, "How old are your daughters, Mr. Bridger?"

"They aren't my daughters. They're my nieces. Their folks're dead."

Impulsively, Inga turned toward her father and said, "Perhaps I should go with Mr. Bridger."

There was a flicker of surprise on the reverend's face. Then he began stroking his beard, and Inga knew he was giving her suggestion serious consideration. She didn't know why, but she wanted desperately for her father to agree.

"I can't pay much, Miss Linberg," Dirk said. "You should know that up front. And the work'll be hard."

She kept her gaze on her father as she replied, "I am sure whatever you pay would be fair, Mr. Bridger, and I am not afraid of hard work. I am much stronger than I look."

"You probably need to talk this over with your pa before you decide for sure."

She heard Dirk take a couple of steps toward the doorway. "Pappa?" she asked hurriedly.

"*Ja.*" Her father nodded. "You could be a help to the Bridgers, I think."

Inga felt a warm pleasure flood through her. She told herself it was because she was doing a good work for someone in need. But she had helped others in the past and never felt this same elation. Perhaps it would be better not to know why she felt this way.

She turned toward her new employer. "It will only take me a short while to pack my things, Mr. Bridger. Would you like a cup of coffee while you wait? It might brace you for the cold trip back to your farm."

Looking a little surprised, he answered, "Yeah, I guess I wouldn't mind somethin' hot before we head out."

"I will see to it then."